D0323803

Also by David Long

• • •

Early Returns

Home Fires

The Flood of '64

DAVID LONG

BLUE
spruce

stories

Scribner
NEW YORK LONDON TORONTO SYDNEY TOKYO SINGAPORE

SCRIBNER
1230 Avenue of the Americas
New York, NY 10020

This book is a work of fiction. Names, characters, places, and incidents either are products of the author's imagination or are used fictitiously. Any resemblance to actual events or locales or persons, living or dead, is entirely coincidental.

Copyright © 1995 by David Long

All rights reserved, including the right of reproduction
in whole or in part in any form.

"Blue Spruce" and "Attraction" originally appeared in *The New Yorker,* "Eggarine" in *GQ,* "Cooperstown" and "The Vote" in *Story,* "Lightning" in *The Sewanee Review,* "The New World" in *Antaeus,* "Talons" in *CutBank,* and "Perfection" in *Voices Louder Than Words: A Second Collection* (Vintage Books, 1991).

Lyrics from "I'm Goin' Down" by Bruce Springsteen, copyright 1984, Bruce Springsteen, ASCAP. Used with permission.

Thanks to the National Endowment for the Arts for their generous support of this work. Special thanks to Roger Angell, Claire Davis, and Dennis Held. To Hamilton Cain, Sally Wofford-Girand, Maria Healey, Mary Vanek. And, as always, to my family.

SCRIBNER and design are trademarks of Simon & Schuster Inc.

Designed by SONGHEE KIM

Manufactured in the United States of America

1 3 5 7 9 10 8 6 4 2

Library of Congress Cataloging-in-Publication Data
Long, David, 1948–
Blue spruce: stories/David Long.
    p. cm.
        I. Title.
    PS3562.04924B58   1995
    813'.54—dc20   94-43345

ISBN 0-684-80033-0

In memory
J.H.L., Jr.

Down with the world behind the world.

—Peter Handke and Wim Wenders, *Wings of Desire*

contents

BLUE
spruce

ATTRACTION

She was fifteen that summer of 1963, living with her mother in a rented house by a stretch of dead water called McCafferty's Slough. It was only a short walk through a stand of aspen to the back door of the skating rink, a huge, watery-green Quonset. She lugged her own roller skates, in a blue tin case with her name, "Marly Wilcox," stenciled on it in nail polish. In love with nothing else just then, she loved the sensations of skating, the swift cuts, the sweat like a cool metal comb delving into her hair. She didn't paw stupidly at the air, didn't grab her arms behind her back like a showoff—they pumped at her sides, thin, efficient, her fingertips tucked together like rosettes. The music crackled from tiny loudspeakers, out-of-date show tunes and syrupy waltzes, the occasional 45 by Duane Eddy or Chubby Checker or Little Eva. None of the boys pulled at her clothes or whipped her into the rails. She gave off a signal, an aura: Hands off, you'll get no satisfaction from me. More likely, they just weren't interested.

Charlie Bitterman was there. Willowy, pale-skinned, with his gauzy shirts, his flop of sandy hair. His eyes were the color of cinnamon toast, his smile abrupt, a little toothy. It was the summer he was going by "Chas." He'd graduated from high school in Sperry that June, and was going out East to study engineering. He was the son of Ike Bitterman, the architect. The Bittermans had sent an older boy to West Point, a daughter to veterinary school in California, and now this last one to Rensselaer. Afterward, he would come and join Ike's firm—the way Jamie Shirtliff and Evan St. Clair had come home and breezed into their fathers' law practices. "It's the pattern," Marly's mother, Jeanette, said. "Time-honored. Old as the world." Marly had been watching him, keeping tabs. He was the most interesting thing going, she'd decided. And she wasn't the only one. She'd caught Mlle. Picard, her French teacher, languidly staring after Charles one winter afternoon—a flush rose to Mlle. Picard's temples, but she had shrugged, smiled, shamelessly dragged Marly into the moment with her, so that it was Marly who turned away, embarrassed, found out.

All that year, until spring, Charles had gone out with Cynthia Lumquist. They'd made a famous couple, no question about it. Cynthia was a loopy, smart-alecky girl, flagrantly blond, with a tantalizing gap between her front teeth. It was a romance oblivious of social standing. Cynthia had no parents, as far as anyone knew—she floated, skirted catastrophe, lived with an aunt or an older sister, emerged at school from an amazing array of vehicles. Her hair was platinum, silver-white like a movie star's.

Invisible amid the horseplay, the clattering trays, Marly had watched the two of them dance to the record player in the cafeteria. Charles danced like no local boy. No flailing, no sappy grin. He kept his eyes shut, his moves cool and minimal. Cynthia stuck her arms straight out over his shoulders, let her fingers dangle while Charles aimed a stream of incantation into her ear. They might have been dancing on the deck of a ship, they might have been the last two people on earth. Eventually, the vice-principal would come and bust up this display—Cynthia would bristle, ready for battle, but Charles always steered her away, unfazed. He might show up in the library later with one of Cynthia's crimson kisses enameled to his forehead.

He had plenty of friends, Marly had observed, but no best friend, and didn't travel in any pack. It was as if he'd siphoned people out of different cliques, one by one. He was smart in an amused, leapfrogging way. Marly had had a civics class with him. He couldn't have cared less about politics (he obviously read only what he wanted to read), but every few days Marly would watch fat, tonsured Mr. Nardi cave in to boredom and address Charles with something like "Mr. Bitterman, how'd you like to give us the succession to the Presidency?" Charles always looked genuinely happy to have been called on. No, he didn't know about that, but what did Mr. Nardi think about *Silent Spring*, and what about this news report he'd seen that the world's population would hit nine billion by the year 2025? He consulted some ink marks on the back of his hand. Roughly five hundred and sixty-two million tons of human being, he said.

Cynthia had broken up with him, finally. After Charles, she had an affair with an older man, Casper Gault, who ran the news agency. The news agency was one of Marly's haunts— she drank sludgy chocolate Cokes, killed late-afternoon hours flipping through paperbacks on the swivel stands. Gault had once played ball for Montana State; he was beefy, with a brick-red face. Marly always pictured him down on one knee, snipping the wire that bound the newspapers and magazines—it made an indecent thump as it released. The thought of lying spread-eagled under Gault, that heaving weight on her—it was appalling, engrossing. Above the news agency was a string of cheap rooms where a couple of the waitresses lived. People claimed that the man who'd had the building before Gault had run girls out of those rooms. That's how it was said, "running girls."

Gault had a daughter in Marly's class, but Marly had never paid her much attention. A pallid, homely girl in wrinkled corduroy jumpers: Ruth Ann Gault. But that night at the rink, Marly noticed her trudging across the dusty hardwood in her oxfords, a strange, earthbound creature among the streaking shapes. Marly ducked into the girls' locker room. Cynthia Lumquist sat worming her feet into her skates, laughing about something. She'd just taken a drag on her Winston, and parked it on the edge of the bench, where it began to sear the varnish. She wore a blue leotard and hair ribbons and a batch of loud bracelets. As Marly watched, Ruth Ann rounded the doorway, came silently at Cynthia with a locker key in her fist, and put Cynthia's eye out.

It happened in an instant, a tiny glint. Cynthia toppled over backward, and Marly, without a thought, threw her arms out and caught her. Someone shrieked. The owner of the rink and his son and some other men shoved their way in through the commotion. Cynthia was peeled out of Marly's arms and carried off, her face in wet paper towels. Ruth Ann was wrestled into custody. Songs kept scratching through the loudspeakers, but the skaters were all packed against the railings. Even the light seemed wrong—thin and gold. Marly scanned the place for Charles, couldn't locate him. Earlier, she'd seen him, watched him taking in Cynthia's arrival, tracking her through the crowd, his face expressionless for once. Now she went out the front door, still in her skates, and crunched into the edge of the parking lot. It was a breathless night. A fog of clay dust eddied in the air, blurring the tail-lights, leaving a film on everything. She looked for his car, his father's pale-gold Thunderbird, but it wasn't there. In a few minutes, they closed the rink. The floodlights were doused, the last knots of people dissolved.

This was the year of the tent worms. They fell from the aspens as Marly made her way home that night, splattering down like the first heavy drops of a storm. She smelled them—awful things, vile, hormonal. She found a few still plastered to her scarf when she shucked it off under the vestibule light. Gagging, she ran to the bathroom and flushed the scarf away—it clogged the line and had to be retrieved the next day with a metal snake.

•　　•　　•

CYNTHIA'S EYES had been honey-colored, but the glass eye was a jazzy emerald. Who could deny her? "Now what are *you* staring at?" she'd say to men, flicking at her bangs. It was as if she'd caught them gawking at her chest. They did that, too. She was shorter and rounder than Marly; she had a good figure, a dreamy, slangy way of rolling her shoulders. She wore puffy angora tops and stretch pants and cowboy boots, or red laceless sneakers. Like her mother, Jeanette, Marly was all torso—Slats, she'd been called in junior high (mercifully, no one remembered).

Charges were filed against Ruth Ann—Marly had to go down to the courthouse and give her deposition—but somehow there was no trial. Caspar Gault put the news agency up for sale, and the family left Sperry for good. Charlie Bitterman was gone, too. Every morning, downshifting raucously,

Marly's school bus cornered by the Bittermans' house. It occupied a spit of ground above the park, a faint salmon color, all flat roofs and eccentric jutting angles, with a few dwarf trees deposited around the lawn. At Christmas, it would float in a bath of blue floodlights. Marly squashed her books against her chest and burrowed down in the seat.

Her own house was an embarrassment: squat and shingled, peeling turquoise, with a glaring tin roof. One winter, an accumulation of cottonwood leaves and fallen-in chimney bricks plugged the heater vent, so that Marly and Jeanette both got dangerous, woozy headaches from the fumes. The landlord was ancient—he appeared every August in the fair parade, a spindly old farmer, piloting a goat cart. Jeanette couldn't stand the sight of him. "We're absolutely not spending another month in this hellhole," she told Marly periodically. Yet they never moved.

Out the back door was McCafferty's Slough, one of the countless oxbows the river had cut, then abandoned. It gave off clouds of mosquitoes in the spring; it smelled of cattails and rotting bark. Later in the summer, algae clumped in the shallows like green tapioca. When the cottonwoods shed, the air was blinding—the screens clogged, great berms of cotton collected in the weeds. But there were turtles in the slough, too, and once in a while a pileated woodpecker. And no traffic, and no yapping dogs, and no neighbors—she and Jeanette could do as they wished down there and never feel spied on.

Jeanette had managed to hold on to some of her father's furniture. There was a heavy sideboard, a gumwood mirror that Jeanette bent and pouted into every time she left the house. The headboard of Marly's bed went clear to the ceiling, scrolled black walnut, with a frieze of dusty cherub faces. Marly's grandfather had been a doctor in Sperry—saw to diphtheria patients, drilled out horrible infected mastoids, amputated fingers. "This wasn't like now," Jeanette told Marly. "They'd sometimes pay in potatoes or cordwood, or send him these pathetic notes." He was a charmer in a black fedora, and the source of all their lanky height. He was also a drunk, Jeanette said, and not averse to injecting himself with morphine. He'd died at fifty-one, his finances in a shambles. She talked openly about all of this. "Why be full of secrets?" she said. Jeanette could be like that, blithe, modern. "You don't know how it used to be, Marly. People suffocated. They couldn't be their true selves."

Still, Jeanette's true self had its own shadowy spots. The subject of Marly's father, for one. He was an indiscretion, that's all she'd say. Poor judgment on her part.

"Yes, but what did—"

"You can save your wind, honey," Jeanette said, fending her off. "It's unfair, I know it is, but I'm not parading that around again. It's just a fact you're going to have to live with."

Well, she'll slip up sometime, Marly thought. Not as to his name and whereabouts, maybe, but how it was, before he got to be a mistake. Something regarding the nature of the attraction. But no, she didn't.

•　　•　　•

MARLY HAD GROWN UP believing there was a cache of money tucked away for her college. When the time finally came, Jeanette admitted it had dwindled. It had been invested rashly, nibbled at. "Try not to hate me," she said. Jeanette could be that way, too. A vein of melodrama could surface; her voice would turn lavish and sentimental.

"Oh, I'm *sure*," Marly said. She and Jeanette might rub each other wrong for days, but their quarreling had no depth. They were companionable, mainly. And, anyway, this news didn't crush her—somehow she'd suspected it. It had more to do with Jeanette not being ready to give her up. Nor did it cancel her vision of herself as one of the ones, like Charles, who wasn't trapped, who had a rightful life to go to. She could wait awhile, it wouldn't kill her.

The September after her graduation, Marly started work at a supper club called Daugherty's. It was out on the highway, the place people went for prime rib or Sunday brunch, a maze of dark, muffled rooms. It was at Daugherty's she ran into Cynthia again. Marly waited tables, Cynthia worked the bar and card room. She'd gotten married, had a ring to flash, but she was the same: flirty and wisecracking, hard to pin down. The winter was endless; on weekends, Daugherty's was crazy with skiers, the lot overflowing with tour buses. Cynthia acted as if she and Marly were fast friends from another life. They went on break together, laughed and complained, drank champagne Cynthia lifted from the banquet rooms. Many nights, Marly stayed late and gave Cynthia a ride home.

The husband's name was Rory Blanchard. He was older by a little, twenty-seven or so, wiry, pale as coconut milk. He'd been in and out of the military. "What's he do?" Marly asked. Cynthia made one of her faces. Apparently, Rory bought and sold—vanloads of this and that. Sometimes deals went wrong and he was required to repossess things. He was often gone. He could be funny in a rough way, and when he was like that—easy with his money, eyes flashing—Marly caught a glimpse of what Cynthia had seen in him. But he could be sullen for no obvious reason; mean. He was always teasing them, plying Cynthia and Marly with jokes. Often as not they blipped right past Marly—there'd be some nasty angle that escaped her at first. Such as the night he said, "You hear them North Dakotans figured out a new use for sheep?"

"What's that?" Cynthia asked.

"Wool," Rory said. He had that grin. His teeth were as big and white as Chiclets.

One evening, the Bittermans stomped into Daugherty's from the cold, and sat in Marly's section. Mr. Bitterman had an imposing head—square, heavy-browed, his hair slicked back in silver furrows as if engraved. Mrs. Bitterman was in fawn-colored suede. She had an airbrushed quality, a touch of a smile, as if she'd spent her life looking out through a train window.

Marly brought their dinners, loitered within earshot, heard nothing exceptional. "And how's that son of yours doing?" she finally got up the nerve to ask, pouring coffee. "Chas? Charlie?"

Mr. Bitterman blinked and glanced up over his half-lenses. Did he know this waitress? His wife tapped her lips with her napkin, looked away. "He's doing fine work," Mr. Bitterman said. "Couldn't be better."

Marly flushed. "Really, well—that's great," she said, ducking, backing from the table. How easily she could be lied to.

•   •   •

SOMETIME THAT WINTER, Cynthia got pregnant. Marly couldn't believe she'd been so careless. No, she could, she could see it perfectly. Why not? Cynthia worked a few more months, then got herself fired. Now it was summer, and Cynthia was enormous. She and Rory lived in an apartment over a three-car garage up on Ash. It had two miserly dormers, an accumulation of spindly furnishings, a miniature stove and refrigerator. The bathroom was an afterthought, a tiny, oblong plywood partition sticking out into the room. Rory hated the place—he vowed to move them onto "his land," a

one-acre lot out in the west valley, which he'd taken in trade
for a Volkswagen bus. Flat, exposed, with nothing growing on
it but knapweed and clumps of Russian thistle. He'd talked
his cousin into digging the cellar hole and setting the forms
for the concrete, but Cynthia had a vision of them living
down there indefinitely. "In the crypt," she called it. Tarpaper
roof, splintery planks laid across the mud, the electrical service on a little pole. No way.

The apartment had a sweet, cloistered feel in the mornings, but after lunch it turned sticky hot. Marly made a point
of never coming by when Rory was likely to be home. She
didn't even like to imagine Rory being alone there with Cynthia, slouching at the dinette, recounting some pointless
transaction. But this particular afternoon Cynthia had called
her, begged her to come over. Marly found her on the edge of
the bed with her feet splayed. She was staring. "This has gotten too weird," she said finally.

"Don't you have a fan?"

"Just blows it around," Cynthia said.

She lay back on her elbows and stuck her belly out. "Well,
I et the watermelon this time," she said.

"You did," Marly said.

"Swallowed the big fruit."

She hoisted herself and made a stab at clearing the mess
from the table. "Rory thinks I'm kind of disgusting." She stuck
her tongue out. "Hey, how'd you like to get me out of here?"

"Don't they want you to just kind of take it easy?"

"Oh, *pul-ease*," Cynthia said.

Marly owned a little black Ford Falcon. She got Cynthia
down the stairs and loaded into it.

"Any place in particular?"

"Just go fast," Cynthia said.

So Marly bought them two cans of pop and took the back roads into the lower valley. There hadn't been a storm or any semblance of clouds for twenty straight days. The first cut of hay had been made, and the wheat was starting to lean over and show the tracks of the wind. Cynthia rode with her eyes closed.

"Any better?" Marly asked.

Cynthia rolled her head back and tried to shake some air down into her scalp.

They swung onto Dutchman's Grade, and Cynthia looked up. "What's that smell?"

"Mint," Marly said. "That's all mint out there, that dark green?"

"How do you know stuff like that?"

"I just do. Anyway, can't you smell it?"

Cynthia laughed. "Stinks," she said. "Smells worse than Rory."

"You're terrible," Marly said.

Cynthia flipped a cigarette from her little plaid case and strained forward to poke in the lighter.

"You want to go back yet?"

"Oh, Jesus, no," Cynthia said. Then, in a minute, she said she wanted to be driven up by the new part of the golf course.

Why not? Marly thought.

A contractor had bought the clover field alongside the new golf holes, and a string of houses was going up. This was the back way to Stillwater. Paper birches had stood in this field, Marly remembered, huge, shivering clumps of them. Up by the road, there'd been stacks of bee boxes, almost too white to look at on a sunny day.

"Slow down!" Cynthia shouted. "Here, turn."

Marly bumped onto the dirt. The gumbo had hardened

into deep ruts, the width of tire axles. She tried to balance on top of the ridges, but slid off. Both their heads banged against the roof.

"Jesus, watch it," Cynthia said. She pointed, told Marly to pull up behind a mound of topsoil, within view of the last house. It was two stories, bare plywood with staging and planks skirting the upstairs.

Cynthia scooched down in her seat.

"What are we looking at?" Marly asked.

"Just hold on."

Marly wiped her eyes. In a moment, she saw Charlie Bitterman creep out onto the staging, wearing a nail pouch and no shirt. It was the strangest place to see him. His upper body had gotten some color, a washboard of glistening muscle.

"How'd you know?" Marly said.

"Spies. Now go get him to come over here, will you?"

"I can't do that," Marly said.

Cynthia squeezed her arm, almost roughly.

Marly got out and did it—bounced up the gangplank into the half-built house and brought him down off the scaffolding. "Somebody wants to see you," she said. "Over in that car."

He squinted past her. His face was leaner, his teeth shone. He tapped her shoulder in thanks, studied her a second. "Marly Wilcox," he said.

Marly hugged her elbows. "Go *on*," she said.

She watched him make his way toward Cynthia, his gait long and springy, the hammer banging against his leg. The sky was white. A few bees plied the air around her.

• • •

IT AMAZED MARLY, thinking of it later, that Cynthia would want to be seen looking like that: sweaty, her hair snarled by the wind, her lap full of that bulky weight. But no, Cynthia always knew her powers. It was a picture Marly couldn't shake. Charles had leaned against the car roof and looked in at Cynthia and let himself be asked question after question in that voice of hers, while she sat rubbing her belly with both hands, the shirt pulled way up.

The baby came two weeks early. Rory was out of state. Marly had expected to be called on to drive Cynthia to the hospital when the time came, but she learned the news from Jeanette, who was rattling the newspaper under her nose. "Isn't this that friend of yours?"

Marly stared: "Discharged, Mrs. R. Blanchard and baby girl."

Cynthia met her on the landing, in a baggy gown. She looked awful, Marly thought—shocking, as if her face had deflated.

"How come you didn't tell me?" Marly said. "Who'd you get to drive?"

"Don't start in on me, all right?" Cynthia said. The baby was sleeping heavily in a bassinet. Her eyelashes were long and fine, as transparent as fishing line. Cynthia had named her Cher. "And don't tell me it's a dumb name, okay?"

"I wouldn't," Marly said. "It's beautiful. And she's beautiful."

Cynthia shook her head tiredly. Then, in one rough motion, she slipped the gown off her shoulders and turned to face Marly. "You believe this?" she said.

Her breasts stuck straight out, hard as marble, cross-hatched with bright-blue veins. The nipples were almost maroon, raw and distressed, leaking milk.

Marly was speechless; she turned away, saw the flowers drooping on the dinette, baby roses in a spray of greens.

"So what's Rory think about all this?" Marly asked. "He must be pretty excited?"

Cynthia looked up from the bassinet. "Who knows?" she said. "He's stranded down in Sheridan."

God, Marly thought. Charles.

•   •   •

JEANETTE WORKED in the Clerk and Recorder's Office. She demanded peace and quiet when she got home—her eyes hurt, she was sick of pacifying people, didn't want a lot of chitchat. That was fine by Marly. But, as evenings wore on, the peace and quiet seemed to eat at Jeanette. Everything got louder—the TV blared, the blower in the furnace wheezed on and off. Jeanette sat on the love seat with a goblet of red wine and flung her voice back over her shoulder. "What's that?" Marly was always having to say from the tiny kitchen.

One such night in early fall, the phone rang, and it was Charles.

"Who's that bothering you so late?" Jeanette yelled.

"It's not *late*," Marly hissed at her. She dragged the cord down into the bathroom and shut the door.

"God, I'm at loose ends," he started in. No "How are you?" Nothing.

She pictured him the way he'd been, shirt off, toughened up. Now he sounded winded, his voice choppy, whiny.

"I think about going back to that school and my heart freezes. I'm not cut out for this."

Why spill this to *her*? What had become of all his tony friends? She listened, stunned, watching a ladybug traverse the window sash.

"None of this was my idea," he said. "I'd rather just stay and work."

"You can't do that," Marly said.

"The point is, why can't I? What exactly would be the trouble with that?"

"I don't know," Marly said. "It's not you."

There was a stubborn silence on his end. "I tried getting hold of Cynthia," he said finally. "But he answered. The husband. I tried three times."

"Well, he lives there," Marly said. "What do you want with her, anyway?" She wished he'd just say it out loud.

"Marly, listen, you suppose you could get out?" he asked her.

"What, me?" Marly said. "I don't think so. It's awful late, and anyway—"

But of course she did meet him. Once the news agency had closed, at ten, the only thing open besides the bars was the Park Inn, a bright, square box up on Montana. Charles was waiting in the window, cupping his face against the glass. He wore a snap-studded workshirt and had a blue bandanna tied across his forehead.

Trying to blend in, Marly thought—he never would. Why bother? She came straight to him but saw at once that it was the wrong place for this talk. The booths were right on top of each other, the lights merciless.

They ended up riding in his car, splitting cans of malt liquor. It had a dark taste Marly liked, and she drank most of it, her back against the door, while she watched him battle himself.

"You know, if I stayed here he'd make sure I got laid off," he said. "He'd engineer it. He'd twist arms."

"Who? Your father?"

"Is that too paranoid?"

"I think if you have the chance you should get out of here," she said. "It's a gift."

"No, it's not," he said. "It's a debt. It's a big, convoluted initiation rite. It's ordained. It's—"

He barely looked at her as he drove. They crossed back and

forth over the same streets—now it *was* late. Marly cranked her window down, letting the wind hit her face, and felt the alcohol's faint buoyancy. He'd worked himself into an impasse, pushed himself right up against it. But he still hadn't gotten at what it really was, what he was afraid of. Was it competing? she wondered. Being found, of all things, ordinary?

She turned back to him. "You can't moon around," she heard herself say, full of spiky energy. It was all she could do not to add, "I expected a lot more from you."

●　●　●

WHATEVER SHE SAID THAT NIGHT, it worked: Charles disappeared back to school. A postcard arrived: two old-time, pasty-white boxers facing off in the Federal Street Gym in Albany. "Knuckling down," it said.

The hunter's moon came and went. It snowed on Halloween, there was a week of slop and gray, then a blast of pure arctic air. Sometimes, on her nights off, Marly babysat for Rory and Cynthia. She brought Cher a mobile of stuffed animals made of calico, and also a couple of crocheted comforters Jeanette had been saving. Cold leaked into the apartment as badly as heat did in the summer. Two space heaters ran constantly. The lights dimmed and flickered, fuses blew. Cynthia never had anything more to read than *TV Guide*, so Marly brought a bag of plastic-covered library books. She pulled a chair beside the crib, laid a hand on the railing, and read *East of Eden* or *Exodus* as the baby slept. "Up to the *E*'s, huh?" Jeanette had teased her.

One night, Cynthia and Rory didn't get home—it was one o'clock, then two. Marly heated a bottle and fed Cher and put her back to sleep. Finally, she went to the window and saw Rory's truck in the driveway. Snow lay on the hood and windshield, as if the truck had been parked for some time. Marly ran down and found Cynthia passed out on the seat, with one arm snaked around the shift knob. She was wearing an unlined windbreaker. "Hey, you've got to *wake up*," Marly said. Cynthia was dopey. She sent her hand up into Marly's face; her nails hooked Marly's little neck chain and snapped it off. Now Marly could see that Cynthia's face was cut—her face was actually sticky with blood.

Rory had hit something with the truck, Cynthia said. Something concrete, some kind of a post.

And where was he now? She had no idea.

"You've got to come upstairs," Marly said. "I can't carry you, you've got to get up." Eventually, Cynthia roused herself. Marly steered her to the bed, covered her. She didn't dare leave. She slept sitting up on the couch, under a heap of blankets. Near dawn, she heard Cynthia throwing up on the other side of the plywood wall.

In the morning, she gave Cynthia some aspirin, and made her bouillon, which she wouldn't drink. Marly bundled the baby and took her out. The day was pearly, with a fine snow sifting down. They walked uptown, under the awnings, and Marly wished she'd run into someone she knew, so she could peel back the flap of blanket and show off the sleeping face. On the way back home, she stopped to have a look at Rory's truck. It hardly seemed dented at all, she thought.

"I don't see you anymore," Jeanette said. Marly started to whip back some smart answer. But it was true. "Sorry," she offered, but let it go at that. She started typing a letter to Charles, read over the half-dozen pathetic sentences. She'd stooped to complaining about the gloomy skies. "It's like living under a trailer," she'd written, which wasn't even original—it was an old line of Jeanette's. Nothing about Cynthia or Rory or the baby. She crumpled the paper, feeling stunted, boxed in. She sensed Jeanette studying her, on the verge of further assessment.

Then one night, mid-March, Charles called.

"Where are you?" she said. "Still in school, aren't you?"

"Still here," he said. "Out in the greater world."

"Glad to hear it," Marly said. It had to be after midnight where he was.

"Tell me how Cynthia is."

"Exactly the same."

"What's she think about us—her and me, I mean. She tell you anything?"

No, she wasn't going to get into that with him. "You any happier?" she said. "You don't sound like it. You sound like you're going to fly apart."

"Me? No, I'm fine," he said. "Straightening it all out."

Somehow she didn't tell Cynthia about the call.

A few weeks later, she went to Cynthia's and found her wearing huge mirrored sunglasses. Tripped going down the stairs, she said. There were tricky shadows, and, after all, her depth perception was weird.

"What if you'd been carrying the baby?" Marly said. "You've got to watch yourself."

Cynthia floated her that wicked, pitying smile. "Oh, I'll be sure to do that," she said. "I'll be sure to watch where I'm going."

•   •   •

EASTER CAME AT LAST, but spring was still sluggish. The cold was gone, but nothing took its place: no color, no hard dry ground. Jeanette had talked Marly into going to church with her, the sunrise service. It was held every year—despite damp, or ponderous banks of clouds—at a farm belonging to one of the members, up on a knoll. There was a card table with doughnuts and cider, paper napkins anchored with a rock. A friend of Jeanette's came and squeezed her and dabbed a kiss on her cheek. "Aren't we honored," the woman said.

Marly made no effort to smile. She stood hugging her arms—why hadn't she worn more clothes? An edgy, unmoored feeling had been creeping over her for days. In the center of this gathering a pump organ rested, not quite levelly, on an old rug, operated by a girl in a pink dress and bulky overcoat. There were maybe twenty other people, holding mimeographed sheets of lyrics for the two songs. Not hymns, exactly. One was "Working at the Real Work." More of a folk song, Marly thought—it was that kind of church. No one sang very loud. How could you with the mountains leaning over you? After that, people began to speak up, thoughts on spring, on feeling hopeful; even Jeanette offered a few words. Oh, God, Marly thought, don't make me have to do this. Jeanette's hand slid down and felt for hers, and, as it turned out, she was not required to say anything after all.

But the feeling lasted, the sense of being called on. That night, as if in answer, she saw Charles. He was alone, wearing an old flapping trenchcoat, striding under the elms on Jackson Street. A block from Cynthia and Rory's. There was still red in the sky, a fading band showing between the houses.

"What are you *doing?*" she said out the car window. "Don't tell me. I know what you're doing."

"It's not what you think," he said.

But it was. It was exactly that—actually, it was worse. He'd left school without telling a soul. He was living in an old panel truck, which he'd taken to parking in a shallow gravel pit down by the river.

In the weeks following, Marly fell into a new routine—not

babysitting for Rory and Cynthia on her free evenings but taking the baby out in the afternoon, so that Charles could go upstairs and be with Cynthia. Why did she do such a thing? "Can't you at least go somewhere?" she wanted to say, but she kept her mouth shut. Cynthia had a way of forcing you to look into her glass eye when she didn't want to be challenged—it was mesmerizing, disorienting. Marly took the baby and rushed outside, light-headed, in a daze; she refused to be there when Charles arrived. She didn't want to see that flushed, ready-to-burst look on him. But how could they count on where Rory was going to be at any particular hour? Couldn't he just materialize in the doorway, lugging home some grievance? It was stupid, dangerous. Next time, she thought, she'd flat refuse.

But she didn't. She climbed back up to the landing, carrying Cher, whispering into her ear, "Sweet girl, sweet girl." She waited in the hot shade, listening for that shrieky, gulping laughter of Cynthia's, praying they wouldn't still be going at it. If she was lucky, when she nudged open the door again Charles might be sitting on the kitchen table in just his cutoff jeans, with his bony knees pointing out. Sometimes Cynthia's legs would still be twisted in the bedsheets, her breasts flopped out on display.

"You're an angel," Cynthia would say to Marly distantly.

Marly sometimes changed Cher and put her down and left without making eye contact with either of them. She dug at herself later: What do I *want* with these people—who are they to me? But other times it was all friendly and conspiratorial. One afternoon, Charles even looped his sweaty, satisfied arm around Marly's neck, and she let herself fall into his hug and relax there while Cynthia rattled around in the bathroom, ran the water, and threw on clothes, as if this were all a reasonable way to live.

"I'm starving," Charles said. "Cynthia doesn't believe in food. Her icebox is a wasteland." He rubbed his bare stomach and stretched, looking about—where had his shirt gotten to? His other sneaker?

Cynthia came out flat-footed, yawning. "You two better beat it," she said. She looked bored to death with both of them.

On his way out, Charles detoured over by the crib and gave Cher's foot a soft tug. He bounded down the stairs, waiting by the flimsy door at the bottom so he and Marly could step out together. She walked up the alley with him to where he'd left the van, under a tumult of lilacs.

"Excuse the debris," he said, leaning in, clearing the seat of paperbacks, stacking them up his arm. *The Phenomenon of Man*, a couple of books by Buckminster Fuller, a thick, comically austere looking batch of mimeographing called *Means of Adhesion*.

"This stuff looks deadly," Marly said, wedging herself in. There was another sprawl on the floor—catalogs, floppy pamphlets, a bunch of steno pads rubber-banded together.

"Absolutely," Charles said. "Mind-numbing." She caught a whiff of Cynthia as he threw his arm over the seat and backed around.

Days like this—not true summer yet, a break before the June rains—the valley floated in a polleny haze. The sun bore down on her bare, freckled legs. Charles drove to a diner called Stell's, out beyond the viaduct. The way he looked, she could never imagine him *eating*. But he ate and ate—hot sandwiches and fries, another order of fries, lemon pie, and cup after cup of coffee. Away from Cynthia, the rest of him surfaced again, shook off the drowsiness.

"Okay, so what's a yurt? What's so great about domes?" she teased him, steering him into what he knew. It wasn't so hard.

"Got a pen?" he said. She had a blue felt-tip in her shirt

pocket. He filled a pile of napkins with his sketches. Marly sat across from him with her iced tea, paying attention more or less, eerily happy. His father hadn't read him so wrong, she realized.

She interrupted him finally, touching his wrist. "You know you could sleep with me," she said.

Charles laughed outright, his long fingers spread across his lips. Not a cruel laugh—as if the idea were absurd, beyond imagining. No, he had thought about it; he already knew. He looked away, out into the shadow of the awning, with the laugh settling into a soft, distracted smile.

• • •

DID SHE LOVE HIM, was that possible?

Now she was provoked, propelled into thinking. She kicked herself—her idea of the future had been unforgivably lazy, worse even than his. She'd thought only as far as Rory catching them in bed. Being caught, and then what? Some shocking scene out of a movie? Rory had been hitting Cynthia from the beginning, why hadn't that been obvious before? The truck, the tumble on the stairs. Cynthia had a dinged-up quality—always sore, dotted with bruises. She'd just lacquered over it, worked it into her act. And she'd lied to Marly anytime she felt like it—that was clear, too. What talk did they ever have that amounted to anything? Wasn't it all just mocking or bitching or Cynthia wanting favors done?

Marly never came straight home from work anymore. She changed out of her skirt and drove, aimlessly, playing the radio; the local station was dismal, but in the late twilight you could pull in CFUN from Vancouver, or WLS in Chicago. Album cuts, inspiring her to an alert, restless mood. She drove, thumping on the wheel, managing to forget Cynthia for minutes on end.

One evening, she crossed the Old Steel Bridge and bumped off the crumbling blacktop onto a sandy lane that wound through the scrub trees. This is stupid, she thought. I won't find him, and, anyway, what if I do? But right away she spotted the truck. There was a wet, smoky fire going beside it. The double doors in the back had been flung open and Charles was sitting inside, with his legs out on the ground. She walked up close enough to touch him. He didn't look surprised to see her in the slightest. "You smell good," he said.

But how could she—fried meat, ammonia rags? "Tell me what you do out here," she said. "No, don't." She slipped onto his lap and kissed him. She hated her lips: They were chapped and thin as a pencil line. They would never have the deep, fleshy feel of Cynthia's. She tried, instead, to make them busy.

Charles put his hands on her back, under her shirt. "You sure you want to do this?" he asked.

"Shut up," Marly said. She pushed him down on his back and wrapped her legs around one of his. He made the long muscle in his thigh hard, so she could press against it. The backs of his fingers roamed up and down her cheek, gently, or patiently—or was he only bored?

"Get my clothes off," she said. "*Hurry.*"

He had a limp air mattress in there, and a couple of backpacks and a mishmash of picky wool blankets and sleeping bags with exposed zippers—and probably, if she could see, dirty shirts and underwear and food wrappers.

But then they were naked, more or less. Marly scrambled on top. From up there, she could see out through the windshield—a smudge of light still showed at the mouth of the valley. Across the river, the birches glowed and shook. Beneath her, Charles was doing his part, trying to act interested.

"I'm too stringy, aren't I?" Marly said.

"No, no," Charles said. "You're—"

It wasn't the same for him, she knew that—she had none of Cynthia's slummy danger. But so be it. "Are you having any fun?" she said. "Tell me."

He gave a pleasant sound. It might have been *uh-huh*.

"*I* am," Marly said. It wasn't sublime, nothing like that. It didn't make her crazy and greedy. Even so, it was sweet work. She wanted to do it forever. She felt like laughing, and then went ahead and let the laugh come out.

Charles raised his hips suddenly, one huge poke, and Marly's head cracked on the dome light—they could both hear it splinter in the dark.

"Oh, Jesus," Charles said. "Jesus, I'm sorry."

He rolled her over. She felt his fingers gingerly inspecting her scalp, felt them slide on blood.

"*Wait*," he said. He rummaged under the front seat, located a flashlight, and smacked it until it offered a coppery light. He shot it first at the ceiling—a jagged, diamond-shaped piece of plastic dangled from the fixture. He made Marly sit up, facing away from him.

There was a surprising amount of blood. He dug a bandanna from his pack, folded it, and pressed it down on the cut.

"God, you must be freezing," he said in a minute. He tried to maneuver one of the loose sleeping bags around her without taking his fingers from her head.

He kept her that way awhile longer. "I don't know," he said finally. "Doesn't seem like it wants to stop. You know, your head's all full of little capillaries."

Marly's chest was goose-bumped, her limbs tingling, numb-feeling.

"You're going to have to get this stitched up," Charles said.

God, just imagine, Marly thought.

Charles shifted around to where he could see her. "We can

think up some story," he said, perfectly calm. He took her hand and guided her fingertips onto the cloth pad, then wriggled into his pants.

"You didn't even—" she said.

"What?"

"You know."

Charles slid out the back. "Keep the pressure on that," he said. "Okay?"

Then she was under the excruciating glare of the examining room, her arm stuck with a tetanus shot, a patch of hair shaved, and eight stitches laced into her scalp. The doctor was short and gruff, and unimpressed with the fumbling lie she'd offered. Charles waited in the hallway, in a turquoise chair. His head was resting on his fists—she stole looks at him through the examining room's open door. She tried to say something, but the doctor shushed her. "Don't get this wet," he said. "And no bending over. Bend with the knees." He demonstrated, had difficulty hauling himself up, and seemed to blame Marly.

She looked for Charles again. His chair was empty.

Released, she hurried out under the canopy. The three red lights of the radio tower blinked in the distance. There was the momentary, sickening smell of the hospital incinerator. Charles scuffed up behind her in the shadows. "I couldn't stand it, watching you in there," he said.

"I have to get my car," Marly said, but the thought of that almost brought her to tears, all that extra horsing around.

"You shouldn't drive," he said.

"I'm *okay.*"

"Then I'll follow you."

He was quiet all the way back to the river. She kept to her side of the seat, her hands flat on the vinyl. She was full of apology—what for, though? The sky was clear and starry, but a wind had kicked up. Thistles were knocking about in the borrow pits; streamers of torn plastic whipped from the wire fences.

Jeanette called out when Marly let herself in at last, but her voice was startled and sleepy.

"It's only me," Marly said, and went into the bathroom. She shook out a handful of Anacin, tucked all but three back, sat on the edge of the tub and swallowed them down. There was a little blood on her arm, already flaky, where Charles had held her. She went to her bedroom, let the shirt fall to the floor, positive that the moment she lay down her exhaustion would disappear and leave her prickling with thoughts.

She woke later, still in her camisole and jeans. Her heart was hammering. It wasn't yet morning, but the sky was a faint charcoal. The wind was louder, thrashing the trees, sending branches scraping down the tin roof. A loose wire slapped against the clapboards. She had to go talk to him again. Too much was floating, undeclared.

She got up and listened outside Jeanette's room, certain that the wind had disturbed her, too. She edged the door open. Jeanette was curled in a sliver of the king-size bed, wound up in the covers, the rest of the bed a chaos of books and papers. The curtains swayed and jiggled away from the sash, but Jeanette didn't budge. Her breathing came in deep, abrupt sighs. After a moment, Marly backed out.

A truck from the Electric Co-op was the only thing on the road. Its yellow light beat in her mirror, receding finally. She swerved down onto the dirt, banged up to the opening of the gravel pit, and flipped off her lights before they showed. The van was there, parked in a puddle of leaves. The fire was out—doused, kicked apart. She stepped past it and walked straight to the back doors and yanked them open. It took her a second, speaking sharply into the dim interior and then feeling about with her hand, to realize nobody was there.

He was down at the edge of the water, his legs over the embankment. The river poured by, churned up with runoff. He'd wrapped himself in a flannel shirt and canvas jacket. Been up all night, she guessed. He had a huddled look—cold, not elegant for a change, in no way enigmatic. She wanted to run and squeeze herself against his back. At the same time, she felt an extraordinary patience; it flooded into her limbs, giving them a graceful and weighted feeling. Hours before, hurrying out of the truck—exhausted, mortified—she'd been hit by the absurd intuition that all their lives depended on her now, even Cher's. By daylight, the momentousness of the night before had washed off, the nervous glitter. It was just true, as Jeanette would say, a fact she'd have to live with.

She held her hair down against the wind and walked ahead, calling out. She had to get right up next to him before his head shot around.

She started to bend over, caught herself, and then squatted as the doctor had instructed. "This is one ridiculous life," she said.

She rubbed her hand on his pant leg and waited until he was looking straight at her.

"Don't go up there anymore," she said finally.

He wouldn't want to talk about this, she knew. He'd prefer to stare at the edge of the sky where a rosy light was appearing.

"Look, I mean it. Don't go up there. That's over. Promise me."

"I can't promise you."

"No, but you *can*," she said.

She let that sink in, as she sat back, warming her fingers under her arms. Out on the river, a boat swept out of the cutbank's shadow—a varnished canvas hull with two figures, one at the motor, the other up front keeping the prow down.

A red setter stood between them, barking noiselessly at the current. Marly watched until they could no longer be seen. On the far shore, the aspens bent and tossed. Even in this first light, the new leaves had that shocking, liquid green. Like parrot feathers, Marly thought. She gave his hand a quick kiss. In a moment, it would occur to him what she was asking. They were joined, they were allies—it was awkward to have to say it like that, she had to admit, but in this she wasn't wrong.

PERFECTION

She waited where she could see the highway, where she could see the lights coming.

Did you have the motor running?

She had on the black Fido Dido shirt and a blue jean jacket. It was chilly—it was October, after all—but she ran the engine for only a minute or two and shut it off, the radio with it. Inexplicably, the radio was making her jumpy.

Why parked there, not down in the high school lot? Wouldn't that be customary?

I told you, the bus was going to drop him off there.

The boy, Storm?

Yes. Storm.

She sat watching the yellow blinker, sagging on its cable, rolling with the wind. Across the street was the Varner Bar, sheeted in red-brick tarpaper. Around the corner, a grocery nobody went to and the post office and half a street of sad-fronted houses. Behind her the moon was coasting past the grain tanks.

I'm not clear on why you were meeting Storm there.

Does that have to be part of this? I just was, okay?

So the bus with the Varner players was coming back from Cobolt and you were waiting there and you were alone?

Uh-huh.

She watched the traffic. Once in a while somebody U-turned and stuffed a letter in the box, but mainly it was cars and pickups sailing straight through, slowing from seventy-five to maybe sixty for the light. A few people drifted in and out of the bar. Hardly anybody she recognized.

Shelley, when did you first see Mr. Poe?

She was thinking ten more cars, then it will be the bus. Then ten more. Of course, because the game had gone into overtime, which she couldn't know yet. She was invisible, a dark car sitting in the dark, with a girl inside singing invisibly and thinking nothing will spoil this perfect perfect night.

Her father had won a trip to Oahu—he and her step-mother, Janet, had flown from Great Falls on Wednesday. Her father sold crop insurance, set up IRAs, juggled debt for the ranchers. What he'd won, actually, was a seat at a company seminar, a write-off. He packed along his golf clubs. Janet took a load of clingy evening wear that showed how long-waisted she was, like pulled taffy. I'd just as soon you didn't stay here alone, he said. That's so ludicrous, Shelley said. Then Janet was all hurt. I wished I knew what makes you treat your father like you do, etc., etc. This isn't a slam against you, honey, her father said. I asked your aunt to stay over, that's all. Common sense. Okay? Shelley contemplated a hard sulk, but abruptly changed her mind. Marta was her mother's sister and it would not be a disaster. Marta would come every night but Friday. Friday, Shelley would take the car to the game in Cobolt and afterward she and Stace would stay at Mary Jo's. Except not actually. That was the one element that bothered her, deceiving Marta. But it was minor. It fluttered away when you weighed it against Storm.

So. But she didn't go to the game. She went straight from school home and sat in the tub, swirling with oil, the blaster blasting, then changed the sheets, installing the blue ones, which would make Storm's smooth dark body look even smoother and darker. She put about fifteen candles on the table by the bed. She'd been sleeping with Storm since early summer. Well, not sleeping. Maybe she'd dozed a little with his arm going numb under her, but this was the whole expanse of night, and in her own bed, where he belonged, *finally*. When she woke Saturday he'd be there, and weird as that would be, it was also the point, wasn't it? So she'd put him on the bus and said, Keep your mind on the game, now, huh? and squashed her breast against his arm, making his face flush as it smiled. The first time would last as long as a milkshake, but the next would be a thing of perfection, long-drawn-out and lush. After that she thought she would like to do it in the shower. The hot water lasted approximately fourteen minutes if nobody'd been using it. Then she went and wrote a fake 800 number on a pad tilted against the clock radio so Storm could see it. When he asked, she'd laugh, That? That's the *Guinness Book*!

Finally the bus grinds to a stop and the door sighs open and there's Storm carrying his duffel. He seems tired, his back slightly off-line, the bag clunky, dragging. He looks up, searching for her, but he's on automatic pilot. When he slides in beside her she sees blood crusted in the corner of his mouth. It's nothing, he says, but half his front tooth is gone, snapped off on the diagonal, leaving a sharp edge. Instinctively, she kisses it, not hard enough to hurt. I blew it, he says. Actually, his kick from the twenty-two sent them into overtime in the first place. He was lifted off his feet, his helmet slapped and butted, and for that moment felt completely aligned, and without thinking of her specifically knew himself to be endowed with a sweet safe reserve of time just ahead. But then after a fumble in the OT he set up from the eighteen, a chip shot, and shanked it right, where it landed out in the shadows of the running track, chased after by grade school boys. And two plays later, with a Cobolt running back en route to the far goal line, a toe cleat shot through his mask and the tooth was gone, swallowed in a knot of blood and mucus. So he says, I blew it, and means, obscurely, more than the kick. It's as if he's betrayed not the team but the gift of weightlessness.

She listens, touching him, but her thoughts are already torn.

•   •   •

DID YOU GET OUT *of the car and go over to Mr. Poe?*
I didn't, no.
You had no idea how badly he was hurt, then?
I knew he was hurt.
But you didn't do anything.
I, no—
She broke herself of counting cars and watched the window of the Varner Bar, where a Silver Bullet sign was blinking slightly faster than the yellow light over the intersection. They'd synchronize for a second, then spike off. For the hell of it, she clicked on the car flashers, then caught herself. *Jesus, Shelley, chill.* She rolled the windows down halfway, felt the cold air on her ear. She was looking straight at the front of the bar when the door opened, the inner door, then the thin screen door. A man was tossed outside. There was a strip of sidewalk, a few lengths of freestanding cement curb,

once yellow, and enough room between there and the high-way for a truck to park, but the space was vacant, allowing her to see.

Describe what you mean when you say "tossed."

He wasn't totally lifted in the air. I mean his feet were on the ground, dragging, but he wasn't in control. The man who threw him out was pretty big—he had on a plaid shirt and I think a baseball hat. The man, Mr. Poe, I think he hit on the back of his head.

So you wouldn't say he fell down.

I'd say the man in the plaid shirt kind of threw him and he landed on his head, back here. She touched her hair, where it was bristled at the base of her skull. That night her hair had still been long, remnant of a shoddy summer perm.

And that's how he hit the curbing?

No. It was out on the tar part, where it was kind of sandy.

He didn't hit on the curbing?

No. Unh-uh.

All right. Now when was the first time you saw Mr. Andrus?

Okay, just after Mr. Poe went down, he tried to get up. He got up on his knees, his back sort of arched like a cat's, then he tried to get up the rest of the way, one of his arms was swinging out to the side, kind of pushing at the air. He looked completely out of it. He was about two-thirds up onto his feet when the door opened again. Wayne came straight out, like he was starting to sprint, and he hit Mr. Poe in the face, straight on. Here. She touched herself again, her hand covering her nose and mouth and chin.

I heard it inside the car.

She stopped talking. How do you make them hear?

It was like he'd been hit with the end of a fence post or a brick or something. But he didn't even see it. He was com-

pletely uncovered—just exposed. *Then everything went out of him, before he even hit the ground again.*

What did Mr. Andrus do?

Went back inside. Then he came out again and he kind of just looked over his shoulder at the ground where the man was and went around the corner and over by the post office and got in his truck and drove off.

Which way?

Into town.

Then what?

Nothing. I watched him and he didn't move and nobody else came out. Right after that the team bus came.

Did the boy—Storm—did he see Mr. Andrus?

I just said, Storm got there after Mr. Andrus drove off.

Did he see Mr. Poe?

• • •

SHE SAID, Look, and Storm looked and said, Some drunk. She told him about it, but Storm didn't want to look. I think he's dead, she said. Storm said, He's too drunk to be dead. As if that meant something.

Do you know Mr. Andrus?

Enough to recognize him, sure.

How is that?

He took my sister out for a while, Karen. Do we need to talk about that?

What I'm getting at, Shelley, you're absolutely certain it was Mr. Andrus you saw?

Uh-huh.

No doubts of any kind?

No, sir.

Plus she recognized the truck. A turquoise door on a red pickup.

After graduation Karen cashiered a year for Stedje's, then shocked everybody by enlisting in the navy—all but Shelley, who saw what her sister was really up to: testing whether she could live in Varner the rest of her life. She had this double edge. She could do what she wanted, go on larks. It didn't matter, she'd be gone soon, no history sticking to her. But she had a hard vigilance, too, because any act, any attachment might be the one thing that locked her in, nailed her down. She went out with some of the older boys, Wayne being one of them, tall and slick-cheeked, but wasn't his face smirky, restless? Nothing I'd trust this flesh with, Karen said, which Shelley remembered because she'd felt herself flinch at the word *flesh* used like that: soft white meat put in someone else's hands. God, you're easy to shock, Karen said. No, I'm not, Shelley tried to say. Anyway, the Karen and Wayne business amounted to nothing, one trip to the steak place in Cobolt and a few aimless excursions in his truck with the swimming-pool-colored door. But Wayne and her father seemed to hit it off. Wayne came over a few Saturdays that summer and helped him salvage bricks from the old Varner Implement building. So before the night outside the Varner Bar, this was her last picture of Wayne: the two of them standing in the hot sun at the end of the flatbed trailer, bricks and hammers in their hands, her father sweating through his shirt, giving Wayne a lesson in how to knock off the mortar without busting the old bricks. They are still out there, the bricks, if anyone's curious, on pallets behind the garage.

●   ●   ●

SHE WANTED TO BE IN THE MOOD STILL. Storm had showered, but even so he smelled like Icy Hot. She lit the candles. He was acting shy suddenly, perched on the edge of the bed, palms together between his knees—he looked like he was sitting in a waiting room. She was telling herself, I'm in control of this. I can make this work. She took her shirt off. Storm was extremely fond of her breasts. She'd managed to log a few hours on the sun porch the second week of September, dry hot Indian summer weather. Her nipples were like mahogany, a little wide but perfectly round, as if drawn with a compass. There was a little wispy hair, which she didn't know what to do about, but it was at least blond, unlike Karen's. Storm stroked her with the backs of his fingers, lifted her breast, let the weight settle in his hand, brought his mouth down. I don't believe you, he said, and that was part of the scenario, pleasing him inordinately, making him just short of speechless with pleasure. Baby, she said. But he said, Don't call me that, okay, Shell? It makes me feel funny. What can I call you? I want to call you something. I don't know, he said.

Then he said, Is there anything to drink, and it turned out there was a bottle of Early Times in the cupboard, also a bottle of Gordon's gin, but the gin was still sealed, so Storm drank the other, mixed with Diet Pepsi. Shelley had a little dope (wadded into the toe of one of her ancient confirmation shoes) but the last time she'd smoked, it had given her the spins, making her think something was wrong with it. And Storm wasn't into it, anyway. He wouldn't chastise, he'd say, Go ahead if you want to. But all in all, she thought, no, not tonight.

Storm lay back and took it easy, letting her ride. She stole a look at herself in the dresser mirror, saw the points of her elbows shining as she tried to muss her hair, but something was too comical about it to be exciting. She did not, literally, think of the Poe boy again until she slid down and tried to kiss Storm a moment later. The upper lip had swollen hard and shiny. The tooth was killing him. She looked down at him and saw the fist ramming into that other face and revulsion splashed through her.

I'm sorry, Storm was saying. She could tell he couldn't concentrate. He was hard as pipe but couldn't come. She said, Baby, then, Oh sorry, Storm, and they went a little while longer before Storm got up and they went into the bathroom and he took about six Advils. Pretty soon he was asleep. Even asleep a crease ran between his eyebrows. She watched a trapezoid of mirror light waver across the ceiling. There was a clammy sheen on Storm's skin. Nestling, shifting—she couldn't find any way to lie against him comfortably.

In her dream she and Karen were straddling the peak of a barn roof, their heels digging into the shakes. It was before dawn, dewy, the wind just kicking up. Karen had a clipboard with sheets of green paper—a list apparently, under the words Secret Shame. In her other hand was a huge aluminum flashlight, the kind that needs about ten batteries. She was pointing at houses, reading from the list. Mrs. Stedje is a luna moth, she said, flicking her tongue, as if this was a juicy revelation. Then the shakes under Shelley broke loose, like avocado leaves, and she was sliding down the roof on her back, head first. *Dreams are moronic,* she wakes thinking, sorting it out. They're reading *The Secret Sharer* in Honors English; it's Janet who's fixated on moths, who's scared they'll breed in her clothes closet and ravage everything; Karen is long gone, on the other side of the world. Only the two fattest candles are still going—there's an alluvium of stinky red wax stuck to her contacts case. It's beginning to be light out. Storm is gone. She hopes, briefly, that he is merely in the bathroom, but when she pads in there she finds no one. There's a faint smell of vomit, but also Ajax. The sink and the floor are shiny, still slightly wet.

•　　•　　•

THE NEXT NIGHT MARTA CAME, bringing Cracker Jack and a video, a mystery with a couple of raunchy sex scenes—

she figured Marta chose it to declare which side of the fence she was on. There was an apartment, silver-blue light from a TV shining on a man's buttocks. Oooh, moon over Manhattan, Marta giggled. Shelley laughed, the first time in twenty-four hours. Marta rolled her eyes. She was still young, in her thirties, had a nice little figure, Shelley's mother always said. She and Janet didn't get along well. They kept up the decorum, but Marta considered Janet drab and worry-raddled, believing Shelley's father jumped too soon, spellbound by desperation.

I'm dying, Marta said, hitting the pause. Shelley's father was a no-smoke-in-this-house zealot. Shelley slipped on her jacket and went out on the back steps with her aunt. Last night's wind had all but gone, and there was a smell in the air, not woodstoves yet, more like wet bark or mushrooms, obliterated a moment later by Marta's lighter.

Used to call these fags, she said. Weird world, huh? So how was it at Mary Jo's?

Storm broke his front tooth, she said, skirting the lie.

Bummer, Marta said. He had such a sweet smile. But he'll get it fixed, won't he?

Shelley nodded. She hugged the jacket around herself and looked around at the sagging skyline. When she looked back at Marta, she saw Marta knew.

Everything okay? Marta asked.

Not especially, she said. She was shaking.

Marta dipped onto one knee and stabbed her cigarette into the geranium pot. We don't have to stand out here like fools, she said, putting her hand on Shelley, leading her back inside.

But she couldn't get warm. All the blood had flooded her chest and face, leaving her limbs suddenly achy with cold. Her jaw couldn't stop chattering. Her heart stuttered. Something's wrong with me, she started to say, I'm having some kind of—

Here, sit, Marta said, touching her, trying to ease her down into the kitchen chair.

But everything was firing at once. No, I can't, I—

Marta's fingers clamped on her, Marta's smell, her hair poured over her. *Shelley!* Breathe out now, honey. All the way, c'mon.

I—

Shh. It's okay, it goes away. Breathe now.

• • •

MONDAY, Tuesday, Wednesday. A fine misting rain falling. She walked to school with her books in a plastic bag. The sky was about six feet overhead, the color of concrete blocks. Storm had an aluminum tooth. Nothing had changed between them, except something had. She sat in class, hearing pages turn, hearing the juices in people's stomachs. *At this breathless pause at the threshold of a long passage we seemed to be measuring our fitness for a long and arduous enterprise,* she read.

Shelley? Shelley?

She looked up sharply. Nobody was looking at her, nobody calling.

The morning evaporated. She skipped lunch. Later, she walked to the practice field, stood out of sight under the bleachers, watching Storm kick ball after ball. Devoid of game, his foot made an enormous hollow smack. He hit ten straight, then missed one, missed again, and another. He stood with his hands on his knees, breathing hard, staring at the cleat-shredded grass.

• • •

THIS IS WHAT SIFTED DOWN to her regarding Richard Poe. He was a slitty-eyed pudgy boy of twenty-three, an af-

ternoon drinker, a pain in the ass. His father was dead. He'd
moved into Varner his senior year and lived with his mother.
No one called him anything but Richard. He hassled people
to arm wrestle, but he had tiny wrists and never won. When
he was semisober, which was most of the time, he was an avid
conspiracist, a quoter of facts and figures from obscure pamphlets. Outright drunk, he got in people's faces, shoved a little, took offense.

But never exactly hurt anybody.

After she and Storm drove away that night, a couple left
the Varner Bar and found Poe still there, knees drawn up to
his chest. The bartender (the man in the plaid shirt) called for
the EMTs. They found a fluttery pulse. They cleared his
mouth, crowded over him with an oxygen unit. It was not
until ten to twelve that the ambulance took him. An hour
later he was on the Mercy Flight to Great Falls, where he died
about six o'clock.

She waited for something to happen.

In Thursday's paper: *Richard Mark Poe, born in Dickinson,
North Dakota, on March 6, 1967 . . . preceded in death*, etc.,
etc. *Cremation under the direction of Barber and Barber*.
Nothing about a service.

Nothing anywhere about Wayne Andrus.

She told Janet she had to get stockings and drove to the
Safeway, but kept going, cutting over to Wyoming, following it out of city limits. She passed the slough, leached al-
kali and busted-open cattails, then the wire gates of the
cement company. Directly across was a small house with
pressed board siding, pale blue. One old cottonwood tow-
ered over it. A branch had come down and lay across the
roof, the dead leaves bristling in the wind. The mailbox said
A. Poe. A. for Alvina. Shelley sat in the car, studying the
house, running the heater. There was one light burning,

back in the kitchen. A few minutes later, it went out.

She looked down at her Swatch. Five to eight.

Five to eight and the house was pitch-dark.

So where are the stockings? Janet asked when she walked in.

All out of nude, she said.

Janet glowered at her.

You can go down and look if you don't believe me, Shelley said. You can just drive down there and fucking look for yourself.

· · ·

YOU'RE AWARE *that your story conflicts with what other people have told us?*

I guess, I don't know. It's what happened.

Now don't misunderstand me, Shelley, I have to ask this. Is there any other reason to be telling us this? You don't have anything against Mr. Andrus, or the family—?

I told you. I don't know him well enough to have anything against him.

Have you discussed this with anyone?

No.

Not your folks, not Storm?

No.

Three items: The airline had lost her father's golf clubs— that was first. He slammed down the kitchen phone for the half-dozenth time. "Those incompetent sons of bitches." Second: Lisa, his secretary, had quit, apparently, simply walked out at lunchtime that Friday he was in Hawaii, never locked up or anything. In her absence, the Mr. Coffee had shorted out, filling the back room with a strident chemical smoke—if the man in the Automobile Club office next door hadn't smelled it through the washroom vent, the whole place would've gone up. Her father spent the rest of the week in the living room, with folders sprawled across three green-topped card tables. His sunburn was peeling. Tell me why any of this surprises me, he said. And third: Though they both acted glad to see her (they'd bought her a rayon blouse with red and green macaws), told her Oahu was a stunner, etc., etc., some grudge, some *seed*, had embedded itself between her father and Janet, and Janet was of course too insecure to take that on, and started in on Shelley instead.

I'm not blind, she said. I can tell something's up with you. I don't expect you to like me, Shelley. But I hate when things go on behind my back.

That must be an awful feeling, Shelley said, not biting, not biting.

Was there any real question about *discussing this with anyone*? Not really.

Another weekend. Saturday was a day game at home. She trooped into the seniors' section with Stace and Mary Jo. The sky was broken now, the light cold and white. Afterward, pizza. Storm was high with the win, twisting in the booth, looking everywhere at once, the black hair falling in his face.

Out by the cars, she asked him, Could we just drive?

There's a party at Koski's, he said.

Maybe you should go to it.

You don't want to go?

I told you what I wanted, she said.

Storm looked at the other cars starting to pull away into traffic.

I'm freezing, she said.

He opened his jacket and tried to close it around both of them but there wasn't enough of it.

Go to Koski's, she said.

You make things impossible, Storm said. He backed away from her. I didn't mean that like it sounded, he said.

She put her fingers through his belt loops and drew against him again.

• • •

THE ONE THING SHE HADN'T TOLD: After Wayne recoiled from the hit, his arm drawn back but the fist still intact, as if his hand would be forever that one thing, he didn't just turn and go into the bar the way she said, but looked around to see what kind of audience he might have. His eyes scanned the empty highway, then froze briefly on the old Impala, which he knew he knew. Did her hair show in the window, that ugly falling-down perm? His chest heaved. Then she saw his chin lift, saw the moon had drawn his attention, had captivated him.

All this gesture meant to her, at the time, was that he was distracted from her, from running over and grinning down into the car. Now it made a picture she couldn't shake from her mind, a man standing with the moon on his face, another man curled at his feet. It made no difference to the moon what it looked at, she thought.

• • •

I'M BOTHERED by why you waited so long to tell us—you know what I'm saying, Shelley? Is there some particular reason?

There's a reason for everything. No, she didn't say that.

It took her three more nights, scattered over a week, before she got out of the car. The wind was ragging at her hair. The bell made a single flat plonk and she had to hit it over and over.

Mrs. Poe's face suddenly filled the square glass.

Shelley realized she knew her. She was one of the cafeteria women. Ordinarily, her face was filmy red from the steam trays, and her hair stuffed in a net. She was the one who sometimes touched people on the wrist and said, Don't take it if you're not going to eat it.

She thought, Now what am I supposed to do? But the woman opened the door, made way for her, arms folded, incapable of surprise.

The house smelled like vinegar. A wall heater glowed in the front room. Under each window stood a TV table full of African violets. Against the wall was an electric piano on spindly legs, a few sheets of music slumped on the rack.

The woman pointed and Shelley sat.

Mrs. Poe stayed on her feet. She was wearing sweat clothes with padded shoulders, a barrel-chested woman, the hair unpinned now, falling straight, ash-blond with heavy bangs.

That's all of them, she told Shelley. Her husband. Her daughter, Rochelle. Richard.

From the kitchen came the clicking of a dog's nails, the rattle of a chain on a metal dish.

Richard found his sister, Mrs. Poe said. She was dead in her crib. This was when we were still living down in Dickinson and his father was working for Peavey's. It was a little room with yellow shades—we had to move Richard out of it after Rochelle was born because it was the only quiet place. It was a nice room for a girl, but Richard still liked it and I sometimes let him sit in there while his sister had her nap. I was hanging up sheets in back. There was always a wind. He came tearing outside, running so hard his arms were going like windmills. I watched him head down behind the elevators— a pack of cats lived down there, feeding off the mice. They were wild, mangy things, and I'd forbidden him to go anywhere near there. What on earth! I thought. What in heaven's name? Then, you see, I forgot all about him. It was dark before we sent somebody down there to find him.

Shelley's face was frozen, stricken. Mrs. Poe was standing over her saying, It's all right. You can hear this, nothing's a secret anymore, and kept on, tugging gently at the flesh of her cheek.

Richard had a counselor in school who said a thing like that would mark him, but I don't know. I don't know what it did to him. He might have been the way he was anyway. Who's to say? You can find a reason for anything, reasons are nothing, reasons are common as flies.

Shelley felt a drop of cold sweat slide down under her armpit.

Tell me the reason for falling down against a curb, Mrs. Poe said. She had pulled a Kleenex from the sleeve of the sweat suit, held it for a moment like a wilted blossom.

•   •   •

SHE DROVE SLOWLY PAST STORM'S, looking at the configuration of lights. It was a plain stucco house, battened down for the night. She kept going, went up Commerce, Varner's three-block main drag, and nosed the car up to the pay phone.

She leaned in behind the glass. Can you get out? she asked.

A catch in his voice, a hand smothering the receiver.

Storm, I need to see you.

Give me a few minutes, he said.

No, it's got to be right now. Hurry. I mean it.

She sat in the car waiting for him. The moon had gone from quarter to nothing and back again. It dodged through broken clouds, hammering the edges silver. She half-expected to see Wayne Andrus's truck cruise by now, as if this was all a movie. She dug a mint out of her jacket pocket. A highway patrol cut through the Town Pump and spun off without looking at her. After that, except for the whanging of a tin sign, it was quiet.

She was parked where she could see Storm come.

She'd watch how he came toward her, how his face behaved at the sight of hers. What is it that couldn't wait? he'd ask, sliding in, a little breathless, his hands cold and dry. I just need you, she would tell him. Well, I'm here, he'd say. No, don't say it like that, she'd say. I've got to have more than that, Storm. Then it would be up to him to say whatever he had to say. It would have to be good and strong, it would need to carry all the weight in the world.

LIGHTNING

"I van, he won't do it," Gretchen said from the daybed. "Believe me, he won't. He's going to let the damn place freeze. You go on up there. While he's gone."

Now that she was like this—plainly crippled, no longer solely identifiable as his mother—Ivan didn't feel the fight so much, the natural urge to dig his feet in. Ivan's wife, Phoebe, sat in the rocker by the east window, one of her fingers stuck in the massive library book she'd been reading to Gretchen. She straightened her neck and gave him a look: *Do what she's asking. How much can that hurt?*

It was mid-November. Ivan and Phoebe had been at the ranch a week. No one had begged them to come, but they'd come anyway—Phoebe had talked to Gretchen on the phone, and gotten the sense, she told Ivan, that things were *this close* to flying apart. So they'd driven up, and were quartered in the log-walled room off the porch—it smelled of chinking and forgotten chenille and a desiccated Airwick hanging from the curtain rod. Ivan had been rising in the sharp cold each morning and going out to work alongside his father. The tools felt remote in his hands. *What am I doing here?* he kept thinking—open to evidence that his father was gratified by his company. But Perry didn't oblige. A film, a gray mood, had settled on everything. This had been the year of the fires, dry smoky winds, two thin cuttings of hay. A few dozen Angus dotted the middle pasture, as animated as glacial till. His father had sold the herd down, Ivan saw—there'd be scarcely fifty calves in the spring.

Perry had been cooking the meals himself, and then he'd hired a woman from up the road to come in, a Mrs. Ankli whom Ivan distantly remembered, but this arrangement had barely lasted a month. Now Phoebe had taken over the kitchen. "I'm sorry all this is getting dumped on you," Ivan said. Phoebe shrugged it off. She threw on sweats, grabbed her hair back in a ponytail, swamped out the worst of it, chewing sunflower seeds, giving off bursts of tuneless humming. After lunch she tended Gretchen in the bathroom, guided her into the dayroom, fixed the flotilla of pillows. Gretchen had lost interest in the stacks of novels spilling from the shelves. "All I want is true stuff," she demanded. Phoebe drove to town the second afternoon, returned with boxes of groceries and a book called *Shackleton*. Gretchen inspected it and lay back. Heroism in the Antarctic, feats of lunatic endurance—it would do. She listened fiercely, not hectoring in the old way. She stared out past the blowing yard, past the fences. Across the river the lodgepole rose up, green-black and prickly, disappearing into the river.

Which thought had led her back to John Andrew? Ivan wondered from the doorway—he'd been stopped, on his way outside, by the cadences of Phoebe's reading voice.

Gretchen's eyes bore into him. She pressed him again, "Take care of it, Ivan."

So Ivan took Perry's Jeep up to the hill cabin, banging over the ruts and shale. The Jeep, too, had deteriorated. The gas pedal had been replaced by a timber nail that caught in his boot sole. The roof crinkled, lacquered over with duct tape. Ivan had watched the day go from pearly to raw; a sleeting wind whipped at the grass. The one wiper made a wan, jiggling pass across the windshield. No one, Ivan guessed—least of all, Perry—had gone near the hill cabin since Ivan's brother, John Andrew, had forsaken it. Gretchen (she'd explained to Phoebe, but never directly to Ivan) had been the only witness to his leaving. She'd been awake one night in July, late, watching the northern lights while Perry snored and twisted the bedclothes. Sleep came flukily, grudgingly— she was stir-crazy, only her thoughts fatigued. So she'd seen John Andrew's truck barrel down from the hill cabin, headlights out, a denser patch of dark careening across the curve of damp lawn, clipping a corner post without stopping—and only a tap of the brake lights at the cattle guard. "That was it," she'd told Phoebe. "That was his grand farewell. Not so much as a horn toot."

John Andrew's own family—Gala and their two girls— had departed early in May, as the greasy buds of the cottonwoods were finally snapping open, the low spots in the hayfields drying and spiking green. After that, the hill cabin became a hermitage, a welter of bad spirits. Ivan knew that in Perry's world you let a grown man alone with his hurt. He would have stayed away, electing to wait for John Andrew down at the main house each morning, then taking in the puffy face, the jerky drifting eyes, and saying no more than, "You ought to not be hitting it so hard, John." *Weren't they a pair*, Ivan thought. But Perry would shun the place itself, as well, Ivan knew. They'd left a taint on it, Gala and John Andrew.

Ivan nudged through the back door and regarded his brother's leavings. A congealed rancid smell rose off the shredded paper trash fouling the linoleum. A windowpane was smashed out above the sink; porkies had climbed the woodpile and scraped through the hole, ransacked the counters, chewed the rubber stripping off the icebox door—it hung open, the bulb blackened.

On the Hide-A-Bed in the front room lay a sleeping bag, shucked inside out—a child's bag, grimy flannel depicting pheasants and hunters. The bedroom door was pocked with boot-heel-shaped gouges. Ivan toed it open, thinking, *Here will be the mother lode,* but the room was empty and unremarkable, except for dents in the carpet where bureau and bedposts had rested, and a scattering of thin cloth strips. Kneeling, Ivan found these to be the scissored remnants of a summer dress. He should run a stream of gasoline through these rooms, he thought. He should stand out in the crushed shale and feel the front of his clothes bake.

Wouldn't a little joyful noise cut loose in his soul then?

But why be that way? You don't hate John Andrew, he reminded himself—actually it was Phoebe he heard. He drew a breath. He pulled the gloves from his vest pocket, thrust his hands in, wiggled down into the crawl space and crawled. He got Vise-Grips on the valve and shut the water off. Upstairs again, he bled the pipes, filled the toilet tank and traps with Zerex. He taped a square of masonite over the sink window, swept the miscellany into a box and carried it outside, dragged the dead fir limbs from the yard, and, bending, blowing, made a fire of that much.

Standing over it, the black smoke batted by the wind, he thought, *If a story can ruin you, can a story save you?*

His brother's unwound from this exact spot, this one chunk of sanctified earth: a grassy bench along the northwestern fence line, where Perry had gone as a ten-year-old to rain stones down on a bend in the West Fork, where he escaped to as a young married buck, so he could smoke and ruminate and still be within eyeshot of the clamorous, red-roofed house down among the cottonwood. Perry would never have explained this in straight language. But had he not led John Andrew and his bride Gala up here one day in April, pointed out the white-flagged stakes driven into the soft grass, had he not announced that he'd decided to build them a place of their own and this was where? Ivan could see Gala drinking in this news, sparkling—she would touch Perry on his bare forearm, lightly, offering surprise, though she wouldn't be surprised, because all things flowed to Gala. And John Andrew would have his usual nothing to say, his big square face projecting a bashful, manly satisfaction—Perry's number-one son caught in a shower of blessings.

In decent weather, you could see it all from here. Zigzagging, shaped like a child's drawing of lightning, Gretchen had once observed. (Like *which* child's? Ivan wondered.) It was river and foothills and barefaced mountain on one side, road and government land on the other. Four old skinny homesteads wired together by Ivan's grandfather, worked since the 1950s by Perry and a succession of hands, men like Arch McPheeter—stocky, grousing old Albertan, dead of a stroke long ago now—then by the team of Perry and John Andrew, with various McKee and Santa boys at branding and haying. But the lower piece, sometimes called The Point—where the hypothetical lightning would come scorching down, a sweet cache of twenty-odd acres, out of the wind, thick with red willow and a few old cedars—had become, lately, the property of an orthodontist from Buena Vista, California. He'd strung electric fence around it, erected an unseemly stone and timber gate at the road, hung a sign reading El Rancho Suzette in corny wood-burnt script. Yet no one had consulted Ivan about this transaction. No one had explained why his father would suddenly divest himself of this parcel. Ivan had simply gone to the mail and discovered a check with a note from Perry stapled to it: *This is your part of what I got for the lower piece. I don't care what you do with it. P. W. C.*

In a proper world, Perry and Gretchen would have retired to the hill cabin, settling into what Perry called "his dotage," which only meant he would sleep an hour later and pretend to take orders from John Andrew. Gretchen would spoil her granddaughters at the Sperry Mall, now and then, and otherwise retreat to the cabin's sliver of loft and read herself into a state of grace. She'd be Perry's college girl again, his unexpected treasure. John Andrew and family, meantime, would assume the main house. Gala would insinuate her ownership, gradually, like a medicine time-released into the bloodstream—first the filigreed curtains would go; one by one, new avocado appliances would appear; Gretchen's words of wisdom *(If you want to cry, go in the bathroom and run the water. —E. Roosevelt)* would vanish from inside the cupboard doors, the yellowed Scotch tape effaced with a razor blade.

None of that would happen now.

In a slot in the hutch, Ivan had found the letters, addressed merely *Cook Ranch* in Gala's childish hand. *You realize there's still items John and I have to deal with, like it or not. Really, I just don't see how you can expect me to believe you don't know where he is . . .* pages of it. Ivan had folded them away, wishing he hadn't looked, wishing to remember Gala in her better days, sleek and smart-mouthed, trailing a fragrance that left him in a condition of heated wonderment.

Hadn't they all taken to her, even Gretchen—especially, somehow, Gretchen?

Ivan had never known precisely whose idea that union had been—John Andrew's (because Gala was the shining daughter of a surgeon in Sperry, emblem of everything he felt lesser than, having been raised out, away), or Gala's (because John Andrew was as handsome as she was, and had no nonsense in him, no waffling, and because marrying him was a rebellion, yes, but one of the right dimension and heft). Maybe they'd loved each other. Early on, at least, before it had begun to cost.

But then, what did any of this matter? Gretchen, by reason of her illness, was beyond living in the hill cabin, anyway. The tingling along her arms had become, over many months, a heavy dead wasting. Her shoulders curled in. Her calves were like slivers of almond.

Who could you point at, who could you blame for that?

●   ●   ●

PERRY HAD GONE TO TOWN AFTER LUNCH—salve and staples to pick up at Equity, a little banking.

"Look," Ivan had offered, "let me go and do that—what do you say?"

Perry cast him a soured look. "Can't wait to kite out of here again, that it?"

"No, look, Dad—" Ivan started in, felt a hot surge of embarrassment, and let it drop.

Some time after the stock sale, before Ivan and Phoebe arrived, Perry'd taken a fall. Barklike scab graced his cheekbone, and something was wrong with his hip. It surprised no one that Perry declined to have it looked at. All week, Ivan had watched him try not to gimp, seen him squeeze away the stab of pain with his left eye.

"How about stopping at the doctor's?" Ivan said.

Perry stood drinking his coffee, a sheen on his temples, his free hand balled under his arm. "No thanks," he said.

Now lights veered up the West Fork road. Ivan thought that the last thing he wanted was for his father to find him there in John Andrew's mess. But it was a Forest Service truck, not Perry's old brown LeSabre. It rumbled by, vanishing into the road cut.

The wind had ebbed and the sleet had become a fine listless snow. Ivan mushed his boot around in the ashes, scattered them. The yard light clicked on, glowed a deep salmon. Ivan went back to the kitchen, reached in and switched it off. He climbed into the Jeep, fired the engine, and pulled eagerly on the heater knob, which gave a quarter inch, but no more.

If his brother's story spooled out from this one point, so, too, did his. Picture the older boy groomed to be Perry, his fingertips dull with grease, his knuckles nicked and infected, the meat of his shoulders hard-packed from bucking bales, his lips as chapped and straight-lined as his father's. Then picture the other boy, Gretchen's by unspoken default, grilled on spelling words and quadratic equations, asked to scratch thirty lines a day in a private ledger, given Peterson's bird book in his stocking, where John Andrew found shells for his Remington . . . All of that, so that Ivan would wow them in the world-at-large. When he chafed under this regimen, Gretchen stood him back against the coat hooks in the mudroom. "I'm going to tell you something I shouldn't be telling you," she said. "I love both of you to pieces, but you're my smart one. You've got something he won't ever have. Choices, Ivan."

Yes, a feast of choices.

The fall John Andrew married Gala, Ivan inaugurated his five-year carom shot through the university. He took Busi-

ness and Society, he took Introduction to Major Religious
Texts, he took Civil War Battles, Contemporary Social Prob-
lems, Soils. He ignored Perry's threats, assured Gretchen
again and again that he was only a handful of credits from
graduating. He thinned down, grew his hair. He tended bar,
worked on a road crew out of Drummond one summer, sold
fireworks, went door to door for the city directory. He missed
a Thanksgiving, a Christmas. Then came four or five years
when he wasn't home at all. He trailed a barmaid to Fort
Collins, drifted east in the aftermath, Omaha, Milwaukee,
then up through the hardwood country along Lake Superior,
taking work when he found it, quitting without rancor a few
weeks or months later. He would just not go in one morning—there would be nothing special about that day, no gripe
or grinding hangover or anything to glorify as wanderlust.
He'd just feel vaguely, sickeningly lost—as though he'd worn
out his welcome.

The first time he saw Phoebe, she was at a round Formica
table in the rear of the Ashland, Wisconsin, public library,
teaching an older man in blue coveralls to read. Ivan couldn't
say why he waited, why he followed her out onto Vaughn
Avenue and down to a bakery, and stood watching her clutch
a white sack of limpa bread to her chest—except that he'd already fallen in love. Compared to Gala, she was big and plain.
Her hair hung. She had thick wrists and skin that blotched at
the slightest irritation. It was idiotic. Yet, as near as he could
pinpoint such a thing, his attraction had begun the moment
he'd seen the man in coveralls shut his book, push his chair
back, and say, with a shy bow, "Thank you again, miss."

And what words had rushed from Ivan's mouth so that
Phoebe seated herself with him, in one of the booths across
from the glass counters, accepting the first cup of coffee?
How was it he'd managed to be right about her? "You were

dazzled by my inner beauty," Phoebe kidded him whenever the subject arose.

"Uh-huh," Ivan answered. "That's what it was." But the memory terrified him. How can you trust yourself? How do you know to leap?

Lights came on outside the main house. Ivan ground the tires in the pea gravel and let the engine die. No, he did not hate his brother. They were too different for hatred, too ignorant of each other. John Andrew had been almost heedless of Ivan, hellbent on becoming the man he was supposed to become. Ivan, for his part, had fixed his eyes on John Andrew, year after year—he knew how his brother looked with a milk glass tipped to his mouth, or what he'd say when he jammed his feet into cold boots. Ivan could see as little as one wrist, flycasting, and know it was John Andrew's. But that was all he knew—he'd simply memorized John Andrew, the way he'd memorized the lay of the mountains, the river's quirks.

How weird it was, Ivan thought, climbing out, that John Andrew should take his place as the absent son.

• • •

PERRY STILL WASN'T BACK. Nonetheless it was dinnertime, and Gretchen was seated at the big table. Sara Dog, the asthmatic setter John Andrew had left behind, was working a path between the kitchen and the buffet, her nails clitter-clattering on the linoleum. Phoebe had tried a curry recipe—the pot had bubbled on low heat all afternoon. She'd put out glass dishes of coconut and peanuts and chopped eggs. She sat, finally, her ears flushed, a fine mist on her cheeks.

Having waited, Gretchen lifted a forkful to her lips, winced, but found it blander than she'd expected.

"What were you burning?" she asked Ivan.

How did she miss nothing, even now? He looked across at

her—her hair was cut like a helmet, the color of galvanized nails. Though she'd been out of the sun for months her skin stayed olivy, buffed-looking. Rills of green vein branched across the backs of her hands.

"I just took care of it," Ivan said. "Isn't that what you wanted?"

His mother frowned, paused. "He was gone before he left," she said finally. "One night the two of them were outside at the table after supper, taking coffee, your father and John Andrew. Your brother had the white mug with the broken handle."

Despite himself, Ivan pictured it: the plank boards gone mealy with weather, the green-gold light splashing through the cottonwood leaves.

"They wouldn't look at each other. John Andrew had his hat off. He kept dragging his fingers over his scalp. Your father sat there rubbing his calluses."

She wasn't so much talking as reciting; Ivan knew enough not to interfere. "Your father got up and started for the Quonset, but he stopped and came over behind John Andrew and talked straight into his back. Then he left, and John Andrew didn't so much as take a breath until your father was out of sight, then—"

She turned her head in that way she had now, squeezing a cough from her throat. "Then looked after him—it was an awful, raw look, Ivan. Like the earth had been cut into. Then he dragged himself back up to the hill cabin and there was only the mug sitting there on the table."

Another cough, two fingers pressed to her mouth. "It's still there. Right outside the window, Ivan. For a while, I couldn't look at it without thinking, John Andrew took that cup down from his lips."

"Oh, now, Gretchen—" Phoebe said.

"But you detach yourself," Gretchen went on. "You see things as they are. A cup sits out in the rain, it catches water. That's what you see."

She looked sharply out toward the kitchen where Sara Dog was wheezing and circling. "Lord, will you put her out," she told Ivan.

Ivan stood.

At the door, the dog swept through his legs, skidded on the glazed incline of Gretchen's ramp, and was gone. Ivan took a few steps into the empty drive. He found himself breathing a downdraft of wood smoke, staring up toward the bench where the hill cabin no longer floated in its pool of chemical light.

Back at the table, he saw Phoebe inspect Gretchen's mostly untouched plate.

"How'd you like some egg custard, Gretchen?" she asked. "I thawed out some raspberries. You don't mind, I hope."

Gretchen gave her daughter-in-law a puzzled, shaken look. Which, in turn, shook Ivan. When the two women were off in the dayroom, he thought, they seemed intimate—traffickers in state secrets. Now Gretchen looked as though she couldn't quite place this woman who'd been rummaging in her freezer.

"But we didn't pick this year," she said, and was quiet.

Ivan didn't know what to say.

Phoebe, finally, asked in a gentle voice, "Do you think we ought to see about Perry?"

Gretchen raised herself, imperial again. "He'll take care of himself," she said. "He's perfectly capable."

Ivan felt a slipping, a little crackle of fear. "Has he been going out like this? Has—"

Gretchen stared.

Okay, then, Ivan thought. *What do I know about any of this?*

He shoved his chair back, feeling Gretchen's eyes still trained on him, as if he were an object to study with an empty mind. A cup with a broken handle, collecting rain.

• • •

BUT AN HOUR ELAPSED, and another. Sometime in the recent past, a satellite dish had been installed—it stood out in the grass by the pumphouse, aimed up toward the mouth of the valley. (Ivan and John Andrew had been raised on the one weak signal that straggled in from Sperry. Ivan had felt perennially out of it at school—"We don't get that," he was always saying.) Now Gretchen was tucked under her afghan, watching a show about the Amazon. A toothy native man was showing off an eighty-pound nugget of gold that God had allowed him to dig from the ground. Gretchen sat steely-eyed, her lips like rinds, but every minute or so her gaze veered up to the mantel clock.

Ivan couldn't bear it finally. He grabbed a coat from the mudroom and bolted out to the car—once outdoors, he realized, rooting madly in his pockets, that he only had keys for the Jeep, and thought, *Shit anyway*—but rather than go back, he slid in and pumped the nail sticking up through the floorboard. He backed around by the nine-bark, rattled out through the main gate, and followed the river in the direction of town. The headlights were caked with gumbo and issued barely a glow. He kept it floored anyway, hammering over the washboard, through puddles of wet, flattened leaves. Wasn't this asinine, to be out like this, his heart quailing? What did he expect to find, ominous tracks shooting off the embankment? His fingers were freezing, the rims of his ears. He knew this place, knew it the way he knew every old thought in his head. But it felt immensely foreign and chastening tonight, and Perry seemed the most inscrutable thing in it.

He slowed to a crawl, bumped onto a stretch of crumbled blacktop that announced the little settlement of Mullan's Crossing. The mercantile sat tall-fronted at the end of the road, flanked by cabins—dark as slabs of granite. Next door, at Reuben's, chimney smoke bent off toward the clouds.

Perry's car was nowhere in sight, but Ivan stepped onto the flat porch, and squinted through the fogged glass anyway. He saw, as he'd let himself hope, that Terri McKee was behind the bar. She was lost in a tattered paperback—one customer was asleep on his forearms, two others were throwing darts in back. No one he knew—and why should he anymore?

He let himself in.

Terri's head lifted, she recognized him instantly, came and flung her arms around his neck. "Ivan!"

Her hair was red, voluminously frizzed, but going to gray, seized up in two beaded barrettes. But she was still a skinny Minnie, Ivan saw—if he looked much longer, he might decide she couldn't keep any weight on. She and Ivan were old allies, fellow sufferers of the endless bus ride down the West Fork road. One spring they'd stolen a day to run the river, and their raft had dumped them into the roiling water at a narrowing called Sculley's Bend. Freezing, his chest heaving, Ivan found himself on the silted rocks, hugging Terri, kissing her face and eyes, her cold, freckled neck, holding her fiercely; it was their joke later, this sudden passion of Ivan's. Their one kiss. "It's okay," Terri had told him. "You were just amazed you were alive."

She had married straight out of high school; eighteen months later, her husband tripped a wire, walking patrol near An Loc.

Ivan pulled away. "You haven't seen my father?" he asked her.

"He was in here," Terri said. "You didn't pass him?"

Ivan felt a punch of relief, which immediately churned over into resentment.

"What'd he do to himself?" she asked.

"That?" Ivan said. "Fell."

"I mean he looked kind of—"

"I know."

Ivan unsnapped the jacket, which, he realized, was an old one of John Andrew's. It even smelled like him, like solvent or smoke.

"My dad didn't say I was home?" Ivan said.

Terri shook her head. "Not a word. You're the sweetest surprise. Sit, huh?" She gave his hand a pat. "I can't believe I almost missed you. We don't stay open winters anymore."

She'd married Leo Leveque a few years ago, Ivan remembered, the last son of the original Reuben—jowly, sad-looking, barely younger than Perry.

One of the men called from the back, but Terri ignored him. "We go down to see his daughters," she told Ivan. "I don't miss it up here. But then I do. Can't wait to get out, then I go kind of crazy."

She reached around to pour him a shot, hesitated. "Oh, hon, what was it you liked?" she asked.

"Anything's fine," Ivan said.

She leaned in. "How's your girl. You still in love—?"

Ivan flushed, sat finally, letting the relief he felt come ahead.

"Lucky boy."

•   •   •

HE RACED PAST the orthodontist's padlocked gate, drew alongside Perry's fence. Off in the dark, higher up, a pulse of yellow caught his eye, then was gone.

Ivan braked and swung onto the property, drove through

the turnaround by the main house, and took the hill, his lights bouncing, dinging off the rocks and blowing weeds. He found his father's car, angled into the firs with its door open. Ivan shut it gently, and called out, "Dad?"

Off in back, by John Andrew's shed, he heard a plastic tarp crackling. He walked clear around the cabin, looking, and finally entered through the same door he'd locked that afternoon. He found Perry sitting on the Hide-A-Bed, smoking, his back to the doorway.

"It's me," Ivan said.

Perry made the springs creak, getting the weight off his bad hip. "Leave the lights out," he said.

"What's going on?" Ivan asked.

"She send you out prowling?"

Ivan didn't answer, but approached, waiting for the logic of this business to dawn on him. He could hear Perry's gravelly breathing, but not quite see how his eyes were.

"Why'd you sell that piece?" Ivan heard himself ask. It had not been on his mind to get into that, but there it was.

"What do you care?" Perry said, rolling his shoulders, stifling a grunt.

"You taking anything for that?" Ivan said.

His father mashed the cigarette into the jar lid in his other hand. He appeared to nod.

"That a yes or no?"

"Ivan," Perry said. "You want something to drink?"

"There's nothing."

But Perry said, "The deep freeze."

So Ivan returned to the kitchen, smelling the Pine-Sol he'd used on the countertops, and found a half-full bottle of vodka among the bags of shredded zucchini and freezer-burnt chicken parts Gala had left behind. He popped a wax paper cup from the dispenser by the sink, then another.

Perry drank off the inch or so Ivan gave him, and thrust out his cup for a refill. Ivan balked, but went ahead. He squatted to set the icy bottle on the floor. Perry lunged and grabbed a handful of sleeve, jerking Ivan's face down next to his own. "Where's he gone to?" Perry demanded. "Try and tell me you don't know."

"You're crazy," Ivan said, shaking free. "You think I've been sitting on that all week?" He felt himself careening. "You think he'd ever tell me anything? He didn't tell me a shitting thing."

"Don't talk that way," Perry said.

Ivan went on, a notch softer. "I'm just stating a fact. I'm the last one he'd come to."

Perry made a move to stand—without thinking, Ivan reached out to help, but Perry was past him and into the kitchen, rocking on the sides of his heels.

"I ought to burn all this," his father said.

Ivan had to laugh. "That was my thought," he said.

"It was you been in here?"

"I just picked it up some."

"I guess to Christ you must have."

"Let's just close it up again and go down," Ivan offered.

But Perry cleared his throat violently and spat into the sink. "You don't know what a black day it was he laid eyes on that girl," he said.

Ivan fished around in the shadow, found the back of a chair and sat. Perry's voice came at him through the dark; he pictured that scene his mother had described—Perry talking at the flat of John Andrew's back. "She got all she wanted," Perry said, "then she didn't want it. What kind of way is that? I don't blame her for getting itchy. You feel what you feel. You think your mother never got an itch. For God's sake, think how she feels now—can't hardly stand up. No, Ivan, I blame that girl for spoiling all this for him. She made him hate it. After that, everything was dead for him."

Overhead, fir boughs scraped on the ribs of the steel roof. Ivan thought of John Andrew drinking in the kitchen here and wondering who in hell he was anymore, every noise acute as a needleshaft—and then the shame and panic that must have come as he understood that despite its buildup of history, his life hadn't ever begun, not really. And Gala, too, before that, killing time in her own fashion, watching the girls, resigned, waiting for something, which turned out to be nothing more momentous than the onset of fair weather. None of it was a mystery, just what happens.

• • •

IVAN LET THE DOG IN. The TV was off, the fire reduced to dull coals. He opened the icebox and stared into it, wondering if he was hungry, then let the door drift closed. What he wanted was to be with Phoebe, lying down with his clothes off, rescued from thought.

Upstairs, he tapped at his mother's door, leaned in. She was in a flannel gown, a dense plaid, buoyed by pillows.

"Don't run off," she said.

Ivan edged in. He'd not been in their room in years. At the foot of the bed, he stood palming the bedpost, old walnut scored like a pineapple.

"He's sitting up there at the hill cabin in the pitch-dark," Ivan said.

Gretchen nodded without surprise.

Ivan wanted to say, I know how you miss John Andrew, but feared her face would snap to life: *No, you don't, how could you possibly know?*

Softly she asked, "Ivan, could you rub my feet?"

He didn't want to touch her. Yet he pulled up the quilt—

her feet were encased in pale pink socks specked with sham-
rocks. Gingerly, he sank onto the comforter and began to
knead, his thumbs on the soles, which seemed to radiate cold,
even through the fabric.

In a moment his mother said, "At first I thought, *Maybe
he'll call Ivan.*"

"John Andrew? You honestly—"

"No, no. I know he didn't."

"He never let loose of anything," Ivan said.

Gretchen seemed to smile. "That's so," she said. "Your father
saw how it was all going wrong up there. He thought if John
Andrew's money wasn't all tied up with ours, if he didn't
have to wait for it. He thought if Gala had a place in town she'd
be all right again—she could have that life and John Andrew
could still do what he had to do, you see. Then that dentist had
been pestering everyone up the road to sell him something on
the river. So your father surveyed off that lower piece and
cashed it out. I thought it would kill him. I thought it was the
last thing on this earth he'd do."

Ivan stared at her.

"But then it didn't change a thing. It didn't make the
slightest difference." She moistened her lips. "He thought he
could stop the bleeding—that's how he talked about it. But
you can't. I told him."

Ivan let his hands relax for a second. But she was right
there, "No, Ivan, keep doing that. *Please.*"

Wind rattled the glass as Gretchen's eyes closed. His father had salvaged this bank of windows from a schoolhouse
up the draw. Ivan remembered lifting them off the back of
the truck, Perry on one side, himself and John Andrew on
the other—hoisting them up to the new gabled room with
ropes. Perry was smiling, clenching his cigarette in his
teeth. Gretchen was up here, where the bed was now, watch-

ing, looking down at them, one summer's day.

"They come back on their own sometimes," Ivan said, but she was asleep.

•   •   •

HE WOKE BEFORE DAWN. Phoebe slept on her back, one hand cupped at her throat. Ivan touched the place on the flannel where her breast was and felt the nipple work its miracle. He found her ear in the muss of hair and whispered into it: "I love you, love you." Her hand slid down his cheek. Ivan swung his feet onto the rag rug and dressed.

The house was quiet. Lacing his boots, out in the kitchen, he saw that the brown Buick had been parked behind the Jeep— so Perry would be upstairs, consigned to sleep, Gretchen beside him.

He set up the coffeemaker, located an old sweater and jacket on a peg in the mudroom, and went outside.

A glaze lay on the fence rails, a wrinkle of ice on the stock pond, broken by a pair of gliding mallards. Ivan walked down to the hay barn and switched on the floodlight. He found gloves that Perry had wedged in the crotch of the timbers, and shook them out.

If there was an off-season, this was it. In a month they'd be kicking bales off the trailer, augering holes in the ponds. And, in another eight weeks, calves.

Ivan noticed that Perry had cut down the rope he and John Andrew had swung on, but a shiny groove still showed on the rafter. He smiled, and let the memory fall away.

An orange cat appeared between the bales. It jumped down and circled Ivan, rubbing hard against his legs.

TALONS

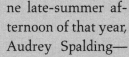ne late-summer afternoon of that year, Audrey Spalding—my aunt Audrey—latched up her white-shuttered bungalow and rode in a taxi to Providence where she intended to have her hysterectomy on the sly. She had dropped us a postcard: *Such heat! Headed up to the San Juans. Give you a buzz when I get back . . .* A little past eight the next morning she took a violent reaction to the anesthesia. Her heart arrested, was started, quit once more, and despite heroics would not take up its work again.

She was fifty-eight.

That was the summer, too, when my parents finally laid their marriage to rest, end of the grueling fresh starts and plummetings. My mother had gone to live with my sister Lil in St. Paul. My father had arranged to be out of the country for six months, overseeing construction of a pumping station for the Saudis. By contrast, it was also the summer—actually, late in May—that Faye and I married, the last forced show of family solidarity. Faye wore baby's breath in her hair, a slippery white dress that showed off her collarbones. When I straightened after our kiss she pulled my head down again and there was laughter. We were toasted, hugged, wished every happiness, and sent off in a gusting rain. Fruit blossoms lacquered the pavement. We were twenty-one, delirious to find ourselves finally cohabiting. We had an airy, one-bedroom flat over Maxine's Dress Shop in West Seattle. *So this is my life*, I thought, taking in the maple dinette, the clawfoot tub brush-painted green, the gauzy curtains sailing and flapping in the cross breeze. Despite her euphoria, I caught Faye doing the same, arms folded, shivering slightly, including me in that questioning look.

The family strewn, it fell to us to attend to Audrey's instructions, typed on blue file cards (using the old Underwood Noiseless I remember from childhood, with the *o* that rose above the line like an escaping air bubble).

She'd left them in her stocking drawer, marked IMPORTANT: Cremation, no service, a small get-together—we were supposed to dust off her bottles of homemade wine, drink what we pleased and divvy up the rest. *Whoever's reading this: Absolutely no tearjerking. I mean it, it was short but I had a great time.* She'd included a write-up for the paper, which ended (so as to needle my father): *Never once voted for a Republican in her entire life.*

She'd left the house clean—fresh linen on her bed, only French's and kosher dills and seltzer in the icebox—but it wasn't clean the way you'd leave it if you thought you might not return. I threw out a shriveled squash blossom floating in a bowl, erased the single message on her chalkboard: *Call M./waterhtr.* Unloading a shelf in the pantry, we came upon two tins of letters from a man named Frank Leland. The first

ones were dated 1955. Gummed to the corner of each envelope was a gold oval that said FRANK'S FRAME SHOP.

"You shouldn't look at those," Faye whispered over my
shoulder. How can you not look? The one in my hand said:
*Sweet, it's unbelievably dreary here. The straits look like
tarpaper. Honest, I don't see how I can bear this much
longer . . .*

But he'd borne it! Years of letters were wedged into the
tins, some ripped open, others scissored off at the end. Now
the worst of it dawned on me: In with the tumble of junk mail
delivered since her death was yet another gold-stickered letter from Frank.

She hadn't told him either.

Faye and I went on piling Audrey's things, we boxed and
carried and mopped. That night we lay on the two halves of
the folded-down daybed, worn out. It had been hot for weeks
and no insects were left to tick against the screens. Out in the
dark a dry wind sifted through Audrey's grape arbors. I
couldn't sleep. I put my hand on Faye. She was tiny and calm,
such a mystery to me still. Her skin was damp under the T-
shirt; I could feel the fine hairs on her stomach.

"You'll have to write him, Sammy," she said.

"Me?" I said, turning, nestling.

"Who else?"

After a minute, I said, "What a stupid thing." I was young
enough I'd never lost anyone to death. I was angry, but it was
anger I didn't know, as raw and chastening as the other feelings consuming me that summer. And mixed with it, like
grains of gravel, was something else—I felt betrayed, straight-
armed away from business of wonderful importance.

My beleaguered parents had shipped me off to spend the
twelve weeks between eighth and ninth grades at Audrey's.
Audrey taught junior high, biology and health, coached

track—I was no mystery to her at all. She read my heart as if it hammered under Plexiglas. She was fortyish, thin as a hurdler, tall, with wide bony shoulders and a solitary's habits. Later on, she wore her hair cropped, almost spiky, still the color of terra cotta—her skull was large and round, warrior-like—but that summer she had two tight-woven braids, bobby-pinned in spirals over either ear, bangs wisping above far-apart gray eyes. Where my own mother had grown peevish, flinching at each day's fresh evidence, Audrey was stubbornly curious. "These two hemlock?" she said, walking with me along the boundary of the old homestead. "We put them down the same year—they were about as high as your head. Now why do you figure this one's twenty feet taller?" I had to offer an opinion regarding soil nutrients, hours of direct sun. "Uh-huh," Audrey said. "Probably right. Then again, maybe one's just stronger. That happens."

Mornings, she tutored me in algebra or tried to teach me bridge; afternoons we pruned the grapes or tied up the peas or swam at Dimaggio's—this was years before the red tide closed our beaches. Audrey's long white arms ripped out of the waves, jerking her ahead. I can see us lying on two towels, her black tank suit drying, lightening, beside me. At night she put me down on the daybed with the radio playing low. "Come on, cut the crap, Sammy," she said. "Tell me you love me!"

"Yes, of course," I said.

She bent and warmed my forehead with her lips. "Roses on your pillow."

Thus Frank came as a shock.

All that summer he'd been in her thoughts. She'd read his letters, filed them in the cookie tin, then—while I slept?—settled into the creaky rattan on the porch and typed hers while moths batted the lampshade. Frank lived two hours north, a ferry ride and an easy jaunt along the water, but Audrey was never absent. No strange man ever shuffled up the steps of the bungalow and squinted in through the screen door, no telephone disturbed the peace at crazy hours. And there was no brooding in Audrey—or if so, it burned deeper inside her than I was privileged to see.

Faye was right, I had to tell Frank, but I put it off. I read the want ads. The rains came, I slid into a low humor. My letters of inquiry shot out like radio messages into deep space. All I'd found was day work, and this came with a jarring call, 6:20 A.M., maybe twice a week. Faye was working for three gynecologists. She left in a nimbus of Canoe, white rayon rustling, new white Clinics going *chick, chick* on the tiles. Home again in the late afternoon, she asked how the job hunt had gone, said, Have faith, Sammy, I love you, don't get *down* on yourself. A couple of times she asked, Honey, did you call Frank yet? I offered a fuzzy reply, slipped my hands under her shirt. Faye giggled, let herself be nuzzled back against the icebox before sliding away, flushed, to see about dinner.

But one raw morning, waiting for a call, I found myself at our window. Down below, Maxine's customers moved heavily against the wind, their heads in snapping scarves. The bell over the door shook, rang distantly through the floorboards. I stood suddenly and retrieved Frank's letters, dumped them on the oilcloth and tore into one. There was his left-handed scrawl spilling down a sheet of legal tablet. *I've been thinking about what you said . . . I've been thinking that it takes an immense strength, a kind of deep in the bone . . .* but I couldn't finish it. I took the bus to where our Falcon sat making rust in the doctors' lot, used the spare key, and drove to the ferry dock.

Frank wasn't at his shop.

"Mr. Leland's sort of retired," a girl in a crimson smock

told me. "Hey, what's this about—?" she asked, as if I might be a snoop for the government. I tried to ease her mind. "You could call him at home, I guess," she offered finally. "If it's like *personal*."

She bent and scratched the number on a sales slip.

I wadded it in my breast pocket, and went back out into the rain. Calling seemed like the coward's choice; I stopped at a gas station and fished the address out of the book.

The house sat on a rocky hummock along the water, glass and weathered shingles choked with blackberry. A wind chime gave a few meek *tings* as I stood waiting, pine boughs dripping on me.

Frank came to the door himself.

He was an old man, his skin as waxy as a Dixie cup, pale and reddish, hastily shaved. Long filaments of hair were varnished to his scalp. He had the eyes of an old bird. My thoughts ground to a halt. This couldn't have been Audrey's lover, not by a breach of nature.

I stuck my hand out. "Sam Church?" I said. "I need to talk to you. About my aunt Audrey."

Panic toyed with Frank's face, still he let me in, ushered me down a little corridor of Simonized flagstones, and then we were loose in his front room, which faced the straits, and before I spoke a word I was confronted by an enormous watercolor of my aunt, commanding the wall over a flowered sofa.

She had the feathery bangs, the two braids wrapped like shells above her ears. She was wearing a yellow-striped sundress I could almost remember. I looked at it for a long time.

"Mr. Church?" he said.

So finally I gave him his sad news. He uncrossed his arms and let them dangle.

He said, "I see, yes—I see," nodding, blinking. He asked if I wanted coffee.

My stomach was on fire. "Well, sure, coffee'd be fine," I said, and Frank vanished around a room divider. I heard water running in the sink, and over the rush of the water Frank crying.

Now the front door opened and two women charged in, the one in the lead engulfed in purple flowers. She could hardly see over the top. "*Frank—*" she yelled, then noticed me, said hello, cool, unimpressed. She thrust the flowers into my arms and wiggled out of her coat. Frank appeared with the coffee. He handed my cup to his wife. I gave him the flowers and he disappeared into the kitchen for more cups. When he'd accomplished that he came back and introduced us all.

The daughter, Sabrina, had the mother's round, disapproving face, the same arched, overplucked brows. I gathered she was living at home again, by default.

"Mr. Church here," Frank said to his wife, with a slight jut of the chin, "is trying his damnedest to talk me into chairing a committee for the hospital auction again this year."

"*Oh, Frank,*" she said, lips squeezing. "I thought you said you'd done enough for those people."

Frank said, "It's nice to feel needed."

There was a clattering of bracelets from the daughter. "Let's please not go through all *that* again, huh—?" she said.

"Frank's too generous with his time," Mrs. Leland said. "There comes a point when you feel you've given enough, don't you think? Some people don't recognize when they're being taken advantage of."

"Gee," I said. "I don't want you to feel like that. I'll just call somebody else on my list."

Frank had begun to look forlorn, rubbing the knees of his corduroys with both palms.

That seemed to pacify the women. As I sipped my coffee, the daughter tapped a Gauloise from its pack and lit up, then slumped back, richly bored, picking flakes of tobacco off her pointed tongue.

Mrs. Leland caught me staring at Audrey's portrait.

"That picture," she said. "You like it? I can see you do. Queer deal. Someone had it framed at Frank's shop, then never showed up to claim it. You couldn't ever track them down, could you, Frank?"

Frank shook his head, no.

"That was years ago, wasn't it, Frank?"

Frank excused himself, not looking at any of us, and padded down the hallway, his steps strangely weightless. I heard a door close. Old man's kidneys, I thought. Minutes scraped by in contorted small talk. No Frank.

A week later Faye and I were in bed. It was a work night for her, late, after one. I was keyed up, rolling over and over, keeping her awake. I couldn't stop thinking of Frank. I hadn't said a word yet about going to see him, but now, in the dark, it was all coming out.

"When I finally got outside it was still drizzling," I went on. "Big dead leaves were plastered all over the windshield. I couldn't wait to blast out of there. Anyway, I slid down into my seat and there he was."

"In the car? Frank?"

"*Yes.* Waiting for me, agitated at hell."

"Think what you'd told him, though," Faye said. "Think of all he'd just lost—"

"No," I said. "I understand that. But you see what he thought? He thought I was going to *spill the beans*. He thought I'd go back in and spoil his secret. Isn't that pathetic?"

I slid up on one elbow. "It's so shabby—he's that old and he's scared to death his wife's going to catch him. What a life."

"Oh, Sammy," Faye said. "Why didn't you tell me be-fore?" She reached up and rubbed my shoulder. "Honey—"

"I had to just about shove him out of the car," I said. "I had to almost get ugly with him. I mean he grabbed me, by the arm, he sat there staring at me, like some huge awful bird."

Far off in the dark I heard a boat horn, fierce and hollow, but close in there was silence except for our breathing.

"You won't be that kind of man," Faye said. "You won't ever be like Frank."

"God, no," I vowed, and lay in the dark, feeling my wife's touch on one arm, and on the other, Frank's, icy, like talons.

COOPERSTOWN

Twelve years after the fact, Isham rents a car, heads north out of San Francisco, and hours later, cuts east toward Lake Estelle. The foothills are burnt khaki, the roadside weeds dry as moon dust. He blasts the air-conditioning on his face, driving pedal-down, no radio, thinking ahead, but not in stringent detail. Then he hits the last rise, crests the crumbling blacktop, and drops down, the town and lake in full view, wavy in the heat, placid.

The near end is developed, a crescent of white stores and motels, lounges and eateries facing the water, circa 1962, but up the shore, counterclockwise, the habitation thins, and where the lake narrows, a straggle of pine woods comes down. Isham ignores the scratch of hunger in his gut, and passes the last gas station where he could stop and ask directions, follows where the road goes. And there, finally, alone on a post, a sign, HEWITT'S MARINA, neat, blue on white.

The building is stucco, a house with an office patched on. In the yard, a few acacias with wasted, rattling leaves. There's a Pepsi machine, the faint stink of diesel. In back, a long flight of white wooden steps leading to the tin-sided boat sheds and a pair of docks.

Isham shields his eyes, squints in through the screen door. There's a woman in the office—a shirt of yellow cotton, glasses in thin gold frames, hair cropped to stiff, dime-sized ringlets. Is this her, Hewitt's wife? Does Hewitt still have a wife? Driving, Isham assumed he'd get a little bump of recognition, but now he can't tell. She is tapping numbers into a calculator perched on one knee, but leaves off, catching Isham's shadow in the doorway.

"It's open," she calls.

He should wave no-thanks and dive back into the car. But he balks, tucks his shirt in, feeling where it's wet against his skin. Then he walks inside.

"Too late to rent a boat?" he asks, buying time.

She guns a look at his plain, hot face, at his clothes, which are wrong for boat-renting—baggy suit pants, wing tips— then she cranks around at a bank of dusty windows.

"You've got an hour of good light," she says. "Maybe more."

Isham digs his hands into his trouser pockets, scanning. No baseball regalia in sight, not a thing. A doorway opens onto living quarters—he can see the corner of a sofa and a blue plastic dump truck, and there's music playing, not the weepy pedal-steel stuff he'd expect, but solo piano tumbling serenely through the scales.

"I should warn you," she says. "The fishing's been off. The lake's way down—nobody's seen it low like this."

"I just wanted to take a boat out," Isham says.

So she catalogs the fleet for him, and Isham, while his eyes

go to the glare on the windows, studies the voice. Just an ordinary voice, a touch raspy, not unpleasant. He's heard it directed at him once before, of course. Righteous, spitting
anger! Three-thirty in the morning, Florida time, the crackle
of long distance. *I know you know who this is.* He hadn't been
asleep. He'd been sitting up with his back stuck to the motel
room's vinyl headboard, trying dismally to see himself as a
man at the top of his game, trying to visualize his right arm
cutting through the bright morning air. Although he'd never
laid eyes on Hewitt's wife, yes, he knew who it was. *You're not
hanging up on me, you sick bastard.* Young, drunk, but not
just drunk. She tore ahead and Isham listened, his palm leaking a toxic sweat on the receiver.

Afterward, striped by the mercury light squeezing through
the blinds, he thought, All right, you take a scalding now and
then, even if things aren't precisely your fault. Which was an
accurate accounting of how he still saw it, not precisely his
fault. But the longer he sat, the worse he felt—how could he
let himself be talked to like that? He threw on pants and a
windbreaker, pounded downstairs to his Blazer, and cruised
the coast road toward Pompano until the night broke. He
pulled off into a turnaround paved with crushed shells, and sat
watching the palm leaves scissoring against the sky.

It was no trick picturing the story she'd reeled out at him:
Andy Hewitt, former boy wonder, in the cage at the Cincinnati camp, missing balls by a full foot. Coaches alongside,
glum and soft as old fruit, telling him, "That's enough for
today, Andy, we'll see how it goes tomorrow. Okay, kid?" Or
that business later in the parking lot. The papers had been full
of it: Hewitt back in his street clothes, whipping a bat down a
line of windshields and headlights, and finally a pop machine,
all of which had led, like water down a sluice, to Carol Hewitt's
being stark alone and sleepless in their rental unit.

Later, after Isham's own tether to the game frayed and snapped, after he became a floating man, it turned into more of a riddle: It's wrong to squander so much of your time thinking about one thing you did. But what if you don't, what kind of man are you then?

Look now, Mrs. Hewitt, Isham wants to say, *Look, I want to tell you a coupla things.* Instead, he dutifully selects a boat and folds out cash so she won't see the *Robert F. Isham* on the MasterCard. But then she's asking his name anyway, and he hands it over, as if it were nothing, air.

No menace registers on her face. She writes, nudges up her glasses, calls back into the house, "*San-dee.*"

Isham shifts his weight, heavy, out of trim in this off-moment. "Look," he says. "Maybe it's too late. Why don't I just—" He shrugs. "Maybe I'll come back in the morning. Why don't I just do that?"

She won't hear of it. "You look miserable," she says. "The wind will make you feel better."

A boy of about twelve eases into the office. Storky, wearing high-tops, a T-shirt that leaves a band of stomach exposed. He has a little O-shaped mouth, eyes like two black beans.

"Honey, take Mr. Isham down to where Dad is," she tells him, and, to Isham, says, "My husband will tell you what to watch out for." Moments later, they are headed around the side of the office and down the long steps, Sandy in the lead, goofily precise, springing off the toes of his sneakers. Halfway down, he whirls around. Isham almost flattens him, stopping.

"You know what?"

"What?"

"There's a town under the lake. Used to be Estelle, before they flooded it. The water's so low you can see houses—they just *left* them. You know what I did? I got out of the boat and walked on the top of this one roof. It was so weird. Don't say anything, okay?"

Isham pictures the gangly boy thigh-deep in water, slimy roof shakes under his feet, and below them, rooms drifting with silt.

"You know what else? There's a cemetery down there, too. You believe *that*?" The boy grabs for Isham's arm. "You want me to show you where? I could."

God, no, Isham thinks.

Finally, he looks out toward the water. An extension has been rigged onto the near dock, slats of white rippled metal on spindly legs. The boats crowd in like feeding cattle. At the far end, there's a lanky silhouette kneeling over an engine.

It hits Isham what folly, what a dance that was in the office. Of course she knew him the instant he pushed through the door. He steals a look back. There she is on the landing, watching, one hand up to block the sun.

It's a look he recognizes. For a time, after retirement, Isham scouted—three seasons, assigned to the Pioneer League. Off-nights, he hit Legion games in mountain and prairie towns—fields with outfield boards that said State Farm, Lundberg's Masonry Supply, Shotsie's Kut & Kurl. The evening sun came at a wicked angle, either in the fielders' eyes, or the batter's—white-gold, full of chaff and gumbo dust. Invariably, in the midst of the hurly-burly, the raffle sales and incessant kid traffic, he'd catch sight of a girl sitting alone, staring over the top of a Coke. Nice-looking in a J.C. Penney kind of way, but deadly focused. Isham knew he could slide over with his clipboard and strike up some talk that would yield a few nuggets of fact he could acquire nowhere else. "So tell me," Isham might begin, "what's he like off the field?"

•   •   •

HEWITT LIFTS HIS FACE from the dismantled Evinrude, sees Isham bearing down on him, and Isham knows *he* knows. Hewitt straightens, wipes his hands on a dock rag torn from an old flannel shirt.

"Andy—" Isham says.

Hewitt angles his head so the better eye aims at Isham, heronlike.

"I was up this way," Isham says.

Hewitt's face constricts into a smile, thin as wire. "Well, no," he says. "No, you weren't."

"Look, I guess it was a mistake."

"You're here now."

Isham can only nod, blotting the sweat off his forehead.

"You met my oldest?"

The boy's head bobs on the long stem of neck. He sticks his hand out, and Isham automatically takes it, but feels the fingers wrap clear around his own, cool as tendrils. No ugly magic in the Isham name for him. He folds himself down onto the dock, swings his legs, glancing away from the grown men, out into the oily reflections between the boats.

"You'd still be playing," Isham says. "What are you? Thirty-five? Thirty-six?"

Hewitt shrugs, still that odd mix of pointy-boned shoulders and spring-loaded muscle.

"You'd be halfway to Cooperstown."

"To tell you the truth," Hewitt starts, but flips the rag down, and says, "No—"

After a second, he says, "There was a time she would've cut your eyes out," nodding up toward the office. "Carol. Would've scooped them out with a melon baller if she got the chance."

"Yeah, I bet."

"How else could she see it, though? I was very messed up. *Bottomed out.* That's the only way to say it."

"Look, now, Andy," Isham says. "I wanted to say—" but Hewitt thrusts a hand up.

"Forget it. You're sorry, you're not sorry, you were doing your job, it was an accident—whatever. Couldn't make less of a difference to me."

The breath sneaks out of Isham. He watches a sailboat in the middle distance; there's not a ghost of a breeze, yet the boat glides along through the fiery light.

"You know what my wife said?" Isham says. "She kept asking me, *How come he just stood there? How come he didn't go down?*"

And Isham remembers what he answered, *Fucking kid's in another universe*—as if that explained things.

Picture this, as a chain of events: Hewitt freezes in the batter's box, and then—skipping ahead to West Palm the following spring—Isham is summoned to the G.M.'s office the last Friday of camp, and learns he's been waived. A few phone calls, no takers, and he's through at thirty-four. Then, high summer of that same year (Isham still believing, deep down, he must be on some sort of leave of absence), his wife, Janey, packs and is gone, the adhesive between them aged to a gritty powder.

This is fraudulent, though, if it starts with Hewitt not ducking. As is saying the pitch was an ordinary high, tight fastball that rode in, as they will (that was management's version: *Life's dangerous*). Or that Isham owned that inches-wide corridor of air space, that he had a consecrated duty to back a hot-hitting neophyte like Hewitt off the plate.

All of that, simply a crock.

It was September, muggy as hell, both teams beyond the

pale, pennant-wise. A game you could hardly stay awake for. Isham walked the first man in the sixth on a fastball and three bad sliders. Then he looked in, the crowd noise a paltry waffling in his ears, and saw it was Hewitt edging to the plate, and the truth of why he threw at him was only this: He'd *felt* like it. By the time his hands came set, he knew, before the delivery even commenced. Already he was savoring it.

To put it yet more simply: He'd wanted Hewitt never to be there again.

And it wasn't just that he could hit, that balls came off his bat like sun off glass. Something was *wrong* about Hewitt. He had a funny, upright stance—bent at the waist as if fashioned from pipe cleaners. His swing looked wholly uncomfortable, a kind of last-second spasm. He was known as a spook around the Reds clubhouse. Touchy, not a joiner, not regular. He looked, Isham thought, like a kid who'd get snared by some oddball religion, or wind up in the mountains hoarding guns. He had a root fire going in him. Isham dug his fingertips into the seams. It was a moment of giddy, thrilling terror.

For an instant, Hewitt's face was full-front, goggle-eyed, the side of his helmet with the earflap angled toward the box seats, as useless to him as childhood prayer. And Isham's one thought, as the ball traveled, was how very weird, how like the way of things, that this should be the one pitch he threw all afternoon that went exactly where he intended. In a rush, the on-deck man, the trainer, the manager Rosetto, and some others were gaggled around. Still on the mound, Isham saw one of Hewitt's feet poking out through all those legs, tremoring.

"What about you?" Isham asks. "What'd you want to do to me?"

Hewitt turns away. "Sandy," he says, softly. "Run up and get some beer from Mom, okay? Hustle."

For a moment, then, they're shoulder to shoulder, watching Sandy lope up the dock, feeling him rock the slats underfoot. A smell washes around them, stale, drifting up from the shallow water and the exposed strip of lake bottom.

"I didn't want to do anything to you," Hewitt says.

"You had to hate me," Isham says. "You had to have *dreams* about me, man—"

Hewitt kneels once more, snaps the head off his socket wrench, and fits it in the box where it goes.

"I don't think about you," Hewitt says. "No offense."

Isham's eyes flick up toward the house. The landing is empty again; she's gone and left them to this. He notices, before Hewitt's voice calls him back, a couple of younger kids, off in a patch of bare dirt, digging. They only show from the chest up, soft brown shoulders, shovel handles rocking like levers. But why not dig a hole? Why not cover it with boards and stay down there where it's cool and private?

"You married still?" Hewitt asks.

"Me? Jesus, no—" Isham says, laughing without meaning to.

Oddly, only the first marriage flashes to mind, the one to Janey. As if the other two were just long weekends—raucous with sex and cajoling and, God knows, all that, but finally stupid and nothing to do with him.

And what *does* anymore? He's forty-five, his finances in disarray. He travels three weeks a month, representing a line of sports accessories that seem an ideal example of things people ought to live without. He owns a seven-year-old Camaro, a third-floor apartment that looks onto a boarded-up grade school. Some nights he forgoes the TV and Tanqueray, and drives to the pool. Changing, he's routinely appalled at the pulpy midsection that greets him in the bank of mirrors, and flees to the water. But his shoulders ache, especially the right, the bursa so drained he can hear the ball scraping *crick*,

crick in the socket—some nights he can barely knock out a dozen laps, and the next day will have to start with cortisone. He stands dripping on the tiles, staring at the Lycra on the long glistening women, and even the itch of desire feels too familiar.

But, strange to admit, that time with Janey, down near the start, playing for Savannah, then Greenville, seems *right there* still. For instance, calling from a stand-up phone, his hair still wet, his voice electrified, and hers, *I heard it in the car. You were getting ground balls, huh? I know, honey. God, will you please please please get home—*

And there was a night he woke on the bus, late, his cheek pasted to the glass. Outside, windbreaks and disked-over fields zipped by, white with moonlight, dead calm. It occurred to him that only three or four of them would make it, ever, and the rest were only fleshing out the squad. A night thought, certainly, nothing you didn't know in your bones. But he rode listening to the breathing around him, the flutter of Spanish, and he thought that if you were looking back on this bus and its contents, you'd see it all spelled out, the many and the few. So that all the hustle, all the getting yourself up, the *keeping a good mental attitude* was pointless.

No, not pointless. Just insufficient.

For the next few weeks, months even—also strange, because you'd think it might work the other way around—he found himself possessed of a brotherly feeling for his teammates. He watched them, amazed, as if they were tricks of light that would be gone when he looked back. And he himself was throwing beautifully, for the first time, really—without thought and without pain. When he ran over a string of pitches, later, in bed, they'd seem like numbers in a code, as inevitable as his own election for greater things. It's been so long since he's felt anything remotely like that. Yet there it is still, all of it, ingrown, down with his thoughts about Janey, his *yearnings*—before he tired her out, before she told him that evening in the seafood place on Sepulveda, *Isham, I'm sorry, but plans change.*

Isham draws a slow, horrid breath, staring at his beat-up shoes. What did he imagine this little face-to-face would accomplish?

The other man suddenly bounces to his feet, inches from Isham. The smallest shove would send Isham sprawling backward, head-first, into the boats.

Hewitt says, quietly, "This is where we went to high school," pointing across the water. "Over there."

Isham turns and stares, but haze has taken the far shore.

"I didn't think Carol would stand for coming back here," Hewitt says. "She had things she wanted, and you better believe they weren't here. But I said, Why don't we just go home for a while, ride it out there? I didn't know what I was saying. Sandy was in diapers. She already had the next one going. I said, Let's just clear out of Cincinnati. You want to know the truth? I was sick of everybody talking about me.

"Carol just kept saying, *Maybe next year, maybe it's just slow to heal.* That's how the doctors were, too. They didn't know—it was all a big mystery of the universe. I had Carol's brother throw some for me. Kids used to come and line up along the fence. It did get a little better, too. I'd nail one once in a while."

The flat little smile overtakes Hewitt's face again. "But, you know, the thing was, it was only Carol's brother. *You* could've even hit against him."

Isham feels the dock shake—the boy back again to chaperone; Isham wonders, suddenly, how you'd warn a boy off sport. Where would you even start?

But it's not Sandy. He sees in Hewitt's eyes that it's Carol, and before he can turn, he smells her scent. Johnson & Johnson, sun-dried cotton.

She hands down a little blue-and-white cooler, as if it's any evening in her life. Hewitt thanks her with a touch, digs into the crushed ice, offers one up to Isham. The can is tall and silver, magnificently beaded. Isham's head feels light, and he can't remember a worse thirst, but reaching, he thinks, *What am I doing, what am I doing taking a beer from these two?*

"I was managing apartments for Carol's father," Hewitt says. "I didn't have anything much to do—get the hair out of the drains, keep the weeds cut . . . I wasn't even twenty-five."

He looks at his wife—she's there. "I'd stopped being angry, but I wasn't anything else yet. You know what I'm saying?"

Isham searches for something to contribute, but only drinks.

"It was after Jenny was born," Carol says finally. "When you got better."

Hewitt nods at her, a private look.

"This place came up for sale," he says. "A guy named Busey used to run it, but then the bank had it. They approached me, they thought I could turn it around. I didn't know what to do—I was still halfway thinking I'd make it back to Cincinnati."

His eyes bear down on Isham, the good and the not-so-good. "Look, forget it. What I'm telling you, it was Carol who changed her mind on all that other. The *ball.*"

There's only the sound of the air for a moment, the slap of boats at rest.

"You don't have to think the same way all your life," Carol says, matter-of-fact. "That's all. Things happen. You grow. You get something different from what you wanted, but then you're happy enough, anyway."

The two men look at each other. Something rises in Hewitt,

razor-quick, but Carol touches his arm, and, that fast, it's gone.

"So, what do you think?" Carol says. "You going to take the boat out anyway? Might as well, you paid."

No, Isham has to go. Has to retrace his steps up the narrow dock, and burn away from this place, has to slide back into that perpetual half-hunger that's his life. But instead, next thing, he is dropping down into one of their boats, a twelve-foot aluminum SportCraft, in his ridiculous clothes, listening to Hewitt's voice instructing him on the whereabouts of snags and gravel bars, and the old town of Estelle, named for somebody's love. Then Hewitt tips the engine into the water and fires it to an idle.

Carol Hewitt is standing by her husband, hip to hip. "Here's the story," she says to Isham. "Some places you have to lose in. That's why they were invented."

And then a foot is pushing him off. Isham has that most routine of thoughts, *Goddamn my life, goddamn every wonder that ceases.* Seconds later, though, the air is rushing, parting for him. It occurs to him the boy had it wrong. They wouldn't leave the graveyard down under the water. Before they'd let the river bottom flood, they'd dig up the caskets and carry them to high ground. There's nothing down there, a few empty shacks, nothing worthy of horror. He hunches forward on the seat, hair blowing, right hand on the throttle. There is actually, now that he notices, plenty of daylight left.

BLUE SPRUCE

L aurel is up in the cool shadow on the porch roof, in dungarees and a sweatshirt, scraping off the pine needles with a snow shovel. Below, an old garden hose snakes across the knobby dirt, its pinhole leak shooting up a spray that fizzes in a slash of sunlight. There's a breath of wind, a commotion in the lilacs. Down the lane, stones are finally warming in their sockets. Between branches, she can see the water tower on Buffalo Hill, the long gravel slide below the golf course, the blinding curlicues of the river.

Eva appears on the walk, church-dressed. "What's this?" she says, squinting. "You're not ready?"

"Not going," Laurel calls down. "Which I told you."

"Well, I guess I just don't believe that."

"Believe it. It's too fine a day."

"After all Mrs. Proctor did for you."

"I'm a rat," Laurel says.

Eva's car—a balky, inherited Olds—is in the shop again, so she is obliged to take Laurel's silver-flecked Prelude. She wiggles in, makes a fine show of adjusting the mirrors and the seat, angling the wheel down, as if Laurel were grotesquely outsized. The lane is just dry enough to send up a thin slipstream of dust that lazes off into the milkweed as she drives away. Go, *go*, Laurel thinks, and once Eva is safely out of sight she claps her hands on her jeans and heads for the ladder. It *is* a fine day. Her heart is rushing with mischief.

Routinely called the Mahugh sisters, they are, in fact, sisters-in-law. Eva was a Bean, married to Laurel's younger brother Eddie. People often take Eva for the older of the two, when, in fact, Laurel is fifty-six, and Eva, who has the raddled face of an ardent smoker, has just reached fifty. Laurel is the less familiar figure in town; before her return, three years ago, she'd spent almost thirty years overseas. She was a civil service employee with the air force, posted mainly in the Far East. She has a rangy, uncomplaining body, and a bantering way men have been drawn to (though not, as it's turned out, for long). But she's had a life, seen a good many things. In Manila, she once watched the head of a young man being carried on the point of a stick down a honeycomb of tiny, sweltering streets. "His eyes were wide open," she later reported to Eva. "You felt he was going to hurl words at you. Oh, and just imagine what they'd be!" Eva waves away such stories, as if they're spurious, told for the sake of shocking her. "That's just your mean streak talking," she sometimes says.

The other Mahughs—two brothers, another sister—have blown to the four winds, Eva says. By this she means: Billings, Casper, Wenatchee. Eva and Eddie stayed in town. For years, Eddie worked under his father, old Warren Mahugh, at Equity Supply, and after Eddie's mother passed away he and Eva sold their place and moved back into his parents' house to look after

Warren. Laurel may have seniority, but Eva has lived under this roof with a husband, which must count for something. She was the one who nursemaided Laurel's father—he was diabetic, nearly blind, and full of staunch, gloomy ideas. Did she ever gripe in public, ever shirk, ever lose patience? Each fall, she'd catch herself thinking, Now, he can't last another winter, can he? and hate herself. Finally, one February, he did die. "Oh, I know how you must feel," she told Eddie, but that wasn't true—she didn't have any idea.

She and Eddie were alone in the house then. What *she* felt was a joy laced with dread. She thought Eddie might bloom, with Warren out of his way, but he seemed, if anything, quieter—a nearly middle-aged man with a long, somber face roughed up each morning by a razor. She waited, she watched him. He was so familiar. He was always checking on things, giving his odd sighs, his barely audible status reports. But he didn't seem to have anything you could think of, really, as desires. "Would you want to take a little trip?" Eva asked him. He didn't think so. Summer came and passed, cool and rainy, hardly any respite at all. "What can I do for you?" she would ask. "What is it you want?" No, she never quite forced it out of him.

One morning that fall, he told her he'd be hunting over west of Swain's Creek. "Who with?" she said, surprised. He'd skipped the last few seasons, and she thought he'd lost the taste for it.

"No one," he said.

"Is that a good idea?" she asked him.

"I don't see that it matters," Eddie said. That was his valedictory. They found him barely half a mile from the truck, seated under a balsam, his gun barrel resting on the front of his jacket, and his head blown to nothing. The jacket had once been Warren's.

"Had he been acting funny?" the sheriff asked Eva.

"No, no. I can't help you," she said. "Go away."

"Mrs. Mahugh—" The man looked exhausted, standing in the kitchen doorway, tapping his hat against his pant leg. But he did go away after a while. It occurred to her later that maybe he wanted her to beg: *Oh, God, no—he must have fallen, he must have tripped over something.* But Eddie was never clumsy, never careless.

Laurel had been posted on Guam, and by the time she could get home, Eddie had already been buried. "She couldn't wait one more day?" Laurel asked, incredulous at the news. "God, that woman—"

One of her brothers took her shoulder. "Eva's awfully keyed up," he said. "You know how she gets."

It was sleeting. Laurel had been traveling two nights, sitting up in rancid clothes. Someone gave her a drink, a plate of cold chicken. Eva had locked herself in her room. The next morning, Laurel drove up to the cemetery alone, and walked through the slop of horse-chestnut leaves. There were her parents, Warren and Grace. There was Eddie, first of the next bunch. "What are you *doing* here?" she asked him, furious. Eddie made no more of an answer than he would have alive.

Laurel stood in the wind, bareheaded, stubbing her toe against the chunks of brown sod. They'd been conspirators, she and Eddie, born fifteen months apart, both of them long and thin. Each had Warren's hatchet nose and faint, almost colorless hair. As they grew up, Eddie taught her solitary tricks he'd learned—how to hot-wire the truck, how to hypnotize a chicken with a penlight. Later on, Laurel taught him dirty limericks (though Eddie would surely never pass them along), and got him to undo his top shirt button and use a little aftershave, and not act so cowed. "Cheer up, Eduardo," she told him. "You can be sweet, girls like a sweet boy." But Eddie didn't cheer up. The muted, flinching part of him took over. Laurel left town. In California, she went to night school and worked days for a shipping company. When Eddie eventually graduated, she phoned him long-distance. "Come and see the ocean," she offered. He sounded enormously far away. "Who knows," he said, "I might just do that." But Laurel knew he never would. A year later, she passed her civil service test—then she was in Okinawa. Had she run out on him, abandoned him? She wrote him now and then, but finally gave it up—he never answered, what was the use? Eva sometimes wrote to her—airmail letters full of dull, dutiful goings-on. Eddie moved through them like a stick man.

Laurel had just put in for retirement when the cable reached her in Guam. She was camped out in her flat, waiting for the paperwork to clear, waiting for something new. She had no intention of staying on in Montana, much less with Eva. Good Lord, what an arrangement. But by the end of the second week, the rest of the family had scattered. Eva was a mess. Untranquilized, she sobbed in place. Dosed, she strayed—Laurel found her on the stairs, cheek pasted to the wallpaper, and another day out in the loft of the shed going through boxes of machine parts.

"God only knows how I'm going to manage all this," Eva said.

Laurel didn't reply. But didn't she, somehow, offer those mealy-sounding words Eva required? Didn't she handle the bank, didn't she fix the first hundred suppers and endure their consumption, didn't she find somebody to cart off Eddie's drill press and the ancient Willys he'd had up on blocks near the chicken yard, not to mention six pairs of curly-soled boots loitering in the vestibule?

The house is gray-shaked and stands alone at the top of the property. Pinewoods rise in back, alfalfa stretches south to the road. A few ravaged plum and crab-apple trees cling to the hillside. Mainly, it's a big, dark place, with a cluttered, wraparound, closed-in porch. "The catchall," Laurel calls this, "the outdoor closet." It reeks of varnish dust and creosote and ancient bug killers; its windows are like the bottom of an old baking dish. The house is further obscured by six towering blue spruce trees, installed by Warren Mahugh himself in the spring of 1929—a gift to his new wife, Eva reminds people. They're historic, symbolic of love: grand, sheltering trees. However, they were planted too close together and much too close to the house—it's as if he'd never envisioned them *growing*. The lower limbs have scrubbed the color from the shakes. The roots have infiltrated the foundation, the septic line, the flagstones in the walk. The trees drip sap, the needles clog the gutters and turn the soil too acidic for grass. They suffocate, Laurel says; they bury the household in an intractable gloom.

•   •   •

EVA HAS A HEADACHE, driving home. The spring sun is vicious—suddenly the world's all glass and stainless steel. The luncheon after Mrs. Proctor's service, held in a hot, fruity-smelling room, was thinly attended, and what could be said, really, about their old teacher Mrs. Proctor, years retired, her mind in tatters? We live too long, Eva thought, that's all there is to it. She finds herself staring, wishing for a beer. Just one, cold as a spike. Her head behind the car's visor, she is nearly to the top of the lane before she sees what has happened.

The trees have been cut down.

They're fanned out from the house, colossal green hulks stretching clear across the lawn. One has snapped off a length of rail fence, the top of another is curled awkwardly against the well house. The trunks have been cut into sections, and two are already limbed. There's a rusty, high-walled truck in the drive. Laurel is standing at the porch steps talking to a man kneeling by a red gasoline can. All this Eva sees in an instant. None of it seems remotely possible.

The man she recognizes as Ethan Wilder, a widower who lives down by the big curve, among a welter of vehicles and sloping outbuildings. She knew the wife a little from church—cancer of the ovaries, Eva recalls. He's wearing plastic goggles and a stocking cap and overalls, woodchips from head to toe. He has grown a thicket of beard—that she notices, too.

Laurel steps forward, arms spread wide. "Shoot me," she says. "I just made a decision. The day had come."

Eva is beyond speech.

Ethan, who has been about to resume the limbing, lets the chain saw hang in one hand, perceiving what he has done. "Oh, now," he says. For all his size—his large shoulders and sloping belly—his movements seem gentle and precise.

Laurel touches one bare, sweaty forearm. "This will all be fine," she says reassuringly. "Really. Don't you worry."

Ethan draws back and tips his goggles up onto his forehead. "Mrs. Mahugh, now I never—" he says to Eva, but she is already striding off into the house. Laurel turns in time to see her kick nastily at the brick propping the porch door open. Ethan casts another look at the carnage. "I best leave this for today," he says. Moments later he rumbles away in his truck.

•   •   •

"THAT WAS THE MOST *SAVAGE*—" Eva says.

"It wasn't either savage," Laurel says. "Such melodrama. You'd never do anything if it weren't for me."

Holding a dripping colander, she steps back from the sink window. "Look at the light in here," she says. The sky has gauzed over since midday, and the room is brandy-tinged, a tough light to nurse anger in.

Eva is still in her funeral outfit, though her earrings have been plucked off and deposited by the creamer. "I don't think I can eat," she says.

"You'll thank me," Laurel says.

There had been a little modernizing after Eddie and Eva moved back in. Eddie lowered the ceiling and laid in new countertops, and now there is a freestanding dishwasher, with a chopping board on top. But the cupboards are old, with chipped glass pulls, and the deep old porcelain sink remains, with a swan's-neck faucet and squeaky taps. Things clatter in this kitchen, voices carry.

"As God is my witness," Eva says, but no threat follows, and there's nothing, really, to suggest that God is going to make her vindication His special project.

"Have a glass of beer," Laurel says.

"I saw your eyes," Eva says. "There was *glee* in them."

"That's me. Lover of life."

It's going on midnight when Laurel finally slides under the covers in the downstairs bedroom. She lies on her back, savoring the cold sheets. There's a Walkman under her pillow, playing some Charlie Parker. She has no intention of sleeping yet. The screens are on, and the night enters deliciously, molecule by molecule. The music is dazzling, druggy. Her last conscious thought is she'd bet money Eva is upstairs in her cane rocking chair, with the lights out, smoking.

And so she is. Eddie had told Eva, years ago, never to smoke in bed. "Promise me!" he insisted. As a boy, he'd seen the Saxon Hotel fire downtown—six bodies laid out on the sidewalk under sheets. So Eva promised, continues to promise. She sits in the dormer, rocking. With the storms off, the night makes noise again—it's as if her ears have popped.

But there's none of that rustle, that *sh-shushing* against the roof peak.

One spring, she remembers, crows took to the spruces, nasty braying things. She had sent Eddie out to scare them off, at five-thirty in the morning. He fired his shotgun in their vicinity—even in full daylight, you couldn't see them back in the branches. The crows flapped off, six or eight of them, heading toward the Mastersons' hayfield. But they were back the following morning, racketing, voices like hacksaws. Eddie slept on—soft simple sleep—he never dreamed, so he said (and never smelled unpleasant next to her, she remembered, only a little stale and sugary). She poked him, made him go out again in his bathrobe and spray more shot up at the crows. He stood back by the well house, a gray figure in the early light. Cones and needles rained down, but no dead crows. Eddie came back to bed. She thanked him, and he said, "Now, don't *thank* me, Eva," and went straight to sleep again, as if he'd been switched off. The next morning they went through the same drill. On the fourth day of it he said in that resigned way of his, "Eva, you're just going to have to put up with it." And so she did. June and July passed, and then the crows were gone, as if they'd been a black mood she'd outlived.

• • •

DRIZZLE IN THE A.M.

Laurel has her coffee in peace. Eva is off at church—this churchgoing is spotty, Laurel has noticed; not a response to guilt but to the creep of chaos. And Eva had to ask Laurel for the car again. "No sweat," Laurel said. "And why don't you gas it up while you're at it." Didn't *that* frost Eva.

Ethan Wilder is supposed to return after lunch, with his boys, but Laurel imagines that's off. The sound yesterday, that was what surprised her. The ground shaking—a great *whump;* made her jump straight in the air. She stood off to the side, awaiting the next. *Whump!* She shouted at him, her heart racing, but he couldn't hear over the saw.

Laurel carries her coffee out the side door. The stumps are oozing. Cones and debris everywhere. She steps back into the grass, getting her feet wet, looking at the house. It needs paint desperately. Maybe she'll have the porch ripped off, a deck put on, some latticework. But it looks naked now—tall and wan, an embarrassing old thing. The soffits are dry-rotted, the shingles are heaped with moss, and where they're not, they're thin as scales.

•   •   •

LAUREL WAS RIGHT ABOUT ETHAN WILDER. Kept his distance all day Sunday, letting the dust settle. Monday, her lilac suit out of dry dock again, she is back at work. She has her pension—decent, actually—but a few months of living with Eva made her hustle a job downtown in a den of lawyers. Shirtliff, the senior partner, stops before her desk this morning, red-cheeked, unsticking filaments of sweaty white hair from his forehead. He's found the sacrament of walking, pounds out the miles swinging little nickel-plated hand weights. "And how's your liver and lights?" he asks.

Laurel has her reputation in this office: utterly proficient, immune to the ordinary tomfoolery, a gamer. "Couldn't be finer," she answers, stretching, mock-languid. Shirtliff smiles, showing teeth. Later, she can hear him humming a bit of sad, lilting melody: "*The days be fast a-wasting, and all the fair maids . . .* something something." But nothing engages her today. Her mind idles, slips off into the sounds of traffic, the moseying of the dusty air. She finds herself in imaginary conversation—not with Shirtliff but with Ethan Wilder. She is smelling the pitch again, breathing the blue exhaust from

the chain saw. She almost calls him, then laughs at herself—
You old bird. At five, she gets into her car, finds it still reeking
of Eva's mentholated smoke. She downshifts at the railroad
crossing, and is startled again at how the house sits up at the
top of the fields, so *exposed.* Then, roaring up the lane, she
sees that the truck has come and gone, carrying away
branches. Only the trunks remain, like fallen columns.

By Tuesday night, the trunks have been cut into stove
rounds and stacked against the wire fence of Eddie's chicken
run. A huge amount of wood—they'll be burning it winter
after winter. The grass is muddy now, tracked by chunky tires
and boot heels, but there's been an attentive raking. All that's
left is eight or ten small mounds of needles and sticks waiting to be picked up. Tuesday is one of Eva's nights to cook.
Supper appears at six o'clock straight up (even this is a con-
cession, Eva insists—Eddie never could wait *that* long). And
here it is: skinned chicken, steamed limas, Minute Rice and
pimento. Monkish portions. There's been a realignment of
the kitchen table: Laurel's chair now faces the sun. She
smiles; this is nothing. "They make handsome blinds these
days," she says. "Little slats—*louvres.*"

"Why don't you go ahead and start," Eva says from the
stove, seeing that Laurel, as usual, hasn't bothered to wait.
Finally Eva sits, gets up for the lemon pepper, sits again.

"Any sweets?" Laurel asks.

"You know better than to ask," Eva says.

"Still peeved, are we?"

Eva looks at her, fork poised. "You make everything—"
she begins.

What's the word she will light on? *Petty? Squalid?* Say it,
Laurel thinks. Render judgment. But Eva fills her mouth
with rice. Laurel watches the muscle in her jaw pumping,
pumping, raising a knob of shadow.

• • •

WEDNESDAY THE STUMPS ARE GONE. Ethan had explained before he'd made the first cut that ordinarily he'd yank them with his tractor and a tow chain. But there was a good chance—old as they were, and possibly grown into the stonework—that he might have to dose them with ROT-X and let them molder. "Or you could leave them be. Some do," he said. "If it was me, I'd want them gone."

And so they are gone, like huge wisdom teeth. The holes are filled in with dark, peaty loam—so fine-grained it must have been sifted through a screen. Now it's been seeded and tamped and sprinkled.

Eva seems brighter that night. Lacks the stuff for holding a deep grudge, Laurel imagines.

By Thursday evening, Eva's car has been restored to service, and she's out in it, apparently. Laurel, home from work, scans the counter for a note, sees none. She changes, and then roams the downstairs, awash with energy. She fixes a drink and takes it to the front steps. It's not quite warm enough to sit out. Nevertheless, she sits, stretching her legs, lightly goose-bumped. The sun is shouldering down through a ledge of cloud, striking the mountains across the valley pink. The pink of candy hearts, she thinks—of undercooked pork.

Up the lane, a moment later, lumbers Ethan Wilder's truck. He descends gingerly from the cab.

"You're an artist," Laurel says, waving her hand at the neat, bare earth.

This embarrasses him—not what she had in mind at all. She touches his chest. "No, look how you've opened it all up—you have no idea the gloom we had here."

But he won't look at his handiwork. He's not in work clothes, either. He's wearing chinos, a checked shirt with a brass-tipped string tie, clean boots. The panels of cheek above his whiskers have a shine.

What's going on? Is she supposed to offer him something? A beer?

"Well," she says, "I expect you'd like to get paid."

"Eva's not here?"

"Actually not," Laurel says brightly.

But there's a moment's sag in his shoulders, a settling of his substantial weight—she catches it. "Would you give her a message?" he asks. "Tell her—" But no, it's apparently not anything he can put into words.

• • •

THE HAYFIELDS BRIGHTEN, the days stretch out, a frail green haze begins to obscure the topsoil along the foundation. Evenings, Ethan Wilder becomes a common sight at the Mahugh house. He listens to Laurel's notions about the renovation, stands outside with her, looking where she points, offers the occasional "Uh-huh, uh-huh, don't see why not," and gets up and measures possible openings. But Eva is nearby, wearing Bermudas and a jaunty navy-striped blouse. She's had her hair hennaed. Furthermore, she's begun to take an interest in the remodeling.

"What do you think about skylights?" she asks Ethan one night. "Wouldn't they be, oh, I don't know, kind of—"

"Stimulating," Laurel says.

Eva coils, but then says, "Yes, I guess that is what I meant."

Of course, the only place you could stick a skylight in an old frame house like theirs is Eva's room, still called—cloyingly, Laurel feels—the master bedroom.

"You don't fool a soul," she tells Eva when they're alone again.

"You can't pick a fight with me," Eva replies.

"No, really. Anybody could see what you were up to out there."

Eva stubs out her Kool and gets up. "Won't take the bait," she says.

•   •   •

ON JULY FOURTH it comes up rain.

"Further evidence God isn't a working stiff," Laurel says.

No rise out of Eva.

"We were wondering," Eva says, later that day—*we:* she and Ethan, there it is—"if you wanted to come down to the lake and see the fireworks with us."

"You're kind," Laurel says. "But I don't believe I'll be able to squeeze that in."

Eva waits by the door, watching the lane, fiddling with her rain hood. "Well, you were invited," she says. "So you know."

Laurel shakes her head. "Look at you," she says.

"I look fine. There's nothing wrong with me."

Lord, what have I wrought? Laurel thinks, once they're gone, but it's not a thought she can bear. The house feels clammy—no place to be. She grabs her jacket finally and drives to the movies, and by the time they're out, the rain has all but quit. She has that flushed, stupid feeling. She sweeps her hand through the beaded water on the car's roof, splashing some down into the neck of her shirt. *What now?* She swings out onto Montana Street, thinking maybe the Dairy Queen, then doesn't stop after all. She veers down through town—*cutting the gut*, isn't that what they used to call it? The lights smear by, packs of tiny fireworks dance and spit in the limited darkness. The traffic curls around the courthouse, low-slung cars like hers, thick with kids, but when they begin to turn out and loop back she goes straight and finds herself alone on the road, fighting back a sudden weakness of heart. She turns onto McCandlish, and takes the long way, past the orchards and the horse pastures, and, for no good reason, past Ethan Wilder's. The house is flanked by a woodlot, down out of the wind. All she's ever seen of it is the spidery antenna coming off the steel roof.

She makes the big curve and crests the hill and pulls over where she can see the whole lower valley, down to the north end of the lake. The sky is low and empty—nothing but black-bottomed cloud, and an occasional minor rocket launched from a boat. Cars are streaming away from the landing—they're backed up a mile at the cutoff to town.

Laurel stands breathing the wet air. Spectacle's over, she thinks.

Next morning, everything lies under a heavy mist. The Mastersons' sheep bleat in the distance. Ethan and his two boys arrive. *Boys*—they are twenty-five and twenty-six, with tool belts and thermoses, and long glossy muscles extending from their shirtsleeves. Laurel moves among them, looking each in the eye. She hands Ethan a square of paper with her work number. "Look, now call me if there's *anything*—I mean it," she says. She's galled at the idea of Eva presiding.

Shirtliff is out of town, and the younger men in the office are grumpy from the long weekend. Laurel forgoes lunch downtown and guns the car home, squinting fiercely. The air is glazed with light now, as the fog tries to burn off.

And yes, the porch roof has gone. The stained, rattling old porch windows are stacked on the truck bed, and the stud walls have been bared. Ethan's two boys are crouched in the wreckage, wolfing sandwiches and swilling cartons of milk. Ethan sits with his back to the shakes, legs splayed, slicing apple and cheese. Eva is standing before them, with her hands stuffed in her sweater pockets. "Can I get you something else?" she asks Ethan.

"Don't hover, Eva," Laurel says.

Ethan collapses his little knife and gets up. "Can't pack it away like I used to," he says pleasantly. The boys yawn and rise. The wrecking bars come out again. Eva trails after Ethan, stepping anxiously, as if the ground were mined. Just beyond the new grass, he stops by a pair of sawhorses and begins jerking nails from the salvaged wood. An easy, practiced motion, a brief wincing sound.

This can't possibly last, Laurel thinks.

In the next days, posts are sunk, cedar decking creeps around the side of the house, and a sliding glass door goes in. Huge, immaculate Thermopanes replace the stingy downstairs windows. Foam is blown into the walls, and one of the boys spends a morning on a stepladder tapping new shakes into place. Ethan is careful to ask Laurel, "How's this look to you now? This pretty much how you had it pictured?"

"Yes, it seems perfectly—" Laurel says. But what? For all the pointing and talking out loud, she hardly had it *pictured* at all. Wasn't it more a craving? Light! Air!

At last, one of the boys—Martin, the lankier, unmarried one—climbs onto the main roof and saws out a long rectangle of shingle and planking as, inside, Laurel watches Ethan cut away plaster and lath and rafters. Eva has smothered everything with sheets. The dust flies everywhere, swirling in with the fresh air. The other boy, Walt, has taken the truck down to pick up the skylight. He's the younger, more subdued one, with an oily faced, hugely pregnant wife. Something about him reminds Laurel of Eddie: the way he turns away as he's spoken to, expecting blame.

Now he's back from Sperry Glass, empty-handed. "Sent the wrong size." he reports.

"Cripes!" Ethan says, the most violent display of temper Laurel has yet seen out of him. "How long'd they say?"

The boy shrugs, starts explaining: The manager wasn't in, there was a question about who'd actually written down the measurements, the company is clear back in *Toledo* . . .

Ethan puts a hand up. "Run and get me that roll of VisQueen," he says. "The black."

Walt removes himself, dodging past Laurel in the doorway. Ethan wipes his eyelids with his thumbs and takes a slow breath, looking around at the white-draped room. *This is her bedroom,* his face says. *These are her things.*

Eva is down on one knee, collecting chunks of plaster in a dustpan. "Eva?" he says, hesitating, then touching her shoulder. "*Eva.* I'll get that."

• • •

THIS, AS IT TURNS OUT, is the first night Eva fails to come home. It's Saturday noon before she surfaces. Laurel is picking at leftovers in the kitchen. "I was this close to calling out the gendarmes," she announces.

Eva gives her that look, her minute tremor of disapproval. "I don't believe that for a second," she says. "You knew where I was."

Laurel scrapes her chair back and slides the rest of her lunch into the compost. "Aren't you something," she says.

Eva sets down her bag, a little green canvas thing with a strap, digs into the pie saver for a fresh pack of Kools, and rips into them. "I'm a perfectly ordinary person," she says. "With ordinary needs. I have no pretensions to the higher life."

Without meaning to, Laurel laughs.

Eva turns. "I know what you're going to try next and you can save your breath," she says.

"What? *Tell me.*"

Eva's eyes burn. "I will not have you spoiling this," she says.

"Now, why on earth would I want—" Laurel begins, by rote. But it's true, she was already casting about for some disparagement, some sly prediction.

"You've said the last hateful thing to me," Eva says, exiting, trailing smoke, her hips switching with vindication. Out into the dining room she goes, and up the stairs, *clip, clip*.

Water runs briefly in the pipes. The house settles into a heavy stillness and the minutes pass. Laurel's legs weave among the chair rungs. It's hot, finally, wilting hot, hot down into the earth.

Is she hateful? Is that all she is, another sour, disappointed soul?

There is at least this: She has held her tongue about Eddie. She has never once gotten into it with Eva, never pinned her down: *Tell me why a happy, married man, with a wife he adores, drives his truck forty miles back in the hell-and-gone and puts his shotgun in his mouth. Explain that away, Eva.*

There is no blaming Eva; there is no story, with its simple satisfactions, to badger out of her. Eva is as baffled as she is.

Laurel stands, unsticks the blouse from her stomach, and mounts the staircase, calling lightly from the landing, "Eva? Eva?" It will be miserable up on the second floor—hotter yet, stuffy, the stale air hardly stirring.

She touches Eva's door and it gives. There's an old-fashioned lacquered suitcase open on the bed, some white things folded inside, a camisole. But—it's crazy—Eva has gone to the opening in the roof and scissored a jagged, three-sided hole in the black plastic. She's on tiptoe, looking out, framed against the sky, with her dark head of hair blowing. From the back and below, she looks as if she might begin to rise and disappear. Laurel has to wonder, just for a moment, if she will hold her down.

REAL ESTATE

The first time Gil stops by, Rosemary is out back where the ground falls away to the slough, spading over sod for a bed of irises. It's all field grass; the roots go down miles, angel hair, clotted with nuggets of clay. A hot, late spring Saturday after no winter to speak of, the lilacs already bloomed and gone, the mud dried, crumbling. Pollen in the air; isolated, glittering hatches of insects. Earlier in the afternoon, Rosemary's daughter Cassie drove off with another girl, who suddenly has her license. They're getting Cokes, renting movies to watch in the girl's basement (*criminal*, after months indoors, Rosemary said, and received two benign shrugs). The girls are both just fifteen, neither of them trouble, but the other one, Liz, seems drifty, flimsy. How good a driver can she be? Cassie's just the opposite—full of intent, impossible to satisfy. She must overpower Liz, Rosemary thinks. In a way, it's a relief having them gone, but all afternoon, though the air's sweet and lazy, and the bulbs go easily into the dirt, there's the intermittent hiss of worry in her thoughts.

Gil's Saab is spruce-green, the engine so refined she hears nothing until the door gives its *chuff,* shutting. She sees him walking about, checking on things, a good-looking man, no doubt of that. Neat through the waist and hips; hard, blue-veined forearms, though he doesn't, as far as she knows, lift or run. Hair buzzed on the sides, boyishly longer on top, black smudged with silver.

"How long's this been dead?" he asks. He's stopped underneath one of the plum trees, fingering the brittle branch ends.

"It always used to have fruit on it," Rosemary says. "I can't honestly—"

Gil moves on, nodding, then hovers near the back porch as if he'd like to come inside. So Rosemary leads him through the mess.

"Ice coffee in the fridge," she says.

Gil smiles, says, "Excellent," as if it's the very thing he's been wanting.

Long ago this was his aunt's kitchen. Aunt Edie, his father's sister. Gil had ridden here on his bike, dropped it in the same stunted junipers where Cassie drops hers. He'd stood here in this very kitchen and let himself be adored.

"Man, what am I going to do with this place?" he says.

Rosemary looks at him, startled. "But you're not going to do anything with it, are you?"

She and Cassie rent from Gil. He asks two hundred a month less than he could reasonably demand. It's an arrangement closer to house-sitting, and it makes all the difference. For one thing, she's been able to have Cassie's teeth fixed, and the other thing about the house, it's *peaceful.* Rosemary was never one for sitting around doing nothing, but this place has surprised her—it invites contemplation, the quiet moment.

Before this, their apartment abutted a tire garage; seven-thirty in the morning, the ratcheting squeal would start, the cars would begin stinking up the alley. Before that, the trailer on Logan, the place in Conklinville that flooded. She remembers one set of rooms her father visited. "How can you put a baby down on a floor like that," he'd said. It makes her skin crawl to think of it.

Not that this is swank: It's kind of an odd house, improvised-looking. The windows don't match, the doors have been trimmed at the bottom repeatedly. There's no insulation beyond sawdust in the walls, a scant dusting of rock wool in the ceiling upstairs. On the other hand, it's *solid,* dense old unplaned lumber, plaster hard as slate. And there's no traffic—the road ends in a rutted turnaround a hundred yards beyond the house. To the north runs a row of Lombardy poplar, grown thick and tall, lovely trees to watch shaking against the sky. This was Gil's grandfather's place before he made his money and built in town. The land was almost worthless in those days, a narrow bench, dropping off to marshland. He'd swapped a saddle for it, that was the story.

Gil is also her boss. He owns the bar and restaurant, Kid Billy's, where she waitresses—one of the better places, along with Daugherty's and the Hotel, to eat in Sperry. He owns it with another man, an "outside partner" named Harvey Cockrell, a heavy, gray-jowled character in his late fifties. He's seldom around, but when he is, Gil's different: extra cheerful and by-the-book. Then touchy, brittle, for days afterward.

Gil sees he's disturbed her a little, saying that about the house, so he backpedals, says, "Well, no, I was just talking. I'd give you plenty of warning, anyway. It's not like I'd jerk things out from under you."

He downs his iced coffee and begins crunching the ice.

Rosemary takes the glass from his hand and refills it.

Then he's off on his aunt again. Died of a stroke, he says.

"Here? In the house?"

"Naw," he says. "Up at the hospital. She was kind of a flake, though. You want to know what she was doing when I came over once? Weighing her boob. No kidding. She had a big tin scale, what you'd weigh produce on? Her dress was hanging down at her waist and there was her tit flopped out on the scale. Freckles all over it, like Sugar Babies. I was maybe thirteen. What do you make of that?"

"I couldn't say," Rosemary says.

How premeditated was this riff about the aunt, she'll wonder later. Or does it matter in the least what his plans were?

He never puts the moves on anyone at work, a fact that doesn't go unnoticed. They've all worked for men who paw, who routinely cut off their angle of retreat. Gil's too uptight for that. He's not insufferably bossy; he has a veneer of being easy to get along with. Wears plain white shirts, laundered out; jeans and Nikes. Some afternoons he occupies a spot at the curve of the bar and talks to people, listens, absorbs information, nursing one green bottle of Heineken. But he's in charge, yes, and no one escapes his temper entirely. Often he seems preoccupied, behaving as if the whole enterprise is tottering on stilts—though how can it be with all the business they do?

He deposits his glass in the sink, runs water in it. When he turns, she can't legitimately say she's caught off guard. He cups her neck, not attempting to kiss her, yet holding her face against his, immobilized. She looks out at the tin of dried mustard, the calendar with her work days scribbled into the squares, the stretched-out beige telephone cord, and thinks of what he's seeing out the other direction, the screen door with its saggy spring, the back porch's dim cowl, the idle shimmer of poplar leaves. His cheek is hard and glossy, but has no smell, no aftershave or residue of sweat. He inhales deliberately, flattening her breast against his shirt, and Rosemary remains in this embrace, if that's what it is, until he has to do something further. He draws his hand up, lifting the weight of her hair, letting the air touch her neck.

"Gil," she says. "I'm so—"

"What?"

"I was working outside. I'm grungy."

"Take a shower," he says. His voice is creamy, utterly reasonable.

She laughs—she can't help it; it's a habitual way of buying a few seconds, of thwarting hysteria. "No, I'm not taking a *shower*. Come *on*. I can't—"

He smiles now, too. The side window hasn't been cleaned in so long the light on his face is flat, blotted by leaf shadow.

"I'm not coercing you, Rosemary," he says. "You don't think that, do you?"

What now?

"It's not like that at all," he goes on, so lacking in menace she believes this is the moment he's being real with her.

Gil's own house is in one of the developments north of the hospital, up in the ponderosas where the flat-lying farmland of the valley is interrupted by a jut of bedrock. Generous lots, secluded—Rosemary and Cassie have driven all through there, sightseeing. He was married once, she knows, during the time he was in California, and now there's a girlfriend, Linda Cameron, who's a realtor. Straw-blond, *tony*, swings around Gil in loose ellipse.

Loose but how loose?

In the shower Rosemary thinks, This is nuts, I know better than this. She throws on her terry cloth robe without toweling off, yanks the sash, runs a wide plastic comb of Cassie's through her hair, pinches the water from the ends, flicks it away. She hurries back to the kitchen to banter her way out of this.

Gil is still by the sink, drinking hungrily, his head tipped back. She watches without his knowing it, thinks abruptly, What's so wrong with being wanted?

Gil turns, takes her in.

What surprises her is her own hunger, revived out of God knows where. Stripped of his clothes, he looks like a swimmer, triangular, bunched in the shoulders, tapering to a tan line suggesting a Speedo suit. There's nothing rough in his manner; rather, he's methodical, inward.

He breaks off after a while and stands at the edge of the mattress, his body running with sweat. Her bedroom lies under the roof peak, facing the road. The window is tall and broad, hinged on the side so that it swings in. Gil grabs up one of her pillows, positions it on the sill, extends his hand to her as if requesting a waltz.

Does she offer even a token protest?

He stations himself behind her, grasping her hips as her forearms rest, almost comfortably, on the padded surface. Across the road is a horse pasture; farther off, a pair of ranch houses, then foothills blurring into mountains, green, then green-blue, then blue. The aspen leaves are rattling, swiveling on their stems. Rosemary watches a cat sashay up the gravel drive and vanish into the weeds.

"Some view," Gil says.

"Yeah, well, for *them.*"

After a moment, Gil answers, "There's no them out there, Rosemary." It's true, they're alone in the world. A burst of wind washes across their skin.

"There," he says. "No, *hold still.* Feel that? Tell me you ever felt anything better than that."

• • •

THE NEXT TIME IT'S A WORK NIGHT, a Thursday,
late. Kid Billy's was steady all evening, just short of frantic.
Early June was always a dead time, a breather, but now that
the valley has been discovered there's no letup. Cars constantly trolling the lot, tourist buses, tables full of people
with matching carnations. She was on with Kitty, Susannah,
ripply-haired Margaret. Didn't see Gil all shift but he's often
out of sight, sequestered in the office.

Outwardly, he's been no different to her, neither partial
nor expressly cool. He speaks normally—has she seen where
the keys to the cellar have gotten to, will she remind Kitty he
needs her change of withholding? Each time he walks off,
Rosemary instantly checks the other women, but nobody notices anything. They're at work, on cruise control. Has he
been to their places? She doubts it.

But now Gil is under her porch light, under its swirl of
bugs and millers; he's calling her name, squinting in, tapping
the glass with his index finger.

She opens up and he's greatly relieved at the sight of her.

She touches his sleeve, half-whispers, "You know my
daughter's here. Cassie?"

He nods, slipping past her into the kitchen. "It's late, isn't
it?" he says. "I'm *sorry*. I wanted to see you, that's all. That's
the whole thing."

"Well, here I am," Rosemary says. "But I'm beat, Gil. You
understand?"

He collapses at the table.

"I guess I could make coffee," she says.

His stare isn't pushy or unkind; neither is it relaxed, settled. When he moves his hand on the table, there appear,
briefly, halos of heat where his fingertips rested.

"Maybe you don't need any more coffee, huh?"

"I'm a little wired," he says. "I admit it."

What is it, what's wrong? It's more than just sex, isn't it?
she thinks, but says nothing. Anyway, you wouldn't go at a
man like Gil head-on.

"Well, look," she says, "Cassie's right in the next room."

"There?" he says, looking at the door. "That used to be
Edie's junk room. What's she want to sleep in *there* for?"

Rosemary shrugs as if there's no accounting for taste.
"Must appeal to her," she says. But why sound so matter-of-
fact? Cassie has precise reasons for loving that hideaway of
hers, closest to the kitchen's heat in winter, the window
canopied by horse chestnut leaves in summer. And it's closest to the door.

"I loved her, you know. Edie," he says. "But she was a
slovenly woman, if you want to know the truth."

"Really?" Rosemary says. "I'm probably no better."

Gil flares at this. "You're *nothing* like her," he says, bringing them to a dead stall.

Finally Rosemary asks, "You want to come upstairs?"
Softly, with as much indifference as she can muster.

He lies on her bed, clothed; Rosemary massages his chest,
through the shirt, then under it, and his breathing slows.
Maybe, the way he's wired himself, this is all he needs. Heat
pulses off him.

She leans over his face to see if he's asleep, then eases her
shoes off and lets herself down onto the bedspread.

After a minute, his legs suddenly lock, his torso seizes up.
"*Jesus*," he says. "Oh, man." He reaches out to get his bearings. "It's pitch-dark in here."

There's a candle on the bureau, but she can locate no
matches among the debris of bracelets and receipts and hair
combs. Instead, she pulls the closet light's chain, cracks the

door, and tiptoes back to the bed. He's stripped down, but still outside the covers, a long, gray chrysalis. It's almost as weird to be the one dressed as the one naked, she thinks as she pulls the jersey top over her head.

She comes almost immediately; it's embarrassing to seem so needy, so easily engulfed. All that panting and biting ridges into her lip, trying not to make noise.

But Gil keeps going, working at her in bursts that last a minute or two, stopping abruptly; he adjusts her hips, lifts them higher and goes again. At some point in these proceedings, the closet door has swung shut. Rosemary is sticky hot now, breathless, her hair swamping her face. The rungs of the headboard have become wedged against her scalp; he seems to realize this finally, and yanks her heavily backward.

"Why don't you *rest*, Gil," she says, nicely.

He keeps at it, reworking his grip on her constantly as if he can't get any purchase. "I can't *see* you," he says, ripping himself away. "It's a goddamn tomb in here."

She sits up, hears his feet rocking the floorboards. "I can't get anywhere with the light off," he says.

"*Here*," she says. "Here, please—"

She reaches out, passes her hand through the darkness, catches hold of him. He's massive, impacted.

●　　●　　●

START OF SHIFT, a few days later. Rosemary is lugging a bucket of ice; Linda Cameron breaks through the glare of the front door, strides the length of the bar, tall and sunshaded, wearing a sleeveless blouse from a catalog—seafoam or kiwi or some concocted name like that. She disappears into Gil's office, the door thuds behind her—it's steel-plated with an extra hasp welded on, leaving a corona of scorched, iridescent metal. Rosemary stares a moment, until the handle of the ice bucket begins to cut into her hand and she sets it down.

That night, coming in through the kitchen, she sees Cassie's light under her door, hears the tape player, calls out, "I'm back." She opens the fridge, examines its unappealing contents, lets the door drift shut, reaches over the sink for a B complex, rolls the gelcap between her fingers, swallows it dry. In Cassie's room the song ends, another begins, laconic, barely audible. Sinéad O'Connor? Cowboy Junkies?

Then a noise comes from outside—a kick, something metallic. Gil making his way around back? She squints out, can't see, kills the overhead light and waves the curtain aside again.

Behind her, suddenly, the door bangs open, the light snaps violently on.

Cassie stands looking at her, mouth-breathing, her lower lip pooched out from the braces.

"What are you *doing*," Rosemary says. "You scared me. I thought—"

"I was just outside," Cassie says. "I wasn't *doing* anything." She's compact and masculine-looking, with her father's thick eyebrows and flat, impatient gaze. She's in overalls, cut off high on her freckled legs. "I wasn't sneaking around."

"I didn't say that, but, honey, where were you?"

"No place. Out on the road. Walking."

"You've got grass all over you. Your hair—"

"Okay, I was lying down."

"Alone?"

"*Yes*, alone. What do you *think?*"

"Sweetheart," Rosemary says.

Cassie draws a breath, ready to give this injustice the full treatment, then changes her mind. She says simply, "I was looking at the stars, all right? Anything especially wrong with that?"

She stands flat-footed, unabashed, waiting to absorb the

next irrelevance from Rosemary, but then the act breaks down, or takes a form that catches them both off guard: Suddenly weightless on her toes, Cassie presses her hot cheek against Rosemary's, holds it there until Rosemary murmurs again, *Sweetheart.* The sound of their skin unsticking, a blur of hair; Cassie pivots and is gone.

Rosemary retreats to the upstairs and undresses, but sleep's hopeless. Out the window, there's the rattle of poplars, the rollick of a sleepless horse across the road. After a few minutes, she finds herself thinking not of Gil, but of Cassie's father, Jack Brothers. The one big love you're entitled to, she used to say of him. Gone to Alaska to work the salmon boats and make his mint. The last faintly plausible rumor of him is nearly ten years old. For a good part of that time, she believed she'd see him again—not a wish so much as a visceral certainty. Awake, as now, she could cast out her radar and sense him, out at the world's edge, his thick legs momentarily planted, his lips chapped, his eyes fighting the sun. Now she's convinced he's dead. Drowned, frozen. She's sure of it. Such a waste. *Jack, Jack, Bo-Jack,* she whispers, a taste of the old incantation, but breaks it off.

Not that eddy again.

She climbs out of bed and sits on the stairs awhile. A little breeze comes teasing through the darkness. Beneath her there's a strip of old carpet runner, big lavish gardenias reduced to bare twine, and beside it, she discovered once, an assemblage of cigarette burns, black glossy runnels in the varnish, one on top of another. Gil's slovenly aunt, with her freckled breasts down inside some nightie. Fretting, dreaming, who can say about what?

Rosemary tips her face against the cool plaster, listens, wills her heart to settle, and it does. Finally the night seems inert.

This is Cassie's last summer not to work. In a year she'll be one of those feckless, smiley faces at the Dairy Queen or Rax or the taco emporium in the mall. Why rush that? But you can't let her run wild, either. Weeks ago, Rosemary made her sign up for a summer school class—Cassie chose drawing, but now seems to hate it. "It's so pathetic. I can't even draw a piece of fruit," she tells Rosemary, as if Rosemary had dreamed it up to showcase her unworthiness. "I'm never going to be an *artist*, it's not like I have *pretensions*."

And when Rosemary won't get sucked into that one, Cassie says, "What you don't seem to *get* is that I'm not a genius." Chin out as if it she expects a slap—ludicrous. *What is it,* Rosemary would like to ask, *why are you acting like this?* But when she sees Cassie's drawings, it's not their imperfection that moves her, but their sheer number. Plum after plum after plum. And farther back in the sketchbook, pages of hands—inelegant, nails bitten down, unmistakably Cassie's, the right drawn insatiably by the left.

●　　●　　●

GIL SENDS WORD he wants to see her. He's at his desk, conversing silently with the Macintosh screen. The office sits in the middle of the building, windowless but for a pocked, painted-over skylight. The walls are a gray pebbly plaster sheathed with corkboard. Licenses, schedules, faint Xeroxed cartoons.

He looks up, orients himself. "I wanted to tell you," he says, "that it's good how you're being."

Keeping her mouth shut. Asking for nothing.

She comes a step closer, cups a hand on his shoulder, and slides down to eye level. I can't live like this indefinitely, she thinks. But she's not prepared to say it, not yet.

"I'm fine," she says. "No problema."

•   •   •

ANOTHER NIGHT. ROSEMARY DETOURS into the bar after work, leg-sore, but not so all-over weary as usual. She's a little revved, actually. Russell behind the bar graces her with a generous glass of Jack Daniel's and then Margaret appears beside her, lays a moist hand on Rosemary's, prelude to some breathless confidence. Margaret the Mermaid, she's called behind her back. Coils of wiry gray-blond hair, a blinking, perpetually unready look in her eyes. Always on the verge of quitting Kid Billy's, wanted to get into color therapy, now it's divorce mediation. "Don't you think I'd be *fantastic* at that?" she keeps asking people.

Even so, she and Rosemary often waste a little time together before going home, but tonight Rosemary frees her hand, begs off with a nod toward the women's room, and once in the back hall, keeps going, steps outside into the lot and climbs into her truck. She sits in the wan, salmon-colored light a moment, her thoughts nowhere, then turns the key, and finds the truck massively dead. Not even that clicking sound. The idea of going back and rounding Margaret up makes her heart drop.

But suddenly Gil is there, windbreaker over his arm, happy to be of service.

"Solenoid," he says after a minute. "Or starter motor, something of that nature." He slams the hood, steps back rubbing the grease from palm to palm. "I'll have Russ give it a look in the morning."

The interior of the Saab is cool, smells of juniper berries. "Where should we go?" he asks, as if the entire night's unfurled before them.

"I need to get back, Gil," Rosemary says. "Cassie's at this *age*—"

"Ah, right, your daughter," Gil says, backing around. He touches the CD player: Bruce Springsteen, the sound painfully close and stark, *I'm going down down down down*. They cruise Montana Street carried along in the traffic's lurching flow, then veer away.

"We could go to my house," he says. "I'd like to show it to you, actually."

Rosemary leans back against her door. "You'd have to bring me back," she says after a minute.

"No problema," Gil says.

Then they're out in the dark of the valley. They slap through an errant spray of irrigation, drop down and cross Schardt Creek on one of the old wooden bridges. Gil slows to an abnormal creep, letting the tires rattle the loose boards.

They enter the long approach road, thread through the maze of houses, headlamps sweeping across outcrops of crumbling shale, slopes of lawn, coming to rest, the split second before he douses them, on the rear end of a red Jeep Cherokee.

"Ah, shit, *shit*," he says.

He throws the Saab into reverse, but Rosemary grabs his hand. "Turn it off," she says. "Quick."

There's a boardwalk skirting the front of his house, a bank of broad Thermopanes, all dark. "She's in *bed*," Rosemary says. "She's out cold."

Gil looks at her, and before he can make sense of what she's saying, she's slid out the other side; he throws himself across her empty seat, puts a hand up to keep the door from slamming.

He catches up with her at the edge of the grass.

"You wanted me to see your house," Rosemary says.

"Don't be funny."

A bloom of heat lightning, out of earshot; overhead, like brushes on a snare drum, the long needles of the ponderosas stirring in the warm air. Rosemary backs against the metal stanchion of a basketball hoop. "Who plays?" she asks. "You? You and her? A little one-on-one?"

He takes her sleeve, catching skin with it. "Let's *come on* now," he says. "I'll take you—"

The thrill is almost uncontainable. She overlays her hand on his until its grip softens. She moves it around to her chest.

"Dare you," she says.

His anger rises, short-circuits.

"You don't dare, do you?" she says. Which brings a flicker of something else, a strange smile, a new accounting of her.

"Shhh," she says. "Can you be quiet as a mouse?"

Who is this talking?

•   •   •

MORNING. CASSIE'S FRIEND LIZ, her ride into town, has failed to show. She's loitering in the kitchen, bumping her daypack into things, working herself up.

"Take your bike," Rosemary says.

"I'd rather walk."

"Walk then."

Rosemary finishes her coffee and stands. "Did you call her?"

"It's her job to call me," Cassie says. She pouts, then realizes how ordinary it must make her look, and darkens her features into a more customized anger. "She's so unde*pen*dable—"

Moments later, before Rosemary can dispense more sage advice, Cassie bangs out the back door and heads off on foot. Rosemary drifts to the front step, waiting to see if Cassie's head will snap around for a final check of her mother's interest. The day is humid, stalled, the sky a bright pewter. Across the road, the horses feed listlessly, their heads between strands of wire.

Rosemary feels sludgy herself. Fat-fingered, headachy. When she looks up again, Cassie has already been swallowed by the meadow's crown. But before Rosemary can withdraw indoors, she sees a black car emerge slowly from that same wavery expanse of field grass. Three heads in silhouette. Government car, Jack Brothers would have said in their dope-smoking days. It disappears into the willows at the turn-around, creeps back out, stops, idles, starts again.

Student driver, Rosemary thinks. That was Friday.

Monday, the same car, the same heads, five miles an hour, hugging the fence line.

Wednesday morning, one of her split-shift days, she hears the anemic buzzer at the front door—only strangers come to the front. She looks down half-expecting that dark, boxy sedan, but sees instead the red Jeep. The ringing subsides; then there's a knuckle rap at the back door. All she has on is underpants. She yanks on jeans, the ratted-out T-shirt she sleeps in, throws a quick frown at her face in the mirror, and proceeds downstairs, barefoot.

"Oh, I know *you*," Linda Cameron says. "You work for Gil, don't you?" She sounds legitimately surprised, Rose-mary thinks. But how can that be?

"May I?" she says, backing Rosemary into the kitchen. The kiwi outfit has given way to western-wear, a shimmer-ing rayon, Navajo turquoise like chunks of rock candy.

"I just stopped by to let you know I'm showing the prop-erty."

"I didn't know it was on the market, exactly," Rosemary says. "That's how I understood it."

"Yes, well," Linda Cameron says. "It's one of those things. A couple from California."

"They can't find anything better than this?" Rosemary says. "You must think I'm a moron."

Linda Cameron looks at her with a blush of pity, a flattening of her lips. "To be honest with you, Rosemary, they're extremely taken with the location. There's not much left this close in, you must know that, and having the slough down below, there won't be any development on the other side to spoil the view. Plus the wife's extremely fond of the Lombardy poplars. You know how people can get attached to things."

"What about the house?"

"I imagine—" Linda Cameron begins to say, but Rosemary doesn't need this finished. They'll bulldoze the house in a second, retaining the ring of old trees to memorialize it; then they'll gouge a new foundation into the edge of the hill.

"You had them in here already, didn't you?" Rosemary says. "While I was at work?" But she doesn't need that finished, either.

For an instant, she cultivates a mental picture of Linda Cameron down on her knees in front of Gil, choking for air, and though this thought should run a current of glee through her, it doesn't. It brings only a sodden, mucky feeling.

•   •   •

ROSEMARY WORKS HER LUNCH SHIFT. Gil's partner, Harvey Cockrell, has been in and out of Kid Billy's for the last week and a half, popping mints, ignoring everybody, holing up with Gil in the office, and today, as she might have predicted, Gil is nowhere to be seen. The restaurant seems noisy and out of sync. Midafternoon she escapes, comes home, slaps her purse down. There's a taint, a pointlessness to everything her eye falls on.

Cassie's class is done at two-thirty, but she's still out. Rosemary briefly denies the impulse, then gives in, drifts into that mongrel room of Cassie's off the kitchen. For once its chaos seems curtailed—all but the desk with its layering of cracked-open paperbacks and binderless school notes and partially unfolded letters. She looks without touching, wonders if anything she'd find there would shock her.

The day has gone cool and still. Through the screenless window, she hears the smack of the first huge raindrops on the chestnut leaves. A sweet, cloistered smell enters with the rain. Lichen, rust, old hiding places.

It occurs to her how lucky she was not to have seen Gil right away. She'd have flown straight at him and been ugly, not caring who heard. Now, for what it's worth, she has the luxury of thought.

She straightens out Cassie's bed and lies back on it, picturing the mat of clouds overhead, the raindrops working their way down from the top of the chestnut, leaf to leaf, out to the drip line, melting into the earth. Hears voices:

It's good how you're being.

I'm fine. I'm fine.

And Cassie: *It's not like I have pretensions.*

Why always say the opposite of what you mean? Why act like nothing's any big deal?

She'd broken Gil down, right in his own driveway, made him squirm, gotten his pants grass-stained and sopped with dew, and her reward is not to take the place of the woman drowsing in his bed that night, but to be booted from her own house, his anyway.

But what if she were to catch him alone in his office: *Gil, I really don't know what's going on with you, I don't know what old baggage you have with that place, with your aunt, what you had in mind with me . . . were you just sort of slumming? It's okay to be wanted—just not so* casually, *not for recreation, you know what I'm saying? But the house . . . I'd rather not leave it, it's good for Cassie and it's good for me. You know how people get attached to things.*

He'd run his tongue over his lips the way he does, nodding, nodding. It's just a money thing, he'd say. He's got an opportunity he can't let slip, needs to *consolidate*. There are whole realms of things she can't know about, a person in her position. Delicate financial structures.

This rain hasn't amounted to much after all, an isolated shower. In a minute, she'll get up and call in and tell them she's sick.

A car pulls up outside, a door slams. There's a jittery moment when it could be anybody. Then Cassie's footsteps on the back porch, her things thudding on the bench. "Hey," she calls out, "anybody home?"

•   •   •

ROSEMARY SITS UP and tries to pull herself together. Better not to be seen darting out. "In here," she says.

Cassie stops in the doorway.

"I couldn't resist making your bed," Rosemary says. "Forgive me."

"You're so thoughtful," her daughter says, the usual sarcasm, but milder, almost companionable, as if they're in on the same old joke, she and Rosemary. Even so, her eyes run a quick inventory.

"Come in," Rosemary says.

Cassie slings off her jacket and acquiesces. She's in her black-and-white mode today, stirrup pants and sloganless tee, hair pinched back in a plastic clip. "Don't you have to work?" she asks. "Aren't you going to be *late?*"

"Oh, hon," Rosemary says, shot through with dread. "Bad news."

And so she tells Cassie they have to move again.

Cassie regards her—anything but devastated, it seems. "So all that was for nothing," she says simply.

"All of what—?"

Cassie makes a face. "That sneaking upstairs."

Instinctively, Rosemary starts to say, "It's none of your business what I do, sister," but she stops herself cold—the last thing on earth she wants is to fend Cassie off.

"I don't know what I was thinking," she says. "I *wasn't* thinking."

Even the pleasure was nothing to hold onto, no grander than the wind on her damp skin that first afternoon.

Cassie pulls out the wooden desk chair, swivels it and parks herself in front of Rosemary. Her face is ruddy-tan, moist and downy at the temples, a handsome, remorseless face. "You didn't want him anyway," she says. "He's a scumbucket."

Despite everything, a flush comes over Rosemary—love, admiration. She lowers her forehead to the back of Cassie's chair, lets her eyes close, the smile wane. What she remembers of those old places they lived is the rush of leaving, turning her back on the flapping plastic, the smells. That wallop of relief; reprieve. There'll be none of that now.

Her daughter's weight shifts in the chair, she feels Cassie's hand descend to her head and begin to stroke her hair, tugging, riffling through it in a choppy, persistent rhythm.

"Oh, don't stop," Rosemary says.

A thought ambushes her: No matter how this turns out, most of their time under the same roof is already spent. She surrenders herself to it, and finds that already it's losing a little of its power to turn her stomach. She feels herself floating through the spaces of this house of Gil's, room by room, then out and above it, looking down, touching nothing. Then remembers the bulbs she poked in the ground that day, and wonders what chance they have.

Some, she decides. Anything's possible.

THE VOTE

Drizzle. But no, Smith-lin decides, once he's out in it, squinting up through thick lenses, more of a cool mist. Not that it truly matters. It's the perception that keeps people home, the threat of an ankle wrenched on slick leaves, a date with futility. He stares at his boat of a station wagon, stifles a jaw-popping yawn. A low turnout will be deadly, precisely what they don't want. He's been awake since quarter to five, listening to the roof, his thoughts roiling. What's he *neglected?* He drives up Third, changes his mind, makes the awkward turn onto Jackson Street and checks in at his place of business, the litho lab he and a partner opened a few years ago. Nothing's shaking, a couple of employees tell him, nothing that can't wait a day. *Go.* He climbs back in the car, veers into the alley behind headquarters and ducks in through the rear, muddying his shoes. The overhead door is still off kilter, wedged in its track. Wind pours under it. Last week the toilet actually froze—

Amanda had to call around and borrow a fleet of space heaters. The whole building is derelict, former glass repair, former bait-and-tackle shop. He dodges through forty feet of campaign leavings, parts the burlap curtain, and slips into the front. She's in already, Amanda—must be *living* there by now. Luther Parnes, too, hulking and rosy-cheeked, on loan from the state party over in Helena. He's parked in his cubicle, studying a miniature TV with the sound off. His PC is lit, but for once no paper's chugging from the printer.

"How goes?" Smithlin asks.

Amanda glances up, back from the void. "Me? Fresh as a daisy." She's short, dark-browed, with billowing hair and a tiny, incessant mouth. Of all of them, except Luther, she's the only one drawing pay, and it's precious little. She's a godsend, people say, a real pistol. They wouldn't have a prayer without her. Smithlin pours himself coffee, doses it with powdered creamer. Why not just leave the prayer part out of it?

Smithlin was one of the younger ones for a long time— there hardly *were* any younger ones when he first started showing up at the dinners. This was fifteen years ago; he'd been in the valley only a few months, hardly knew a soul, had just found work in a print shop. They congregated in the basement of the Eagles or the Sons of Norway, or sometimes one of the banquet rooms under Daugherty's. A few attorneys, a carpet dealer, a guy from the Job Service, a few shopowners and teachers and what-have-you, but mostly they were old farmers and union people. Smithlin ate his spaghetti, his beans and chicken, drank his Tang, anted up for innumerable raffles, shook hands with the visiting firemen. Nobody asked him what he was doing there. They were genial, gotten up in a mishmash of styles, from sober to raffish, but underneath, they were angry and principled and, it seemed to Smithlin, moral. They took him in.

"It's so damn peaceful in here," he says after a minute. "I'm disoriented."

The center table's been cleared of printed matter and pencil stubs and wadded-up Dorito bags. There's a vase of white carnations, compliments of somebody. Next to that, a tangle of plastic Groucho glasses, marked *Candidates Only*. The rest of the table is consumed by a fan of paper napkins and an immense box of doughnuts no one has yet touched.

Between the backwards-reading posters on the plate glass, Smithlin sees his man, Ebersole, loping up the sidewalk, topcoat flapping. He bursts in, stands blotting a sleeve against his steaming head. "The great day dawned brilliant and fair," he announces.

"Spare us," Amanda says.

Smithlin looks him up and down. "You okay?" he asks. "Get any sleep?"

Ebersole nods.

"You look a little raw."

"You can sleep later," Ebersole says. "Isn't that right? That's what Pam's always saying: *Plenty of sleep at the other end.*"

He smiles his wide smile, peels off the overcoat, takes in the cornucopia of doughnuts. "Aw, man, look at this," he says. "I'm in trouble now."

Ebersole owns a dome of balding forehead, wiry, somewhat erratic hair. He's Smithlin's age, early forties, yet sturdier, lacking Smithlin's baggy jowls, his tendency to obsess. Had a bad go-round with marriage back there somewhere, Smithlin understands, without knowing the fine points. Companionable as Ebersole is, there are things he won't go into, and so be it. For most of the time they've been friends, he was unattached, a little skittery as to dating. Then this Pam materialized. She works at the courthouse, down in the

Assessor's Office. A calm, striking woman—olivy, with huge, Mediterranean-looking eyes.

As to the candidacy, Smithlin had tried recruiting him the past two elections—arranged meetings with the state people, goaded, massaged his guilt. "I can't picture it," Ebersole kept saying. Smithlin backed off and waited. When a man wasn't ready, he wasn't ready—that's one thing he'd learned. "Why don't *you* run?" Ebersole asked in self-defense. "Lack the temperament," Smithlin had to answer, which was shorthand for a covey of small truths about himself. "I do better out of the lights." And what accounts for Ebersole's leaping this time—other than Smithlin's intermittent nagging, and a general, accrued disgust? Pam, it must be. She's focused him, made him buoyant, fearless.

Ebersole teaches chemistry at the high school, which gives him a pool of former students, and means, too, that he had those late summer weeks to hit the doors. The district covers most of Sperry's city limits, extends north to the subdivision by the water tower, zigzags south as far as Farraday Slough. Seven precincts, all told, mostly stable on the East Side, but the west is full of multiplexes, lots of unregistereds, lots of transients, people with grudges. Ebersole was tireless, his doorstep manner superb, it turned out—acted like he was born to it, scratched out copious notes on his steno pad, phoned people back, never soured, never rose to the bait. Smithlin had to hand it to him. Even the incident with the schnauzer. "Look, it was an *old* schnauzer," Ebersole insisted. "Barely drew blood. Couple little pinpricks, big deal. And anyway, we got the vote, right?"

Smithlin circles, checks the street again, peeks over Amanda's shoulder at the legion of names, all color-coded. So insanely much to do, weeks and months of it, and now it's been done. They've got a cadre of poll watchers and phone jockeys in place, but it's out of his hands now.

"You might as well go drive somebody," Amanda says finally. "You're driving *me* nuts. In fact, I want you both out of here."

Ebersole looks at her. "That do-able?"

From his cubicle, Parnes says, "Nope, not the candidate, I wouldn't recommend that."

Amanda says, "Hush, Luther. I checked it out." She turns to Ebersole. "You just stay outside the actual polling place." She hands him a two-page list and steers him toward the front.

She grabs Smithlin's arm on his way past. "Hey, don't look so cheerful," she says. "And sweetie? Have your boy wipe the custard off his cheek, okay?"

•   •   •

SCATTERED ACROSS TOWN, like late-blooming bulbs, are three hundred and eighty-seven EBERSOLE yard signs, the small kind, light cardboard on lath. The morning after Halloween, Smithlin had to cruise around the potholed streets and reinstall a good third of them. Another forty of the big ones anchor strategic intersections. You see them a block away: half-sheets of three-eighths plywood, white sans-serif letters, just the name, against a loud red. (Ebersole had lobbied for a blue script and a slogan. Smithlin had to put his foot down. "Scrap the message," he said. "The thing with the signs is, you're getting people comfortable with your name, that's all. And the other thing is, you want them bright as fire engines. Think how goddamn *gloomy* things look in November.")

In the car, Ebersole says, "Had a kid yesterday, fifth period? Stood up and told me they took a poll, and he was real sorry to have to inform me, but I came up one vote short."

"Everybody's a comedian," Smithlin says.

Ebersole smiles. "Wysocki," he says. "That's what I flashed on."

The Spooner-Wysocki race is legend, a cautionary tale. Four years ago, Jerry Wysocki actually *did* lose his house race by a single vote. There was a recount, and eighty-six untallied ballots turned up—which split forty-three, forty-three. It was freakish. Still, that wasn't the point. Wysocki's district had been winnable, but he'd dogged it. You don't dog it and expect to win. It was shameful.

"We hustled, though, huh?" Ebersole says. "Tell me we outlegged them, at least."

"Yeah," Smithlin says. "I'll give you that."

Sixteen hundred votes it will take, by Smithlin's count. You'd think you could come up with that many. The incumbent is a man named Lloyd Grilley, who runs a Christmas tree operation off Foothills Road. A shambling, self-righteous old bastard—down in the legislature, he's garnered the nickname Grumpa. Yet, astonishingly, no one's made a dent in him in five terms. He wouldn't appear in public with Ebersole. Why lower himself? He hung back, then flooded the TV with his spots: *Lloyd's one of us!* And worked the radio call-in shows a few mornings. Smithlin hears that snide, dumbed-down voice, and his bile rises, that old affronted, panicky feeling races through him.

He corners onto Seventh and pulls to the curb opposite the Grosvenor, a three-story, elm-shaded retirement place. No door-to-door allowed in there. The best Smithlin could arrange was tea and sugar wafers in the rec room—only a handful showed, but man, did they know their legislation.

A chunky woman in her late sixties waits out front, and nearby, a slimmer, older gent in a bolo tie and rust-colored Dacron. Ebersole pops out, gives his arm, guides them into the back of Smithlin's car.

Ebersole swivels on the seat. "Spared that rain, I guess," he offers. "You folks reside at the Grosvenor long?"

The man relates a brief, disjointed story about the sale of his implement company in Plentywood.

Smithlin maneuvers the car up to the gymnasium door of the Agnes Bjorneby Elementary School, and his charges get out to vote. He toys with the radio, finds nothing palatable. It's all boom-boom-boom—he's not in the mood. A side door opens and the younger grades stream out for recess. The playground's suddenly awash with neon jackets. "Like watching a fish tank," Smithlin says, but Ebersole is quiet.

Smithlin doesn't have children himself. He has one sister, an RN back in Haverhill, Massachusetts, where they grew up, but she's almost twelve years his senior, and they've pretty much lost the thread. "What is it with you?" she used to write him. "When are you going to find somebody?" What could he say, that wouldn't sound flip or pathetic? Ebersole, on the other hand, acquired an instant family when he married Pam. Two daughters with fussy names, Mirabella and Danielle. They look nothing like him, dark-eyed and bird-boned, but when the four of them are out somewhere— at the mall, say, Ebersole and Pam with coffees, the two girls nursing swirls of frozen yogurt—you can see how they belong together. Ebersole talks about them in amazement, saturated with relief. So maybe that's the real difference between himself and Ebersole, Smithlin thinks: Ebersole lets himself be blindsided, one way or the other.

"Here they come," Ebersole says. "That didn't take any time at all. Must be *deserted* in there."

"Tom?" Smithlin says. "The middle of the morning's always thin, okay? And listen, those two? They're not together. I mean, they're not married to each other, in case that's what you thought."

"Really?" Ebersole says. "God, I must be losing it."

Smithlin looks at him in the rearview. "You know what I'm kind of enjoying? Seeing you come unglued."

"Thanks for sharing that with me," Ebersole says. He pats around in his pockets, sighs audibly. "You got a mint or anything?"

• • •

AS MORNING PASSES, he and Ebersole are back to Bjorneby School twice more, then twice to Precinct 15, which votes in the lobby of the Oldsmobile dealership. This is Smithlin's own precinct, and when there's a break, he slips in, exchanges a quiet word or two with their poll watcher, votes, hears his name spoken aloud as the ballot disappears into its lockbox. He steps outside, walks past a double row of new trucks, new Cutlasses and Ninety-eights with their drooping pennants. The sky seems lower, more socked-in, if that's possible. He and Ebersole drive uptown, grab lunch—meatball subs, coffee—then swing by a Mini Mart so Ebersole can dash in and buy a packet of Tylenol, some gum.

"Who's next?"

"Wohlers, Frieda."

A gray-and-black house on the East Side, mid-block. A touch of gingerbread at the roof peak, a bicycle with a child's seat chained to the porch railing, lilacs and clumps of drooping bridal veil.

"Right," Ebersole says. "Duplex. Single mother upstairs. No answer down." Smithlin doesn't doubt for a second that he remembers every door.

Smells have gathered in the entryway—a damp, puttylike scent overlaid with something burnt.

"This the one here?" Smithlin asks.

Ebersole presses the buzzer; the door slivers open. "Mrs.

Wohlers?" Smithlin says. "We've come to drive you to vote."

Her front room is taken up entirely by a crank-up bed, a television, a clunky dark-stained wardrobe. A cactus has grown from a clay pot on the floor clear to the ceiling and then sideways along it, creeping toward the light fixture.

Smithlin introduces Ebersole, then himself.

She is tall, Mrs. Wohlers, nearly as tall as Ebersole. A lifetime of back trouble, Smithlin imagines. Her coat is buttoned up to her neck, a kind of gray, nappy wool. She's carrying a rather bulky purse of black patent leather.

"I can't manage stairs," she says.

"No," Smithlin assures her. "No stairs."

Her precinct votes at the old hospital building, now a warren of county offices: Extension Service, Public Health, Council on Aging. Smithlin has reconnoitered it. There are no stairs, only a long, possibly treacherous hallway of buffed linoleum, leading to the former chapel, lined with Votomatics.

It requires a number of minutes to walk Mrs. Wohlers to the car. On the ride, bolt upright, she says nothing.

Smithlin eases his car under the brick-and-steel canopy, what used to be the emergency entrance. He shuts down the engine, walks around to Mrs. Wohlers's side, but the instant he bends and sees her through the glass, he knows she'll never make it. He cracks the door, squats. "I've got an idea, Mrs. Wohlers," he says. "Why don't we see if you can vote out here, in the car. How would that be?"

He looks back at Ebersole. "Mr. Ebersole will be happy to keep you company. I'll just be a second."

The lights are on in the chapel, but it still has a subdued, reverential look. Smithlin wades in, addresses the table of election officials, and finds himself, too late, face-to-face with Bunny Koch. They know each other, or Smithlin knows *her*, certainly. He's stared across the ramparts at her enough times, at planning board hearings, at the last redistricting. A husky woman with stiff, ash-blond bangs. Cool, indelibly patrician, married to Dr. Edwin Koch, the orthopedist.

Smithlin plunges ahead.

Yes, they have a detachable Votomatic, for the handicapped, and no, so long as an election official's present, there's no reason Mrs. Wohlers can't vote in the car.

They walk back together. Mrs. Koch marches out through the double doors, catches sight of Ebersole, frowns indulgently, touches Smithlin's arm. "Tell your companion to take a little walk," she says.

Smithlin ducks his head into the car, exchanges quick whispers with the candidate, and Ebersole strides off through the parking lot.

The plastic tray is arranged in Mrs. Wohlers's lap. Mrs. Koch climbs in back, leans bulkily forward, gripping the seat, to where she can see the proceedings.

"What's all this?" Mrs. Wohlers says. The tray slides a little. Smithlin reaches in to steady it.

Mrs. Koch starts in, "Now, this first item concerns the levy for the high school."

Mrs. Wohlers listens, the punch pin, on its chain, resting in her hand. She seems almost unaware of what it is.

"You can see the holes all right?" Smithlin asks.

Her hand moves, the pin finds a hole.

"Fine," Smithlin says. "Now we can turn the page."

Mrs. Koch reads the next item. They work back through the booklet—commissioner, smoking ban, several very obscure initiatives Smithlin himself was surprised to find there and hasn't a clue about.

"My purse," Mrs. Wohlers says.

"Right here, down by your foot," Smithlin says. "Do you need it?"

"I'm all—" Mrs. Wohlers says.

Through the windshield, Smithlin can see the candidate leaning against a rust-pocked propane tank, talking with a maintenance man, who's gesturing emphatically up toward the roof, stabbing the air with his finger.

"This next is your state representative," Mrs. Koch says. "Mr. Ebersole and Mr. Grilley." She names their party affiliations, her voice frostily neutral.

Mrs. Wohlers takes up the punch pin once again, plunges it into the dimple marked GRILLEY.

Has he seen this correctly? Has Bunny Koch seen? Oh, absolutely. What a wonderful dark joke.

After this, Mrs. Wohlers votes for a district judge, then utters something in a voice so low Smithlin can't hear.

"Excuse me?" he says.

Mrs. Wohlers says, "I'm so tired."

Soon, Mrs. Koch is gone, and Ebersole is back inside the car, his face glossed with sweat. Smithlin hits the ignition.

"I'd like to thank you for coming out to vote," Ebersole says to Mrs. Wohlers. He's blinking, yanking the turtleneck away from his throat—it's sweltering in the car. "It means a lot to me, I can tell you that. You'd be surprised," he continues on, "the impact one vote can have."

Smithlin hopes, urgently, that Ebersole will let it go at that. Mercifully, he does. Mrs. Wohlers steadies herself against the dashboard, and they begin the trek home. "Is that snow?" she asks finally.

"No snow yet," Smithlin says.

It turns out, once they're back in her entryway, that Mrs. Wohlers has forgotten the key to the apartment.

"You're completely sure," Smithlin says. "Could I?"

But her purse is virtually empty. A package of tissues, a used-up nasal mister.

"We'll have a look at the back way," Smithlin says. "Wait here."

The back door, opening onto a glassed-in porch, is locked. In fact, Smithlin gathers from the way it's stacked up with water-spotted cartons, the back way isn't used at all. He glances at his watch. An hour and thirty-five minutes this errand has consumed.

Mrs. Wohlers has laid her hand on Ebersole's sleeve for balance.

"What about upstairs?" Smithlin asks.

Ebersole shakes his head. "Out, I guess."

They're utterly stalled. Mrs. Wohlers is as still as salt. Smithlin's mind ought to be racing. Pocketknife? Loose window glazing? Someone to, for God's sake, *call*? But these thoughts pass by dreamily, in a mist. What if they were frozen like this forever?

But then Ebersole reaches down and tries the handle. Miraculously, it turns, the door falls open. "Ah," he says, "there we go."

•　　•　　•

"YOU BELIEVE HOW DARK IT IS?" Ebersole says, shaking his head. "Ten past five." And still six weeks to the shortest day, Smithlin thinks.

He double-parks, drops the candidate outside headquarters. Ebersole bends to the window. "Drink?" he asks.

"No," Smithlin says. "Thanks."

Ebersole nods. "What do you think? You got any vibes?"

Smithlin touches his hand. "I'll see you back here," he says, and pulls away.

His apartment has a cooped-up, gassy smell—he's scarcely been in it for days. He cracks the kitchen window, reheats the last crinkly square of lasagna he lugged home from a potluck on Sunday. After a while, he reaches for CNN—the polls closed a half hour ago on the East Coast. But what's the rush? He retracts his hand, lets it fall. In a moment, he peels back the curtain to look down at the street. Chestnut leaves scratch across the carport's steel roof. He cups his hand on the glass. Is it snowing?

There's no sense in going back until nine, at the earliest. He showers, shaves, locates a fresh shirt. And no use, either, in calling up the memory of past election nights, the trays of warm cheese, the eventual giving up, then the dreary post-mortems. He cleans his glasses on a kitchen towel, holds them to the light. This business with Mrs. Wohlers? He'll take it to his grave.

By the time he arrives, his cheeks hot from the walk, head-quarters is already jammed, and the noise has an edge. Luther Parnes is stationed by the greaseboard with a walkie-talkie mashed against his ear, and with his free hand is squeaking up numbers with a blue pen. And it looks like they're doing all right—or maybe better? McCullers has already won. Their two incumbents, Munro and DeSmet, have held their seats. Alicia Fritz is leading. They've even managed, amazingly, to pry loose the governor. Smithlin holds a Diet Coke to his face, drinks a long, stupefying gulp. The phones ring, one on top of another. More people jostle their way in, holding up Crock-Pots, jockeying foil-covered plates through the hurly-burly. Who are they all? Smithlin catches sight of Amanda. She's put on lipstick, a dress—black with shimmery tinsel and a bit of a scoop in front. She's laughing, waving. Somebody waltzes by in Groucho glasses.

Ebersole's first precincts come in about even, and there follows a span of forty minutes when the numbers don't budge. "What's going *on* down there?" Ebersole keeps asking. Luther shrugs, shifts his weight back and forth. Long blasts of static issue from the walkie-talkie.

"I can't stand this," he says to Smithlin. "I'm going to run over and see what the story is. You want to?"

It's only a few blocks to the election department—the air would straighten them both up. But Smithlin tells him, "Let's just wait. Let's just hang on, okay? A few more minutes?"

Finally, the logjam lets go. Votes from those mongrel West Side precincts pour in, two-to-one for Ebersole. And in a rush, it's over. Raucous whoops, a tattoo of camera strobes. Smithlin's hand is pumped, a bottle of beer thrust at his chest, which he holds for a moment, then sets down. Pam Ebersole brushes by him, squeezes his shoulder, whispers, *Thank you, thank you,* leaving a pulse of scent in his vicinity. He watches her slip through the commotion and find Ebersole and press herself to him. Her hand runs up along his neck, the bracelets falling, collecting soundlessly on her forearm. Ebersole spins, kissing her, tears on his cheeks. Smithlin moves out of the fray, finds a desk to sit on, something solid to collapse against. What's going on, he wonders, out beyond this racket—which armies are regrouping, what walls of water coming down?

JOSEPHINE

H e remembered coming in late from a trip. Two weeks east of the mountains, winter. The roads had been plowed, but few cars passed him. He'd duct-taped a piece of cardboard box over the radiator; even so, the heater blew feebly. His breath collected on the windshield, leaving only a hole the size of his face to see through. Still miles from home, he descended Homestake Pass and stopped at a bar on the outskirts of Butte, nearly too stiff to stand. He opened the heavy door and stepped into a wall of steamy air. The bartender charged toward him, round-faced, malicious. "*You!*" he said, arms gesturing in wild circles. "This man's been buying your wife drinks for three hours. What you going to do about it?"

He could see now that the only other customers were a man and woman perched on stools, with their coats mounded nearby. They chuckled lightly and looked away. That was how it was at that time in his life, always outside the joke. He accepted a mug of coffee, wrapped his hands around it, a blush rising on his cheeks.

His wife was up waiting for him. He dropped his bag and embraced her. She was wearing a chenille robe, some bright color. Fuchsia, maybe. Her face was scrubbed, her watery brown hair loose against her shoulders. They stood on the floor grate, the only warm spot in the house.

She hardly slept while he was away. With no seniority at work, she didn't get off until eleven. She'd told him, many times, "I can't stand coming back to a dark house."

"I'm sorry," he said, and he was. "Can't you leave the TV going, or—"

But of course she'd done all those things.

She backed off the grate and stared at him. "I bought a dog," she said.

He scanned the floor, but she said, "It's an outside dog."

She spun and went out through the kitchen, her sandals slapping her heels. He followed, out to the garage, back to a low, added-on space where some earlier renter had over-hauled engines. It was cold and oily, but she'd rigged up an extension cord with a bare bulb hanging down.

The dog lay under the bench, curled on fresh straw. A coon hound, black and tan.

She'd gone to the pound, she explained. "I hadn't slept in two nights. I mean, not *any*. This was the only big dog they had."

He didn't know a blessed thing about dogs. It appeared to be full-grown, but all skin and bones, and shaking.

"Jesus, it looks cold," he said.

His wife hugged the robe tighter around herself.

"I don't know," he said. "I don't think this is much of a northern dog. It doesn't have any *fat* on it—"

"I'm sorry. I didn't have a choice."

After a moment, he said, "Can't you just get them to give you something to take?"

But they'd been over that ground, too. "I won't lie in there *drugged*," she said. "That's not sleep."

"You'll get over it," he said. "I can't see it going on like this forever. It'll pass, don't you think?"

She said, "I didn't want a fight."

He touched her shoulder, turned to face her, to say something better, but his movement frightened the dog. Its tail whacked the plank wall. His wife knelt and ran her hand over the dog's drooping ear. *"Shhh,"* she said. "It's okay now."

"Does it have a name?" he asked.

"Josephine."

"Jesus, you're kidding. *Josephine?*"

"That was her name," she said. "I can't help it. I can't just start calling her something else. She's not a *puppy*."

And so, finally, he remembered, they'd gone back inside. He was still cold from the car, cold in his bones. He wished he could take a bath—they had no shower, just a shallow tub that left his bony knees pointing into the air. But he brushed his teeth, stripped down, and joined his wife in bed.

He felt her arm; it was all goose bumps.

"Lots of people live alone," he said.

She said, "I'm married. I don't want to live alone."

In a minute, she said, "I shouldn't have to be afraid all the time."

Once in a while, he asked her, straight out, "Do you want me to go in and tell them I can't travel because my wife can't stay alone? Do you really want me to say that?"

His first good job.

He'd installed deadbolts on the doors, screwed stops in the only two windows that opened, bought her a twenty-foot cord for the telephone. "What do you think's going to happen?" he sometimes asked.

He knew what she'd say. There'd been rapes—a student in the education department, an eighty-year-old woman who ran a tiny grocery near the fairgrounds, a towheaded fourth-grader whose body was found in a culvert.

Wasn't it better to say it out loud?

He reached for her under the covers.

"Could I just sleep?" she asked.

But it was so good after they'd been apart. He would ache for her. He couldn't believe that anything could take him outside his body.

"I'm sorry," she said. "It's okay, isn't it?"

He lay in the dark, eyes open.

When they'd first rented this house, a pair of spruce trees had stood out front, shading the window where they ate breakfast. But in the summer's drought, the trees had died, one, then the other. Raking trash and sticks one evening, everything powder dry, he'd leaned an ear toward one of the spindly trunks and heard a stream of beetles beneath the bark, an army on the move. A week later, he'd come home and found the landlord and his pasty-faced boy chainsawing the spruces into firewood. The only tree left on the lot was a willow, out back, victim of ice storms and cruel, random prunings. Its branches stirred in the cold, peppering the bedroom window with shadows. He imagined how they'd look to someone who couldn't sleep.

"You don't know what it's like," she said.

"You know, things bother me, things get to me—" he began, but he knew it wasn't the same, and he didn't go on.

Through the beaverboard walls, he heard a low *wuh-woof,* then the clicking of the dog's toenails on the cement as it paced and paced. In a few minutes, his wife was asleep. Her back rose and fell with huge soundless breaths, as if she were recovering from a great exertion. Later in the night, the willow branches hung still, and it began to snow, a thin dry snow that nevertheless accumulated.

Toward morning, he got out of bed, and walked through the house with a blanket draped over his shoulders. He'd slept maybe an hour, and that hour had been anything but restful, a procession of road dreams, the car hitting black ice and sliding away under his hands. In the first light, the world looked snowbound, inert. He slid back the elaborate deadbolt and went out to check on Josephine, called her name. She'd retreated to the straw, but snapped to her feet at the sight of him, showing her teeth.

One winter years later, paralyzed in her hindquarters, the dog had been put to sleep, and they hadn't replaced her. They'd had their kids by then. One born less than four pounds, with a heart the size of a maraschino cherry. How it had worked! He seldom thought of their life before children, not unless something reminded him, as tonight, walking on the outskirts of a strange city, he'd heard the yodeling of a hound. What had become of those fears? He remembered them, for a moment, as one remembers old enemies, almost fondly.

PERRO
SEMIHUNDIDO

Early March, no bulbs, no seductive stench of damp earth. Under the dock pilings the stones are webbed with silt, still exposed to the air. It will be weeks before the lake begins to fill. The only promising sign is the gold haze in the willows—that and the way it's staying light. Past seven tonight, and there's a steely glow on the water, a frieze of heart-stopping pink along the far shore. Faith breaks out of her stare, dumps her bag in the back of the Subaru, slams the door. She accelerates up the gravel drive away from the Lodge, gets as far as the blinker, and hesitates. The neighbors' horses watch from the fence, chewing, blowing jets of breath.

Think of us, they say.

The note she's just left for Rick is nine parts falsehood. He doesn't like a woman who worries (his wife Lana was a champion of fret and premeditation, a real sourball, he says), so Faith told him nothing about this trip in advance, nor about the uneasiness that's nagged her for weeks.

Cabin fever! she wrote. *Back in a couple days. Hold the fort, dear heart.*

And underneath that, *There's a big thing of chili in the fridge, cookies in the freezer. Tollhouse. —F.*

Nothing about the true subject of tonight's mission, her brother George in Seattle.

The *dear heart* is fiction, too, but where's the harm in that? Rick's a decent man, not a mess of thoughtless habits. Slim, boyish in the western manner; watery blue eyes, a chop of graying mustache. Dependable in bed, if silent, a little squeamish. Richard Summers: former smoke jumper, bartender, shop teacher. He has a grown son and daughter in Oregon, and no desire to start again, though Faith hasn't pressed him—despite her age, thirty-nine, despite not having ever resigned herself to being childless, she has barely floated the subject with Rick.

Even the *cabin fever* is a benign little joke. Faith owns Spruce Lodge, hidden in a quiet bay on the big lake, not a lodge at all but a dozen cedar-sided cabins, a boat landing, a patch of weedy lawn with a volleyball net and a flagpole. Booked solid through summer and hunting season, more erratically in winter—cross-country skiers, stray couples, now and then a solitary pilgrim. After New Year's, they are often alone there. Furious cracks rifle through the ice; some nights even the firs explode with cold. The Lodge feels like an outpost then, and human companionship seems miraculous. She curls against Rick on the sofa; they talk, they plan, but his ambitions are mainly behind him, she can see that. She has discovered his secret: He's happiest glazing windows, manning the snow blower, mortaring walls. If she loved him it would all be fine. No, it *is* fine, it's just not enough, not the right thing. What does she mean by that? She can't say.

Driving now, headed toward her brother, she watches the last color leach from the sky. At the first turning point, she chooses the back way through the mountains: Dewpoint with its one closed-up bar, the cutoff to Camp Niemi, then Adrian Springs, stretches of barren road where someone has nailed bluebird boxes to the scraggly fenceposts. On the downslope outside Edwina, she roars up behind an old hay truck traveling blind under a weight of round bales, blows by, and doesn't see another soul for an hour. It crosses her mind to pull off and let the stars pelt down on her head, but she can't bear to stop even that long. She joins a two-lane highway at Jupiter, crosses the river on a low silver-painted trestle bridge, enters a canyon alongside the railroad grade, and not long afterward catches up to a string of freight cars—lumber, empty flatbeds. Almost close enough to touch; she leans over, cranks down the far window and lets the cold air rush in with the noisy charisma of the train.

● ● ●

THE HIGHWAY NO LONGER WEAVES through the lightless gorge of Wallace, Idaho, old silver mining town, infamous for its whorehouses; the road swoops overhead now, the last stoplight on America's interstate system gone. The whores gone, too, for that matter. Well, no, probably not.

A cherry Danish in Kellogg, a refill of her thermos, a walkabout in the side lot. Under the canopy, a Highway Patrol car has pulled up on the slant, blocking the path of a green Firebird. Inside, three young Indian men stare forward as if they're at the drive-in movies. A fourth sits impassive in the back of the cruiser, his braids looped over his shoulder. She watches this tableau, wonders if it might involve her. Five minutes pass, ten; nothing happens. West of Spokane, out in stubbled range land, she tunes in a show of fifties jazz,

Thelonious Monk—the music leaves her arms tingling, her thoughts of George coming in dreamy shards. She glides through the hovering beds of ground fog as if onto a dance floor suffused with dry ice. Later, the rise into mountains, Snoqualmie Pass, the winding descent. It's an hour shy of dawn when she reaches the city.

Months ago, George had written to tell her he'd moved. A terse note for George, no mention of what the trouble was. His old place was located on Queen Anne, the airy top floor of a manorly brick building. He'd lived there since the early seventies. Graceful rooms, not quite austere, altogether George-like. Outside, a terracing of slate roofs and treetops, then the bay with its sulky gleaming and, farther off, the orange cranes of the container yards, the mouth of the Duwamish. Maybe there'd been some squabble over the lease; maybe he was plain sick of it. Who could say? Yet the new address, once she tracks it down, is over in Ballard, a ragtag neighborhood.

She parks at the curb, nonplussed. The house is brown-shingled, a squat-looking bungalow with an odd collection of dormers upstairs. Two little slopes of hardpan in front, a row of battered hydrangeas. No lights on. She drives away, circles back, looks, drives away again. There's a grocery at the end of the block, the front window espaliered with duct tape, a black dog nosed into its doorway, out of the wind. Two blocks farther downhill George's street dead-ends in one of the arterials. A double-jointed bus sails by. There's a Burger King, a Hardee's with a smatter of step-vans and ladder-laden trucks, a Color Tile, a car lot festooned with dreary streamers.

She settles on an old tin-sheeted diner called The Raven; The Raven for the ravenous. She takes a booth by the steamy window, orders oatmeal, a stack of toast, V-8; peels off her glasses, stretches out across the spongy vinyl and tries to knead some life into her calves. There's a lunacy, a clattering hyperreality to everything. The waitress emerges like a wraith from the highlights on the fluted chrome, wan, rib-thin.

"Was I *staring?*" Faith asks. "*Sorry.* You know how weird it is when you've been up all night?"

The girl nods solemnly. "Yes, it happens to me all the time," she says. Her voice is the size of a pearl. She lingers, as if there's more to say, more confidences to trade. The backs of her knuckles graze the tabletop. *How do I look to her,* Faith wonders. *Warm and fleshy, blindly welcoming?* She tries to smile, offers the girl's hand a conspiratorial pat.

Her hunger proves shallow; the buttery toast sends a wave of queasiness through her. She slips off to the bathroom and endures a minor confrontation with her face, fluffs her bangs—they look frowsy, her eyes red-rimmed and hot. "You *are* something," Faith thinks out loud, scoops a palmful of tap water and tosses back a pair of Advils. She makes her way back to the booth, glimpses the waitress again, and impulsively throws down an outlandish tip, then ducks outside, wondering where this wallop of generosity has come from.

The morning air is raw, the sky ragged with light. She thinks of George waking in his apartment, only blocks away. It's all she can do not to run.

•   •   •

THEIR FATHER WAS IN HIS FORTIES when George was born. He'd operated a well-drilling outfit, owned some business property in downtown Sperry. An inveterate barterer and deal-maker, a bulky man, shaggy-browed, sometimes loud and teasing, but often darkly elliptical. Ambrose Wicks. Faith's mother was half his age, half his size. Alice Petry, pronounced *Pet-tree*, come all the way from Simcoe, Ontario. She'd done the books for him before they were married: a pretty, blandly good-natured Methodist, daughter of a florist.

After George, she'd lost a baby, then came a span of ten years, then, unexpectedly, Faith.

By her junior year in high school, her father was ensconced in the Lutheran Home up on Buffalo Hill. He'd become treacherous, unmanageable. He'd be found weeping in his car, out of gas in some unlikely venue. Once they'd put an end to the driving, he wandered off afoot, down the alleys of the East Side, into people's garages. He scared children, set dogs to dancing angrily at the end of their chains. In his own home he shambled about undressed, a bearish mass of springy gray hairs. Faith was afraid to be alone in a room with him. There was no telling when he might erupt in some insinuation: *Look at you.* His lower lip would hang down. *Looka-chu.* She had a secret horror that she'd keep on growing, becoming huge and hairy like him. She'd put on four inches in the last year; her bones ached—she thought she could hear them straining, cracking like fiberglass. She was already long through the middle, her breasts low-slung and doughy; she wore flat-soled sneakers, sweatshirts and loose baggy jumpers, kept her arms knit in front of her.

There'd been a time when she was her father's darling, though, surely she was right about that? When she was hardy and tomboyish, in plaid flannel and jeans, her sandy hair braided and bobby-pinned up under a Red Sox cap she'd ordered through the mail. She'd kept him company on his rounds, passed him sugar doughnuts in the truck, trailed him into the cellars of his buildings downtown. The Mode O'Day, Penniman's, the Christian Science Reading Room. Under the sidewalks there were passageways; the light seeped down through glass cylinders embedded in the cement, wavery, sea-green, the light of dreams. He stood beside her in these catacombs, immense, his hands the hands of a stonemason. Was another girl in Sperry so blessed?

It would be comforting to blame her slide from favor on his illness, the senility or whatever name they were putting to it, but he'd begun to lose interest before that. An adolescent girl wasn't what he'd had in mind, apparently. The moods, the unspeakable creeping femininity. She finally sought out her mother, who wouldn't get mixed up in it, wouldn't take sides. "Honestly, Faith," she said, "you make too much of everything." Her friends were no better. Louisa, Annette, Sass. "Wish to God mine would leave *me* alone," one of them said. Cool, shrugging; as if it was natural to feel this repugnance. So Faith dropped the subject.

By this time, George was long gone. He'd been a quartermaster in the army, stationed at Fort Lewis, outside Tacoma, then a purchasing agent for Swedish Hospital. He was big like their father, but more handsome—broad-shouldered, substantial through the middle, not in the least boyish. His hair was black as shoe polish, combed in glossy furrows; he favored sheer white shirts with suspenders, high-waisted trousers with pleats when no one wore pleats. Holidays, long weekends in summer, he rode the Empire Builder home from Seattle, squired Faith and her mother out to Daugherty's for a fancy meal. Her mother became dewy-eyed and passive when George was around. Virtually collapsed in relief.

It was all Faith could do not to be that way herself.

She hated visiting the Lutheran Home, never went on her own, but George could charm her into it. Their father would be parked by his window, glumly watching the parade of golfers. Always the same pilling cardigan, the same protest when he looked up and recognized his children: *It's a sin what your mother did to me, some fair-weather friend she was.* Bitter, but somehow half-hearted. (Was it true their mother hadn't tried hard enough to keep him at home? Who could judge?) George mollified him with a bag of hard butterscotch candies. On his better days, cribbage was possible. Sometimes he turned voluble, recounted heroic bouts of well-drilling, the acres of guck he'd pulled out of the earth, the legion of know-nothings he'd put up with in his time. Old Fred Dyer, Eldon Stoltz, the three McClendon brothers. George listened, nodded, patiently tallied their hands. Faith sat by the radiator and feigned a glorious disinterest, thinking, *He never once asks about us!* And a second later, chiding herself: *It's too late for that. Let it go. Let it go.*

She could stand these sessions because afterward George gave her the rest of his day. They bought ice cream at the news agency and drove into the lower valley to one of the old steamboat landings on the river.

"Is this where they come parking?" George asked. "I believe it used to be."

"I wouldn't know about *that,*" Faith said, although of course she'd been there with boys, had her blouse unbuttoned while the wind ransacked the cottonwoods overhead, had the experience, once, of walking back to town on one shoe.

The muddy bank was riprapped with old car bodies. Two rows of pilings stuck out into the water and barn swallows twirled among them. Nothing gave her such pleasure as to sit there with George; it was almost unbearable. He was different than she remembered. A grown man—worldly, seasoned, as if the city were a sharp brine. Somewhere he'd acquired the gift of mimicry; he had their mother down cold, the slight lisp, the repertoire of slightly archaic expressions: "Best not to delve into things *overmuch.*" He could do Mrs. Barnhardt, ancient firebrand of the high school cafeteria. His Richard Nixon left her squirming, telling him stop, she'd pee her pants. He asked what she'd been reading. *On the Beach, Franny and Zooey,* didn't mention the romance novels. What did she think she'd study in college? Probably keep on with her French, she said, wouldn't that be all right? Her brother nodded. And was anything troubling her, any worries dampening her soul? No, of course not, she said. But a little coaxing and out it all came, the mortifying particulars of her life. Without warning, her eyes pooled with tears. George nudged up her glasses, wiped with the big flat part of his thumb, then blotted it on his shirt, where the gauzy fabric turned briefly invisible. He did nothing to dissuade her from this excess of feeling. Later, alone, as she replayed these talks, she understood that they'd not been as meandering as they'd seemed. She saw how he'd drawn her out.

She thought: *I must be on his mind all the time.*

Then she was at the university. A loose plan had been hatched for her to study in France for a year, but by then she had a boyfriend, a journalism student named Teddy Sangster. A dark, sexy boy; impatient. She loved him furiously, left school to marry him. Naturally it was George who gave her away, who took command of the rehearsal dinner, jollied the Sangsters—staid, suspicious people—with rounds of black Russians. Who tapped his glass and stood to deliver a lavish toast in praise of Faith. When he was a little drunk, his words had a lovely reckless sound. With Teddy rubbing her leg under the table, she heard her rise in the world cataloged, from scabby-kneed girl to student of French culture to bride. It was all deeply ludicrous; she was a fake, savagely made up and poured into the wrong dress, too clingy and bare, exposing the wrong parts of her. Yet she shut her eyes and let herself float in a brief delirium, borne on her brother's voice.

After two years, Teddy abruptly changed his mind. He was stir-crazy, he said, couldn't adjust to settling down. It didn't fit the image he had of himself. The whole thing was an ugly mistake. Stung, blind-sided, she didn't have the first clue about fighting to keep him. How could she be so ill-equipped for loving someone? The worst of it, somehow, was the thought that she'd let George down. A needless fear, of course. George wrote a sweet letter, named an attorney, offered practical suggestions. And it was George, too, after she'd been working at the credit union for a few months, who said he knew of a man with some cabins for sale. Their father had been dead for a year by then, and their mother had abruptly removed herself to Ontario, that farmland along Lake Erie where her people grew flowers. The house on North Wyoming had been sold, frantically remodeled by the new owner, even the yard torn up, the hedgerow bulldozed, replaced by a batch of gangly saplings. Faith passed it on her way to work, stared in shock—it was as if their time there had been a trick, a spell that had worn off.

"I hate to think of you treading water," George said over the phone. He almost sounded put out with her. Her cheeks burned; she started to protest . . . but what *did* she want? She had no idea, no plan, so she'd agreed to have a look at the Lodge. George walked her through the arrangements, cosigned the note. And he'd been right—it suited her immensely. That's the George she prefers to think of, gallant and rock-solid, who seemed to know her better than she knew herself. What he's been up to lately is more of a mystery. She still gets a letter now and then, but he skipped his usual two weeks at the Lodge last August—postponed once, then begged off completely—and failed to come for Thanksgiving or Christmas. His excuses weren't just vague, they were *wispy*—it was as if he'd put no thought into them at all. She's been trying to reach him, off and on, since February, but of course he has no answering machine; the phone rings and rings. Sometimes she's convinced she simply misdialed and tries again, then feels foolish, embarrassed. Finally, a week ago, she fired him off a postcard, one of those brazen summery shots of the Lodge she'd had printed up by the boxful (*The scenery is here, wish you were beautiful!*). On the back, in her own stubby handwriting, "How you?"

•   •   •

NOW THERE'S A LIGHT ON DOWNSTAIRS. The driveway is two dimpled concrete tracks, buckled like sheet ice, leading back toward a storm door and a darkly cowled staircase reeking of solvent. She climbs to the landing, rings her brother's buzzer, hears its tiny refrain within, and whispers *Come on, George*. Thwarted, she thinks to look in his mailbox, down at the foot of the stairs: a Seattle City Light bill, a tool catalog—a wad of inconsequential stuff, but no more than a day or two's. And no sign of her postcard. So he must be around, coming and going at least. She roots in her purse for paper and pen, leaves a message.

She drives downtown to the docks and takes a time-killing ferry ride to Vashon Island. She joins a few hearty souls out at the rail, watches the city shrink behind the boat's wake. In a few minutes, cheeks numb, she retreats to an inside table, lays her head down and feels the deep rumble of the engine. One fall, she remembers, George gave her a dinner party at the old place. Such an odd cache of friends he had: two ex-lovers, Merrit and Annie; another woman, Annie's spidery friend Therese, nimble, grasping; a single man named Paolo; a couple of others she's forgotten. George made a cassoulet, lit the apartment with dozens of candles. She loved watching him oversee this enterprise, attending to everyone, his toed-out walk, strangely graceful. He seemed so at home in his big body.

Paolo, who ran a gallery downtown, had talked about a painting by Goya. A huge, mustardy fresco: *The Dog*. The dog was apparently swimming—a gray splotch of head with frantic, disbelieving eyes.

"The Spanish call it *perro semihundido*," Paolo said. "The half-submerged dog."

A perfectly decent evening, yet unsettling somehow. Once they were alone, drunk on dinner wine, then Calvados, she asked George finally if he was gay, came out and said the unsayable.

He gave no sign of being affronted, acted as if she were long overdue in asking.

"Nothing so exotic, I'm afraid," he said.

They sat up and drank a little more; the candles burned down.

"*Semihundido*," he said after a while, and they both laughed.

Faith was next to him on the sofa. She felt what she'd felt when she was much younger, his gravity, the immense pleasure of being near it, drawn up to the warmth of his flesh.

"Man, you must think I'm an awful hick," she said.

"Oh, Sweetie," George said. "No, *no*. Couldn't be further from the truth."

Later, they folded out the sofa. George disappeared, returned with a pillow under each arm, fluffed them for her, murmured good night and went off again to his own room. The light shone under his door for some time; then she slept, waking near morning to the sensation of her brother standing over her, which, letting her eyes adjust, proved untrue.

●　　●　　●

WHEREVER HE SPENT THE NIGHT, her brother must be at work now. After those years at Swedish, he'd gone over to one of the vendors, Puget Sound Medical; not long ago he changed companies again, and she realizes she doesn't know the name of the new one. But surely he'll come home after work? So it's suppertime before Faith makes her way back to the bungalow. She inspects his mail: A few additions have been wedged into the tiny box. From the bottom of the stairs, she can see her note, still swiveling from its clip.

Now she considers bothering the downstairs people. She goes around front before the urge fades, up onto the dusty porch. Through gaps in the blinds sees a young girl in jeans and pink ballet skirt, spinning on one foot—ten maybe, Asian, hair spinning like a short black rotor.

Faith rings; then she's flooded with light, standing before the girl's pretty young mother. The man upstairs? She hears him on the stairs, once in a while spies him taking out his trash, his recycling. A ghost. No, sorry, she has no idea, can't help.

So Faith finds herself checking into a Super 8, succumbing to a twenty-minute shower. She dresses again: turtleneck, long sweater, black leggings. Sits on the bed, combs out her wet hair and hastily rebraids it, then, impulsively, pulls the phone into her lap to call Rick.

"I thought it might be you," he says, a little breathless. "I was outside."

"Were you worried?"

"Should I have been?"

"I'm over here seeing George."

"Ah," Rick says. "I thought you were off with some boyfriend." He's kidding. Rick loves jokes, the kind you hear and pass along. *What's Irish and comes out in the spring? Paddy O'Furniture.* His own tend to be modest, never wounding.

"So your brother's wining and dining you, is he?" Rick says.

"You know how he is," Faith answers, stretched out on her

back now like a snow angel. "Nothing he wouldn't do for you."

Outside, it's dark again. Her shoulders ache, but she's overshot the need to rest. In the car once more, the layout of this complicated city returns to her in small illuminations. She discovers a multiplex she remembers, buys a ticket and greedily watches a movie, shucked down in the seat, anonymous among the scattering of university students. It's the kind of picture Rick would hate—all talk, minor revelations, with snow sifting onto cobbled streets. She hugs her knees, stares until the last credit has scrolled into oblivion, wanders out to the lobby and orders a monster cappuccino, then sees another movie. It's garish and violent and thought-quelling—Rick would tease her for watching some parts through her fingers. By the time it lets out, it's after midnight; there's another show starting, but waiting undecided in the lobby she's touched with a chill, a breath of reality. She trails outside in the safety of two young couples, takes refuge in her car, jams down the door locks.

Saturday morning, she wakes from a welter of dreams, collapses back among them, and wakes again, stiff-necked and sour-mouthed. From bed, she dials George's apartment, but already this seems a formality—even the rings have a vain, fluttery sound. *Get up, get out,* she tells herself, and so she dresses and spends a few hours poking through shops, buys earrings, a gaudy floral shirt for Rick, picks up a *Paris Match* at the Market's news kiosk and forces herself to read French in a café overlooking the waterfront. Her unease rises and falls, minute to minute. Late in the day, she checks the motel for a message. Nothing. Then, with dusk settling on the city like spent fuel, she drives again to the bungalow, chagrined, intent on snatching down the note and hurrying away. But there's George's car, a venerable and stolid Dodge. And from the dormers, the suggestion of light.

•   •   •

SO, YOU'VE FOUND ME, his face says.

She squeezes against him, puts her lips to his cheek, then pulls back, ready to give him a hard time, *Why didn't you get ahold of me, you bum*— But he's already headed back to his chair, his cloth slippers shushing on the rug.

She's been visualizing his old place, she realizes. Her first sight of these dim, beveled rooms is as dispiriting as the look on his face. The only light trickles in from a half-opened closet beyond his shoulders.

"You're just sitting in the dark up here? That's no good."

He flops his shirtsleeved arms against the chair, as if to say it's not his fault, evening simply snuck up on him.

"What can I do?" Faith asks. "Can I make us some coffee?"

Her brother wipes his face, looks as if he'll stand. "I'd rather you didn't see me like this," he says. "Could I have a rain check?"

Apparently, he truly expects her to leave. Instead, she steps into his slot of a kitchen, flips on the light. The counter is clean and spare. There sits his little bag of coffee beans, folded over, rubber-banded, and there his miniature grinder. She thinks she'll cry. The prospect seems almost a relief, but how pointless.

"Are you going to make me badger it out of you?" she says. "You're dis*turb*ing me, George."

"That wasn't my intention."

"What is it, then? What's the trouble?"

A look crosses his face, frank annoyance, *Now this*. He sags, sucks in a resolute breath and shoves himself up from the chair. "Would you come down to the car with me?" he asks, retrieving his crinkled suit coat from the sofa.

"Of course," Faith says.

But at the door, she has to touch his arm and point to the slippers, then wait as he changes into regular shoes.

At first it seems as if he means to drive around aimlessly, putting her off, but then she thinks she recognizes landmarks of his former neighborhood. Old gates, pebbly retaining walls, snarls of blackberry. "This is where you used to live, isn't it?" she asks.

George eases into a parking spot without answering. He rocks the car as he gets out; Faith trails after him, up to the top floor of the building, waits while he twists his key soundlessly in the lock.

Inside, there's a nurse at the table reading under a gooseneck lamp. She glances up at George, surprised to see him, but not very.

"She asleep?" he asks her.

"I don't think quite," the nurse says.

George puts a hand on Faith's back and sweeps her through the double doors.

The figure in the bed stirs, the mattress whirs a few degrees more upright.

"Lucy," George says. "I'd like you to meet my sister."

•   •   •

THE WOMAN, this Lucy, lifts her head so that Faith can see the silky glint of tubes emerging from her nostrils. Faith steps closer, extends her hand, and has the tips of her fingers squeezed.

"She's paid us an unexpected visit," George says.

"The famous Faith," Lucy says.

Faith nods, smiles.

What on earth is going on here?

In the bad light, it's hard to tell how old the woman is, but certainly she's years older than George, a tiny thing, barely a wrinkle in the sheet. Her hair is short and lank, her skin eroded at the eyes and mouth.

"What time is it, George?"

"It's not late," he says. "Eight or nine."

"Is *that* all?" She regards Faith. "I hate to sleep," she says. "Hate it like the devil, can't . . . bear to have the time stolen from me. But I have no energy. None."

Her head drops back among the pillows. That dark bundle tucked like a hen in the crook of Lucy's arm Faith now recognizes as the telephone.

This had not been a bedroom when the apartment was George's, but a sunroom. Leaded casement windows, philodendron on runners of twine, green-painted wicker. Faith remembers drowsing in a delicious stupor here one afternoon, the feeling of sanctuary. Now the plants have gone, along with George's furniture; the room has an astringent, camphorish smell. Outside, the lights of downtown, the harbor's black space. It must be why she wanted this room, Faith concludes. The long, light-stricken view to combat the closing-in.

"And how's your paramour?" Lucy asks between shallow, raspy breaths.

"Ah, well, my *paramour*—" Faith says, playing along, trying to match the gallows humor in Lucy's voice. She has to squelch the desire to air every doubt she has about her lover. The famous Rick.

"You need one like this one," Lucy says. "This prince."

Faith casts a look at her brother but his attention has fallen to the shadow pooling at his feet.

"We can't stay," George says in a moment.

"You just got here. Am I mistaken?"

"It can't be helped," he says.

Lucy looks at the two of them—the gaze is piercing, voracious: *What good are you if you won't divert me?*

George braces himself against the mattress, bends and lowers his cheek to Lucy's lips.

"I'm going to see you tomorrow?" Lucy says.

George gives a shake of the head that could mean anything.

Faith murmurs an awkward goodbye, and waits at the outer door while George has a word with the nurse, and then they are out in the must of the stairwell again, down two flights, soft, out-of-sync footsteps, across the flagstones to the street.

They're blocks away, out on the Aurora bridge, before he says, abruptly, angrily, "She smoked like a gangster. Her fingers stank, they smelled like rawhide, like a smoked goddamn *ham*." He sniffs at his own index finger, retracts his lips, disgusted. "It's not like she didn't know," he says. "They told her what would happen—she'd always had rotten lungs. She was told and told, but it was always *c'est la guerre*."

"Did we have to run off?" Faith says. "It wouldn't have killed us to stay a minute."

George ignores her. After a while, he says, "You don't know the first thing about it, Faithie."

This old endearment startles her, fills her with a creepy, invaded feeling. "Yes, but why *don't* I?" she says. "I can't believe you'd keep all this to yourself."

He turns partway toward her, says grudgingly, "She wrote for the newspaper. She had a column. Lucy Graves."

"That's *her*?" Faith says, brought up short. For years, George's letters would arrive with one of those long strips of scissored newsprint tucked in—maybe a comment or two inscribed in the margin, *How she loves to fillet the high and mighty!* But nothing more. No suggestion that he and Lucy had ever so much as met.

"She was crazy about privacy," George says. "It wasn't good enough to have an unlisted number, she had to be the mystery woman, the queen of misinformation. She'd look you straight in the eye and hand you some utterly fabricated story. It was a compulsion, a sickness. But if you wanted to stay in her good graces, you put up with it, you forgave. Even her *name*, for God's sake. She told people she'd been married to someone named Graves, an older man who'd rescued her from a hideous childhood. Her own family was from Michigan, so she claimed. A pack of ogres and philistines and child molesters. Even I believed that, or at least I believed there was some little nut of truth in it. But I happened to run into a man—and this was completely by accident—a guy who'd grown up with her. It was over in Omak, just the other side of the mountains. Her father was the postmaster. Floyd Graves, a perfectly okay guy, apparently. His only other child was a boy who'd been shot up in the Battle of the Bulge."

It's begun to spit rain now. George fiddles with the wipers; they make a heavy, disconcerting clunk on each pass across the windshield.

"And where do I fit in?" he says. "How did I manage to get embroiled in this business?" He fixes her in a quick sideways glare. "I was another of her secrets. Her young man. Her young friend."

He tries to let it go at that, but a block or two farther on he says, "Of course she had other ports of call, don't think she didn't. Weeks and weeks might go by and I'd hear not one blessed word out of her. You'd think I might've minded it. You'd think I would've voiced an objection. But I did not. There was something illicit, *glamorous* . . ."

His choice of words appalls him—his finger goes to his

mouth as if he can scoop them out like a wad of unchewable meat.

"Even when we traveled," he says, "she had to have her own quarters."

They're up on Market now. Sluggish, stop-and-go traffic, brake lights flaring in the rain. George curses softly, makes a veering, unsignaled right into a grid of parked-up streets. Discreetly, Faith squeezes the armrest, stiffens her feet, feeling the slaps of water against the Dodge's undercarriage.

"Things started going wrong for her at the newspaper," George says. "They said her outlook had soured. The columns had lost their charm, gotten shrill and unfunny. They tried to get her to retire—oh, there were great shouting matches. Finally they just yanked the column. Pulled the plug on her."

So, Faith understands all at once, Lucy's broke. Broke and sick and out of fancy friends. All but George.

This prince.

She reaches for his sleeve—a reflex, an offer of allegiance.

He wants none of it, asks, "So where was it you were staying?"

"Super 8," Faith says, but thinking he means to go straight there, adds, "But I've got my car. Remember?"

He shakes his head at his lapse. The rest of the way he's quiet. They pass the little grocery at the end of his block. He slows, the car bottoms out on the hump in the drive, the lights play down the tines of a ruined fence. He shuts the ignition off, collapses against the seat as if he's driven back from the moon.

•   •   •

THE RAIN COMES HARDER, a full-blown downpour hammering the roof. George rolls his shoulders, squirms inside his suit as if it's shrunk.

"I'll get back here after seeing her," he says in a minute, "I'll get undressed and try to get a few hours' sleep, and there she'll be on the phone."

Then, suddenly, he's doing Lucy's voice, a roughened, oxygen-starved falsetto: "I can't, I can't . . . tolerate this . . . George, can you hear me, I'm scared to death, I'm not going to live through the night. *George, are you there*—?"

It's merciless, dead-on.

"Sometimes I let it ring," he says.

"But you can't not answer, George."

There's a tug at the corner of her brother's mouth, dismissive, mocking. Now he's going to do *her* voice: *You can't not answer*, as if she's still sixteen, woeful in her ignorance.

Something just holds him back.

"You know what, Faith?" he says at last. "Why don't you go home." And when, a moment later, she's not out of his sight, he says, "I mean it. *Please,*" his big face radiating heat, fogging the glass.

"What planet are you on?" Faith answers. "You don't think I'm going to just hop out and leave you? In this rain and everything?"

But a sick panic is splashing into her throat, caustic, ammonialike. "It's *me*, George," she says. "Don't you see how messed up I am for you?"

Hasn't he always known it, though? Hasn't he basked in it? She thinks of how they used to drive him to the train in Stillwater, she and her mother. Waiting on the platform in the summer dusk, chaff and diesel smudging the air; then the moment when George picked his bag up, bent and placed a kiss on each of their foreheads, and finally tore himself away, their mother calling after him, "You're an angel, George."

Faith cracks her window—the car's so clammy she can hardly breathe. The rain hasn't let up at all; she hears it

202 🌲 David Long

splashing from a busted downspout, slapping the ground erratically, dinging on something hollow like a coffee can. She sticks her hand out, cools her fingers, then applies them to the artery in her neck, letting a trickle of water escape into her shirt. In the mountains, she thinks, this would be a wet, obliterating snow. Rick would be out on the glassed-in porch, watching it fall through the yardlights, wondering if he would need to pull on boots and plow one last time, or go knock the heavy clumps off the arborvitae. She can see him perfectly: the baggy sweater, the three-day beard, the look in his eyes—patient, guileless. If she were there this very minute, she'd sneak up behind him, lay her chin on his shoulder, and tell him not to go out. *It'll melt . . . stay here.* She'd flatten herself against his back, rock from breast to breast until he covered her hand with his, lifted it to his lips. Later, in bed, she would notice that he had taken the trouble to shave.

She turns to George, opens her mouth to say she can't believe how mean he's gotten, how constricted in his heart, but he knows that, too—isn't he taking a malicious pleasure in it? And so she says nothing, scoops up her purse and gets out, skids down the slick incline to the Subaru in a rush of relief, reaching a hand over her head as if it will keep her dry.

Drenched to the skin, she starts the engine for heat, rakes her hair, dabs her glasses with a wadded-up Kleenex. After a while, she drops the car into gear, fighting off the urge to look back up the driveway, where she knows her brother hasn't budged, where he's no more than a blur behind the glass.

EGGARINE

My father walked with a cane all his life. He'd been born with a withered leg, and it had grown into a bony shank, the muscles like long whittlings of white wood. He wasted no effort trying to hide it. Summers, we drove to Stallings Pond, and he swam in front of God and everybody, stroking to the far buoy and back, then made his way up the sandy beach to the changing room in his puckery blue-plaid trunks, coaxing the leg along like some ne'er-do-well cousin he was responsible for. Now and then, my mother presented him with a new cane; they collected in the closet under the front stairs, bamboo or oak or fiberglass, with crooked necks and red rubber tips like pencil erasers. One had a roly-poly nude carved into its grip, which my father pretended to find amusing and scandalous. But the cane he relied on was more of a walking stick, a straight shaft of some close-grained hardwood, topped with a fist-sized burl polished by the weight of his hand. When he drove me to school, the stick rode on the seat between us. When he saw me after an absence, he waggled it in fond, silent greeting.

He had the face of a trawler captain, angular and gray-eyed, but in fact he worked in the offices of Nashua Paper, a job he'd miraculously acquired back in the heart of the Depression. His name was Aaron Joseph McCauley, but he was known by grown men as Joe, Joey by his brothers and my mother. He was forty when I was born, and I was his only child. He was a thoughtful, fastidious man, not one to pick at old wrongs or air his views on human comportment often, and so he'd shocked me one Saturday morning when he turned away at the sight of our former neighbor, Harley Grimm. "He's a louse," was the sum total of his explanation. I extracted from my mother the information that Harley had involved himself with a young woman from Lancaster and forsaken his family.

Mild, moon-faced Mr. Grimm. The adult world astonished me.

"You surely know," my mother added, "that walking out on people would top your father's list of sins."

I did know that.

We lived on Burnham Road in Pepperell, Massachusetts, in a house known as the Loomis Place, after its original owner, a farmer and timber contractor named Asa Loomis. It stood on a foundation of granite fieldstones, with McIntosh trees to the south and in back a hayfield we rented out, set off from the neighboring fields by tall hedgerows swarming with grapevine. It had lightning rods and chipped green shutters that keened when the wind blew up from the pine woods. There were rooms in it we never filled, bedrooms that remained closed off, disavowed. Other Loomises had modernized it a bit—upgraded plumbing and wiring, applied dour wallpaper layer on layer—but there were places, behind doors we never closed, where the old plaster showed, as hard and stained as crockery dug from the ground. You could feel the restraint in these efforts. "They were a frugal tribe," my mother said. Gradually, my father had brightened the place with carpet and drapes, cut down on its clattering echoes and leaks of air, but he had his own frugality, or caution. It had nothing to do with Calvinism, everything to do with his deep fear that all would be taken from him.

We each spent great quantities of time alone, but the kitchen was where we convened as a family. Off the far end was a pantry my mother archly referred to as the root cellar—passable for canned goods, but too dank for anything fresh, a meringue pie, say. She expected to meet raccoons in there. My father explained the impossibility of this; she didn't care, it was *unsavory*. Otherwise, the kitchen was a comfort, long and low-ceilinged, with a trestle table and a gaping, stone-hearthed fireplace. Sunday mornings, by the time I arrived downstairs, grumpy with sleep (those years I was a starved-looking teenage boy, when my life had first begun to seem a strange, provisional artifact to me), my mother would be on her umpteenth cup of coffee, scissoring articles from the *Globe*: Glenn Gould, Harry Houdini, Viking runes, accounts of inhuman strength or sacrifice. What was *that* all about? You have to take an interest in things beyond your own petty self, she'd say. Pay attention; a lot's going on. She'd shake her head in mock-dismay. How had two such alert, early-to-rise types produced me? "Close your mouth, at least," she'd say. "You'll catch flies."

My father would be at the cutting board, shaved and dressed, his hair neatly center-parted, his cheeks glossy with witch hazel. "And how's his nibs this morning?" he'd ask. "I hope you're hungry. I hope you're ready for something truly splendid." He was in the midst of fixing an "eggarine," a kind of Denver sandwich he'd invented, his one-morning-a-week glory in the kitchen. He broke the eggs on the lip of the bowl, worked the whisk, began to hum. Waiting, I saw his gaze stray to the meadow, to the pine-serrated skyline he never could seem to believe was his.

• • •

THE SUMMER I TURNED SEVENTEEN, I went to work for a house builder, cleaning up trash and running supplies in a battered Ford truck he refused to license. I was paired with an older man I hated, named Warren Thibault. Slouchy and rank, not a drinker, but erratic and full of gripes. He wore a T-shirt and worsted vest and oily green pants, with a massive black leather wallet stuck in the back pocket and chained to his belt loop. I drove, avoiding the main drags; Warren rode with his knees against the dashboard, talking without letup—about Buck Owens or the price of scrap copper or his wild, no-good daughters. He'd veer into Scripture apropos of nothing: "I am the Alpha and the Omega. Who is and who was and who is to come, the *Aaawl-Mighty*." His voice was high and stubborn, with a hitch—it was mesmerizing, and I couldn't protect myself from it. We kicked off our load of rock lath and splintered wood; then Warren scavenged the dump, poking at things with a curtain rod. I waited in the breezy heat, bored, slightly guilty about not earning my pay. Afterward, he directed me up the hillocky lane that led to his house—not the shanty I'd expected but a stark old frame house in the woods, once yellow. At the rumble of the truck, a curtain drew back from one of the tall downstairs windows, but no one came to greet us. Warren slid out with a yip of pain and began throwing his booty off into the weeds, banged the roof with a length of pipe, hollered, "You, get out here."

Warren had a story he told. After the war, he and his
brother, a character named Bernard, had been hired to plant
trees and seed the lawn surrounding the new hospital in
Lowell. They'd done it all themselves, he said, a mammoth
job. They'd dropped fish in the holes where the bushes went,
as the old-time farmers had; they'd sown the grass seed
under a full moon. It sprouted luxuriously, grew like a thick
pelt. If I didn't believe him, I could drive down and see it with
my own two eyes. I was already sick of this story when, in a
panic one day, the builder detailed Warren and me to rake out
the topsoil and plant grass around one of his spec houses.
Warren refused the spreader, called me a know-nothing. He
waded into the soft dirt, broadcasting seed from a paper bag,
letting it blow where it would. He set the sprinklers and we
left. They were still going the next day. What grass did grow
came up in funny tufts, in the eroded furrows where the
water had run off, and in the deep prints Warren's boots had
made.

One afternoon, the two of us baking inside the cab, Warren started on his daughters again. Nola and Marilyn. They
were rotten, they'd wind up in hell. "You don't believe in hell,
I know you," he said. "Just like them. You're too smart for all
that, ain't you?" He poked at me. "Ain't you?"

I said nothing.

"What's the worst thing you can think of?" he asked.

"Cut it out," I said.

"*Ha.* You and them, you're just the same. You can't think
of nothing bad enough."

We came, at last, to the gully where he left his car. I let him
out, wickedly relieved. I drove home, showered, and fled into
the evening, passing my father partway down the gravel
drive. He was hiking along in his old canvas jacket, rocking

against the stick. The field beyond him was dense with gold-enrod. He looked at me the way he was always looking at me, caught between speaking and not.

"You off somewhere?" he asked. His capacity to be surprised seemed limitless. "Your mother wishes she saw more of you. And myself, as well."

"Yes, I know," I said.

He nodded, put his head down, walked on.

Out on the tar road, I floored it. Sunlight strobed through the colonnade of maple trunks; the stone walls melted by in a blur. I roared down the middle of the narrow road, whumped into the air at each rise. The tires chirped, the oil pan rang off the blacktop. No one was ever coming the other way—no moving van, no station wagon full of sandy kids. I drove and drove, but nothing the evening brought lived up to its first luscious minutes. Hours later, as I neared home again, Warren Thibault wormed his way back into my thoughts, with his smell of kerosene and rot, his talk of the quick and the dead. I let myself in, tore my clothes off and lay on top of the sheets. The house was hot; the air stirred in secret eddies. I'd never been afraid of sleep, but I was now, afraid of my plunge into nothingness. I got up and pulled on gym shorts and wandered through the downstairs, touching things. In the kitchen, I planted my bare feet on the slab of granite by the fireplace and drank a tumbler of milk so fast the nerve in my forehead burned. I pictured myself running outdoors and fleeing in the car again, but the thought filled me with desperation. What good was it, where could I go that was not still the earth?

•   •   •

MY GRANDFATHER MCCAULEY had fallen to the Spanish flu that hit New England the winter of 1918. He was thirty-one. He'd taught at a business college in Worcester.

Before him, the McCauleys had all been farmers or teamsters—he was the novelty families sometimes produce. He'd stranded four boys and a young wife who'd taken none of his classes. My father was the youngest; his steel leg brace skidded on the ice, clunked up and down stairs. My grandmother was lost, a tiny woman overrun by moods and furious superstitions. She found work in a store selling yard goods and dress patterns. Her older boys slipped out of school one after another, and my father was on his own. He might have burrowed in and not come out, but an Englishwoman in the apartment upstairs took an interest in him that my grandmother apparently allowed, or was too put-upon to stop. She baked him scones, forced an odd raft of books on him, badgered him into having opinions. Mrs. Watts, whose husband had died in a train accident. "You must persevere," she said. It was her incantation; it resonated in him, took on the stature of a commandment. He finished high school, put himself through college at night, tutoring, working a few hours a week in a Western Union office, borrowing.

It was 1934. Perseverance or not, there were no jobs. He didn't know what he was going to do. Day after day, nothing. Then, one night on the train, a man named Ben Saterlee bought him a drink and they fell into conversation. The Saterlee brothers owned Nashua Paper, which had been founded by their great-grandfather. Well, Ben said, times were lousy. You couldn't argue that. It was like a contagion, the way it fed on men's souls. Ah, but maybe not everything was black and hopeless. You never knew, did you? They drank; the towns winked by. An affable, careless soul; my father's benefactor.

My parents first crossed paths at the old Hotel Excelsior in Fitchburg. My mother and her sister, Alvie, and Alvie's husband, Carl Upshaw, were out celebrating some stroke of fortune. One of the wives in my father's party knew Alvie from somewhere. My mother was in green, her hair waved, a deep cordovan in direct sun, almost black in the dim atmospherics of the lounge. She had high, arching brows, a sturdy complexion. He wrote her name on a two-dollar bill, folded it into his wallet. He didn't call. Months later, they turned up on a jury together, and my mother acted as though she'd never laid eyes on him. He produced the two-dollar bill; there was her name, Rose Stergios, in his draftsmanlike hand. "All right then," she said. "Buy us a drink." She was twenty-four, smart, restless. She'd been living in Alvie and Carl's spare room, working for the phone company, with thoughts of taking an apartment in Boston, studying acting or art history. There was no money for such a thing, but she would have him know she was not some ordinary girl trapped behind a switchboard.

The Loomis house had stood vacant for months, the hay uncut, the apples left to freeze on the ground. My father had noticed it on one of his Sunday excursions. He'd parked at the road and hiked up the lane and stood regarding it as if it were a huge wood-sparred ship at anchor. It was impractical and prideful, a reach, but necessary for just those reasons.

My mother lost her first pregnancy. When she conceived again, she hoarded the news, passed the date of the first miscarriage, held out a week or two more, until he could see for himself; but the outcome was the same. And a third time, and then years elapsed. At thirty-six she was pregnant again; they located a doctor in Cambridge who put her on a regimen of estrogen and bedrest. She was due on April Fools' Day, and made it nearly into March when I was born. Her reproductive history—the experience of miscarrying, those ghost siblings of mine—I couldn't bear to know about it, couldn't bear not to. Why hadn't she tried again? "Too old," she said. "Didn't care to tempt fate. Anyway, you were a mir-

acle; what more could I want? Has it been such a burden,
Jay?"

She liked it if I bantered back, showed some spark, so we
could be delivered from this impossible business. Sometimes
I caught her staring at me as if I *were* miraculous, and there-
fore exempt from judgment. Mostly, I puzzled her—how had
I gotten so moody, why were my talents so hard to divine? I
couldn't answer. I could no more express how it felt to be so
singular in the world than my father could have described his
disappointment at not having populated that big windy house
of ours.

• • •

ASIDE FROM READING, my father had no pastimes—
cared nothing for televised sports, joined no group he didn't
absolutely have to. What he did, mainly, was keep the property up. He trussed the gravid branches of the fruit trees;
laid walkways of herringboned brick and sand; built lattice.
He rode an old Graveley mowing tractor that pulled a bank
of cutting reels, crisscrossing the knobby grass by the hour,
meditative, his back straight, his left leg propped up. His
arms were surprisingly thick, furred with sandy hair that
caught the flecks of cut grass. When he finished, he piloted
the mower up the dirt ramp into what remained of the
Loomises' great shambling barn. It had no weather vane, no
rooster or codfish. The cupola had disappeared before our
time, and some of the shingles had kited off in the wind, letting in needles of light. Its hay had turned to a powdery
mold, the manure to a fine, pungent dust.

On the back side, where the ground was flat, he'd installed
a basketball hoop for me. I liked team sports no better than
he did, but I became obsessed with the monotonous pleasure
of shooting foul shots. At the first bang of the rim, pigeons

would come unstuck from the rafters, and stream out through a hole in the loft. Sometimes I saw my father at the window of his workroom, but its glass was as milky as wax paper, and it was impossible to know what he was looking at or what he might be thinking. When the ball had bounded into the barberry bushes one too many times, I'd leave it there and join him inside, and be enlisted to crank the grinding wheel as he drew the sickle blades across it, or reach him down the copper oil can with its comic *plick-plock* sound. There in the barn he was in his element—so I thought, or maybe that was only what my mother said, joking, faintly ironic. But one afternoon as we started down the ramp together, I noticed how his gait quickened, how his cane hand gave an extra shove and the cords in his neck went taut. So he had his own superstition: He wouldn't turn and look back into the barn. Amazingly, he felt the way I so often did— scrutinized, insubstantial. The feeling welled up in him out there where the Loomis men had gone about their work. And yet, he could throw it off, too. Nearing the house, seeing my mother's car parked in the sun, he restaked his claim on the here and now, on the brilliant green day.

We were irregular churchgoers. After the browbeating she'd taken in girlhood, my mother wouldn't set foot in any church, unless it was for a wedding, and even then she clutched her purse in her lap, looking trapped and set-upon. But my father did go now and then, honoring an internal timetable I wasn't privy to, and when he went, I went, though he didn't require it. He favored the austere meeting-house of the Congregationalists, with its whitewashed walls and blandly tinted window glass. I sat beside him, studying the quavery inscriptions, IN LOVING MEMORY OF LORRAINE GILCHRIST, FREDERICK MAY, PRISCILLA SMITH-PETERSON. He sang;

he closed his eyes appropriately; he abided the sermons with a polite detachment. Afterward, we retired to the cellar for cider and sweet rolls, and he came to life again, chatting with men from town, his free hand around my shoulder, no heavier than a woolen scarf. At home, he'd color his talk with scripture. "Mary pondered these things in her heart," he might say, meaning that people ought to make of things what they will. But he had no stomach for evangelism, nor would he drag God into the fray as Warren did. He never terrorized me with the specter of a snoopy, vindictive deity. Asked about the afterlife, he'd have shaken his head, said it was too private a business. He might have added, "Let us hope for the best."

•   •   •

SO LONG AS IT WAS in the hands of the Saterlees, Nashua Paper had been lenient about retirement. My father let it be known he'd work until he was seventy, but the company seemed to falter in the late 1960s; new managers were hustled in, weaker divisions sloughed off in panic. His friend, Ben Saterlee, was long dead. The other Saterlee men had gradually retreated to their summer places in Falmouth and Cape Ann. Their sons hadn't gone into the business—they taught college, designed books, practiced sports law. Finally, like the other old family firms—manufacturers of shoes and hand tools and hardwood chairs—Nashua Paper was sold. My father was asked to retire at once and did, without ceremony, without complaint.

I'd always thought of him as old, an envoy from a time beyond reach, but, oddly, he seemed no older at sixty-nine than I'd ever remembered him. No weaker, no less cheerful—no more profligate with advice, either. I was out of college by then, living in Atlanta and working for a company that drew up market profiles for radio advertisers. My mother called almost every Saturday morning, pretending it had just occurred to her to see what had become of me out in the greater world. She grilled me on my eating habits, my love life. When she ran out of steam she passed the phone to my father. In his reticent way, he, too, inquired after my well-being. How was that job of mine?

"Not bad," I said.

But it *was* bad, as stupefying as the two before it—the one writing copy for a tool catalog, and the one at the auto club. Must've been home sick on Career Day, I used to joke, but the humor had gone out of it. The job was like a long, dead stretch of interstate; most days I found myself disheartened, beating back panic, ashamed. I went into none of that with him, and he didn't pry. We said our goodbyes for another week.

• • •

ONE NIGHT, the third summer after his death, I stepped from the shower to the ringing phone. It was after midnight, still sweltering in my apartment. I'd never heard her sound so beset or weepy. She'd had a man out to look the house over, she reported. The main roof would have to be reshingled before it could take the weight of ice again; the wood below was mealy as well, down into the timbers. And not only that, maple roots had invaded the septic line, which would have to be dug up.

Hadn't he *done* that?

"Oh, yes," she said. "But somehow he got talked into using Orangeburg pipe, which is the absolute worst, apparently. It was so unlike him."

She had more: The taxes had grown truly monstrous; Mr. Violette had moved south and she had no idea who was going to plow the road; there was no end to it. It was insane to keep on. "I'm just rattling around in here," she said. "It's a mausoleum. You know what I want? Brand new. No more rotten fruit in the grass. Oh, Lord, Jay, I tell you honestly—you think I'm not en*titled*?"

What was I to make of this barrage? I'd dreaded such a call, but gradually my guard had dropped. She'd managed her grief magnificently, people said. She'd purged their room of his suits and razors and drawers of old socks; she'd bundled the canes and given them away, all but the burl-headed stick, which stayed in the vestibule, as if someone might need it. I wondered if she didn't use it herself on her walks, but it never seemed to have budged from where it rested among the boots and slickers. She spoke his name with a crisp matter-of-factness—I had no idea what she really felt. Meanwhile, my own grief murmured and tugged at me, came like chanting just over a hill.

I tried her first thing in the morning, then from work. At lunch I shouldered my way to a crowded kiosk, ate a few bites of sandwich and tossed it in the trash. I thought of trying her friends, asking if they wouldn't mind driving over, but all this seemed hysterical and disloyal, and I let it pass. By evening she was home, herself again. I'd have to forgive that awful outburst. I *could*, couldn't I? She had no intention of getting rid of the house—had she given that impression? Oh, no. "I had a weak moment, which I've weathered nicely."

"Sure?"

Yes, yes. She paused and gathered her forces. "We're tested, Jay," she said.

The next time we talked, and the time after that, there was

no panic or melancholy in her voice; it was bright and quick, caught up in things.

•   •   •

IN OCTOBER I FLEW INTO LOGAN, rented a car and drove out Route 2, peeling off onto 2A at the penitentiary in Concord. Boston had spilled farther into the countryside. There were colonies of custard-yellow townhouses where I expected orchards and horse pastures; old red diners and ice cream stands had been bulldozed away. The sky was heavy, pewtery. The hard cold had already come, hitting the maples and butternuts, picking some clean, leaving others ablaze. I pulled into the drive and honked. My mother was waiting on the flagstones by the back door, hugging her arms to a down vest I didn't recognize. She waved, marched down to plant a kiss on me.

Impatiently, she led me through the wet grass, stopping once to light up a Pall Mall. She'd quit for years but had gone back to it. *Why not?* She smoked like the girl reporter in a Forties movie, one eye clamped down, raking her free hand through her hair, which was thinner and no longer so red but still tumbled down in curlicues. She pointed: The arborvitae bent under a cascade of mossy shakes; a muddy trench angled out toward the drain field, disrupting the rail fence. She'd let a sweep of lawn revert to field grass. The woods hovered behind the mist, subdued, blue-green. She hooked my arm and brought me inside, into the kitchen. There were the new countertops, the cabinets, cream and terra-cotta; the new double sink, the blinds. I began to mouth my approval. But no, wait, she said, and stood theatrically aside to reveal her prize: She'd had the pantry ripped out. "That miserable sink-hole. Gone, *poof*." In its place was a glassed-in bay—a sun-room. She waved her hand at the floor dismissively. "Still waiting for the tile people. Promises, promises. As you can see, we're at a standstill."

She'd dragged a kitchen chair and an old maple table out onto the subflooring, where they stood like stage props. She smiled, but seemed let down, as if showing me hadn't been half the fun she'd expected.

The next day we hauled trash, swabbed things down, did a big shopping and restocked the cupboards. Midafternoon, she disappeared upstairs for a nap. I found a pair of rubber boots and drifted outside to mulch her iris beds. The day had turned raw, and the light came in steely shafts. Was I doing my best by her? I couldn't tell.

That night I told her to dress up a little, I'd take her out. "We can go to Butterfield's," I said.

"Closed up," she said. "Somebody new took over and they went out of business."

"Someplace else, then."

No, she had all this stuff in the icebox.

"A little celebration," I said. "What can it hurt?"

She considered the idea, frowned, gave in.

So we found an old inn on the road to Groton and sat by the window and had our drinks. It was early but getting dark. Outside, wrought-iron chairs had been upended on a low stone wall. Now and then, a stray shot of wind rattled the birches by the walkway, spraying the terrace with black leaves. "Confetti," my mother said without emotion.

She eyed the menu at arm's length, said she couldn't de-cide, settled on a cut of prime rib, bloody rare. She seemed heartened when it arrived, smeared it with horseradish and ate in determined bites.

"I don't hear so much about your friends," she said. "I saw that Parquette girl the other day, that went to Barnard? On her third marriage already. She looked so *proud* of herself. I was sorry to see it. And that Ricky Gaylord you thought was such hot spit? Amounted to absolutely nothing." She coughed against her fist. "Well, I suppose we ought to stay off that," she said.

"Please," I said.

Other diners had come into the back room by now, for which I was grateful. Evening had finished blackening the windows. My mother studied me. "There's nothing wrong with you, honey," she said. "It's not a race."

I hadn't intended to mention this, but after a minute I said, "I had a dream last month: Dad and I were drinking in some out-of-the-way little bar. It was the afternoon, deserted. He was buying, of course. His hat was lying on the next stool. We were talking and there was a lull, and then he smiled all of a sudden—a big exaggerated smile, very comic—and he squeezed my shoulder and said, 'Well, I guess you could've used a little more *guidance.*' And then broke into wails of laughter."

It was the strangest thing for me to tell her, for we'd lost that kind of intimacy.

She looked away. "I don't dream much anymore," she said after a minute. She tossed back her coffee, ready to be gone. Then, for a second, she lost the focus in her eyes; her back sagged, her elbow bumped a teaspoon onto the floor.

Next morning she shuffled out late, wearing jeans and a paint-splattered sweatshirt. She seemed brittle, couldn't keep track of what we were about. The day after, she blacked out and fell. Over furious protests, I ferried her to the hospital in Fitchburg. Well, she was simply tired, that was all there was to it. A little more beaten down than she'd realized. Who could begrudge her that?

They held her for tests.

I sat by the bed. She took my hand, squeezed it in bursts.

"Christ, Jay," she said. "I'm an old wreck."

I told her she didn't look so terrible. "Just tired, like you said. Who wouldn't be?"

"I *am*. You don't know the half of it. I'm worn *out*. It comes on in such waves, it crushes me. I can't stand not having him here."

She rolled away, appalled at herself, and was quiet a long time. I thought she'd dropped into sleep.

"I'll tell you what I wish sometimes," she said. "You want to know? *Do you?*"

"Come on," I said, touching her through the bed linen. "Don't talk like that."

I left the hospital, crept down Prospect Street, past its terraced, slate- and copper-roofed old palaces, and circled the upper commons. I felt empty. Hungry, headachy. I took a roundabout way home, back roads I remembered distantly from driving with Warren Thibault that summer. In no time, I was lost, trailing around some lakeshore. A wind had come up. The headlights stuttered over dark, wet-shingled summer cottages. The road was little more than a deer path, crumbling blacktop slicked with maple and sumac leaves. Eventually, it dead-ended in a gravel pit guarded by shot-up car bodies. I lay my head against the wheel. The rain hit the roof in heavy spatters.

• • •

I'D GOTTEN ALMOST UP INTO NEW HAMPSHIRE— I was another hour finding my way home. I'd forgotten to leave lights on; the house loomed like a wall of black rock. I leaned under the dripping overhang, trying keys. The air had a rank, saturated smell—moss, frost-killed geraniums. Inside the vestibule, I stripped off my soggy shoes and stepped up into the kitchen in my stocking feet. The floor gave off a stony chill. I upended the box of scraps the carpenters had left and started a fire in the kitchen grate, kneeling and blowing on it. The smoke rose, bumped off the old flue and began spilling into the room. I reached up and tried to wiggle the plates open but found them fused. How long had it been since she'd used this? I made a few blind jabs with the hearth tool, and then it gave, raining down leaf stems and soot and flakes of fine rust that spit in the flames. The chimney drew at once. Cold air rushed past my ankles. I sat back on my haunches, wiping my eyes. I couldn't bear to go upstairs. What was I going to do with myself all night? I got up and poured a drink, had a swallow, backed away into the shadows of my mother's new sunroom and collapsed.

It was past midnight, on toward one, when my father wandered into the light. He wore his tan cardigan, a broadcloth shirt, chinos. His hair shone like monofilament line. He stopped by the fire, sniffed, held his palms out, bent and dropped a couple of birch sticks onto the coals and straightened them with his shoe. Satisfied, he tipped his head and glanced out through his bifocals at the lay of my mother's new cupboards, nodding. He gave no sign of having seen me. He pulled open a drawer, shut it, opened it again, admiring the glide of the rollers. He tried another. He reached in and fingered the utensils, as if reacquainting himself with them. Finally, he drew out a small black-handled paring knife, and touched the blade gingerly with his thumb.

Why had he come back? The old stories are always about vengeance, but that felt wrong—vengeance wasn't a hunger I could associate with him in the least. His hunger had always been to do for us.

I watched, not quite in a trance, afraid to stand, as if a current of air might disperse what I saw. He opened the icebox and picked out a bell pepper, hauled down the cutting board and set about dicing it into minute diamonds. His fingers were the whitest things in the kitchen, soft and immaculate. Next he found an onion, cupped it pleasurably, shucked the outer skin with a noisy rip.

The last time I'd seen him up on his feet had been a breezy Saturday with a high, dense sky. He was desperately ill. My mother had done battle with his oncologist, insisting my father be granted a brief furlough home. So they'd wheeled him out and seated him in the car, and we'd driven from under the hospital canopy into the spring sun.

"This charnel house," he said. His voice was a dry rasp, unrecognizable.

"What?" my mother said, hands on the wheel.

He didn't repeat it.

On the road to Pepperell, she suddenly pulled over at a nursery. Rows of wooden flats had been carried out into the air. Leggy tomato plants in peat pots, geraniums, phlox, blowing slightly, giving off waves of color. She coaxed him out of the car, pointed, made cheering talk. He lagged. His cane dragged, spiking into the wet sawdust. His free arm swung like ballast. His eyes scanned from side to side, without hope. For an instant, I believed I saw what he did: everything shriveled, bare stalks under a withering sun.

"Joey," she called.

He seemed not to hear.

"Am I your girl?" she asked. She put her hand on top of his, on top of the cane. "Yes, I am," she said. "Wild horses couldn't change that. Do you understand?"

Watching, I thought of Warren Thibault, of the riddle he'd implanted in me. What was the worst thing I could think of? What was the worst thing my *father* could think of?

Now he held the spatula at his side, calmly chewing his lip. In a moment, he switched off the burner, buttered the toast, laid on the egg, cut it on the diagonal. He reached for one of the good plates, grabbed a fork and deftly rolled it up in a blue paper napkin.

It all seemed plain as day then: He didn't want *anything* of me. Whatever distance he'd traveled, whatever had attracted him to my mother's kitchen, it was his own affair. I was as remote from it as I'd been from his life at work, from his illness and all the rest.

Yet there he was. Humming, buoyant with purpose, coming ahead with no cane, no limp. I smelled the pepper, the sweet margarine. The plate clicked to the tabletop. How could I go through with this, how could I watch him eat his meal?

But he refused to sit. Instead, he looked at me, his head backlit and glowing. "Jay," he said, "come and eat."

THE NEW WORLD

1 November 1940

oward evening, McCutcheon's cleanup man, an old Swede named Tomasson, stood in the lot behind the store, burning trash in a drum. It would be dark in an hour. The fog would roll back over the valley, as it had each night for a week—by sunrise, hoarfrost would coat the windshields fingernail-deep, the power lines would sag in glinting arcs, as if by some fluke you could see the electricity itself. Tomasson fed in the refuse, spent receipt books and shavings and tiny crushed boxes. He watched it burn, watched the flecks of ash rise and disappear against the sky. Now and then he tamped it with the charred end of a pole. Two paperboys scuffed out of the alley, caught sight of the fire, and detoured. They eyed Tomasson, but Tomasson only gnawed at his upper lip and showed no interest in running them off, so they edged in, and then the three stood a few moments, feeling the heat on their faces, Tomasson scarcely larger than a twelve-year-old himself. "Any glass in there?"

one of the boys was thinking of asking, hoping for a minor explosion. But before he managed to say this, Tomasson collapsed. His eyes crimped, his knees buckled, his hands locked onto the pole—it seemed for a second he'd vault with it, miraculously, up and clear of the valley. But his legs gave, and the pole flew to the side, cracking the nearer boy across the knees with such quickness it took him a moment to realize he hadn't been struck on purpose.

• • •

MCCUTCHEON WAS IN HIS OFFICE at the rear of Sperry Hardware. The door was shut and his forehead lay on a stack of shiny-covered catalogs. Earlier, he'd returned from upstairs, where he'd evicted, or tried to, one of two solitary lodgers (the other being Tomasson) in rooms behind the Opera House. Winded, McCutcheon had crouched on the landing and scratched a note against one pant leg and forced it under the door: *Won't carry you one day more. M. McC.* But back downstairs, he felt none of the relief he believed he was entitled to. He sat up, kneading his face. By now the office had grown too dark to be found sitting in. The back window was so matted with alley grit it scarcely let in light—all he saw, dull as November sun, was a glow where the trash fire burned.

McCutcheon's father (known as Old Malcolm) had come up the lake to Sperry by steamboat in the year 1900, bearing the proceeds of monies invested down in Silver Bow County. Within days he'd dreamed up the notion of a hall to preside over. He secured land at the corner of First and Montana Streets and put up a two-story brick structure: commercial space at street level, Opera House upstairs. Not grand, but a fixture from the first. The high school rented it for theatricals and winter proms and graduations. McCutcheon, sweating in a wool suit, had been handed his own diploma up on the Opera House stage—so, another June, had Lila Dare Mc-Cutcheon, his only child, class of '29.

Old Malcolm had presided with abandon. He offered roller skating (and sold skates by the bushel basket, the new kind with ball bearings). There were band concerts, wrestling matches, union dances, military dress balls. He brought in road companies from New York and Chicago, presented speakers. And there was the time, long ago, he procured them an elephant. A gray Saturday, spitting snow. The animal was led down the ramp of a freight wagon and up the front stair-case of the Opera House, then hidden backstage, where it waited, rocking foot to foot, its trunk letting out a riffled sighing. It was a dwarf elephant, or not full-grown—though its eyes looked ancient, lost in crosshatched smudges. It stood no higher than Old Malcolm's derby, harnessed with red silk, its tail done up in red silk bows. Old Malcolm was delighted. He loitered backstage, running a hand over the dusty, sour-smelling hide, chatting up the animal's train-weary keepers, and finally demanding that his son be allowed to sit atop it. Though shortly to balloon into a man of Old Malcolm's heft, McCutcheon was undersized as yet, moon-faced, with a fis-suring voice. There was no escape; he allowed himself to be hoisted up and led in a tiny circle behind the swaying curtain, mortified.

Old Malcolm was a glad-hander, a booming public man, an optimist. McCutcheon's own view was a man could afford to be cheerful when his life's labors had been rewarded. Even Old Malcolm's death was transfigured into minor legend: by heart attack, while in the bathtub, scrubbing for an evening with a twenty-four-year-old beauty named Cora Baskins.

Neat getaway, people said.

McCutcheon's one dream, when he was young, was to be as

well regarded as Old Malcolm, but his own time, the years since Old Malcolm's coronary, was no time for dreams, unless it was the one *everyone* had, of shucking weight, of finding a place where people weren't so strapped and stooped over. But he didn't think of this often, or with any sense he might actually do it. It was enough keeping the hardware company open, the rest of the block rented. A Hupmobile dealership had gone in and out, ditto a confectionery, a run of other marginal enterprises. Meantime, McCutcheon had lost his wife to Bright's disease, and Lila had careened into a witless marriage. The high school had added an auditorium with sloped floor, deep proscenium stage, and seven hundred velvet-backed seats. Throw in three movie houses and the new Elks, where people went to dance.

Then, three Februaries ago, a short had burned out his stage. McCutcheon was heading home from a card game when the alarm sounded. He ran back, slung on a canister, and went after the flames himself. The next day he shut down for repairs. Winter dragged on. One of Old Malcolm's compatriots poked his face into McCutcheon's office and said, "If I was you, I'd get up a Friends of the Opera House." McCutcheon felt a gust of fatigue at the thought, and somehow knew, before spring ever blew into the valley, that he wouldn't open again, not anytime soon.

When this mood had visited him before, when he felt as though the next thing would land on his chest and suck the breath from his lungs, he'd haul the boat trailer down to Graves Landing and fish a willow-shaded stretch of river. He'd stay until the light was gone, then drive home and fall quickly to sleep and not wake. Other times he might disappear to the old Gladstone Hotel in Missoula and be someone else for three or four days. A little poker, a little companionship, no questions asked.

But even diversion felt like work now, felt willed and tainted. The mood wouldn't go. At forty-eight, he found himself still ruminating on Old Malcolm's life, picking at it for instruction, but the genial, ruddy-faced Old Malcolm grew harder to call to mind. What came instead was the picture of McCutcheon himself jimmying the bathroom door and finding him, the lather dried on his chest hairs. Each time in this reverie McCutcheon bent and unstopped the tepid water; each time his father's huge torso slumped as the water coursed out through the pipes.

Get the hell up, McCutcheon told himself, but before he could take a breath and slick his hair back and go forth between the aisles of useful goods, he heard a pair of boys shouting in the alley, their hands slapping furiously on the steel door.

• • •

"You've gone mean and stingy," Lila told him.

Her drinking voice, McCutcheon thought. "Spare us how I am," he said. "Get the radio, will you?"

Lila sprawled in the captain's chair by the fire, arms tossed back over her head, looking so much like his wife it pained him. Rangy as a cat through the midsection, the same sleek nose and squared-off chin, the black half-moon eyes that watched him not straight on but ten degrees sidelong. What made it worse, Lila couldn't have been more *unlike* his wife if she worked at it, which was possible. Where Hazel Dare had been a serene girl, growing into a steady, unflappable woman (McCutcheon's one joy, his ballast), Lila grew up near-beautiful, short-tempered, contrary. On her, the off-center stare meant a sizing up, a clenching before she started railing at him, for sins he barely comprehended—the sin of heading the Downtown Boosters Club one year, the sin of giving her hours, of having no imagination. *I should be so lucky*, Mc-Cutcheon thought.

"What in God's name does she want of me?" McCutcheon had asked his wife. "Patience, Mal," Hazel told him, as if in due time all would be revealed and put right. But then Hazel was dead. And Lila, whom he'd sent to Missoula to start music school, was without warning married to a clarinet player in a jazz combo, a man in his *forties*. At first Mc-Cutcheon knew only that she was AWOL from the dormitory. It was weeks before he heard from Lila herself, charges reversed from Vancouver, and by then McCutcheon had convinced himself she'd contrived the whole business to get back at him, for a lifetime of seeing to her needs.

"Don't you think about showing up here," he shouted (freezing, only pajama bottoms on), knowing, even so, he'd receive her without complaint, should it come to that, which of course it did, months later, 1932, October. No call first, she walked home from the Intermountain depot lugging one pasteboard bag, headed to the kitchen and fixed supper, eggs and rounds of Canadian bacon, not a word about the clarinet player.

McCutcheon ate, thinking, *What has to come out, will*, the approach he imagined Hazel would've taken.

Finally he cleared his throat and said, "I'm glad to know where in hell you are."

Lila nodded, carried off the plates, and their truce was begun.

But that wasn't quite right, either. Maybe she was holding her tongue, or maybe she'd just lost the need to go after him. He offered to make work for her at the store, but she instead finagled a job at the high school. "Unbelievable," Mc-Cutcheon said, hearing this news. "You couldn't wait to clear out of there." Mornings she strode off as she had, but minus

the green bookbag bouncing at her shoulder, minus the clus-
ter of girlfriends. Tuesdays and Thursdays she took in piano
pupils, never many. Otherwise she read novels and made spo-
radic stabs at keeping the house up. McCutcheon believed
this would be short-lived, recuperative in a way he didn't
wish to explore. But couldn't she start over at the university
after that, couldn't she marry again, decently? As for that,
Lila didn't go out much—and the men she did date all had
something wrong with them. One was recovering from tu-
berculosis. Another was nineteen.

Somehow, eight years slipped by.

Too, there was her drinking, which waxed and waned in ac-
cordance to a cycle McCutcheon never deciphered, something else to either take in stride, or not. Late one night,
McCutcheon had been wakened by Neils Jessup, a farmer in
the south valley: Lila's Buick had kept on straight where the
foothills road made a sharp right at the section line. Heart
racing, McCutcheon grabbed a jacket, hiked through a misting rain to the store and got the flatbed, and when he arrived
at Jessup's saw the tire tracks slashed into the wet lawn and
the Buick inert against a wooden flagpole, the top of which
had splintered off and struck an upstairs window. Lila was in
the kitchen, a towel at her head.

"You all right, honey?" McCutcheon said, trying to pull
her hand so he could see, but she shook him off. The man was
Tomasson's age. Once Lila had been taken to the seat of the
truck, Jessup followed McCutcheon around to the driver's
side and told him, "If it was my daughter, I'd be shamed to
death." He walked to his porch and extinguished the light.
McCutcheon drove them back, livid—at Jessup. He allowed
himself the pleasure of picturing the flagpole's finial busting
in and scattering the man's miserly dreams. He made a pact
with himself not to give Lila a bad time over this incident,

and felt a startling surge of well-being overtake him as, nearly home, Lila finally slept against his shoulder.

But he *did* feel ashamed. He couldn't keep himself from cornering her a few days later, asking, too loud, "What were you doing out on the goddamn foothills road? I mean it, Lila—all boozed up?" The bandage was off, the stitches out, a gap left in her brow where the hair wouldn't grow again. She blew smoke and gave McCutcheon that breathy, self-mocking laugh she'd acquired.

McCutcheon persisted.

Lila glared at him suddenly. "You don't have a clue about me," she said.

McCutcheon wished to say, "Well, that's not entirely true, but why don't you just tell me . . ." Instead he found himself rigid, humiliated. He tore into a speech about how he expected her to pay the damages, and how goddamn fortunate she was Jessup had called *him* and not the sheriff, and was about to say more, all of it best left unsaid, when she rose and trailed from the kitchen. But she did pay, to the penny, and thereafter demanded to pay McCutcheon twenty dollars a month room rent. McCutcheon threw up his hands at this, took the money rather than argue, and tucked it in an envelope inside a book of his wife's still wedged into the headboard of their bed, meaning to give it all back to Lila on some appropriate occasion, though a couple of times he had borrowed against it, most recently to have the roof reshaked.

Mean and stingy.

He stood, heavily, got the radio himself, and was greeted with the dolorous voice of one of the candidates for district judge.

Tonight's little flare-up with Lila had to do with McCutcheon's saying no, he hadn't planned on driving over to the hospital and looking in on Tomasson.

"I'm not going near that joint," he said again. "It pains you so awfully much, you go."

Lila didn't move for a while, then stood, slinging the ice cubes from her glass into the fire, where they hissed.

Now Christ, McCutcheon thought. *Why the fascination with Tomasson?*

As for himself, McCutcheon had phoned for the ambulance, then he and Dewey Fritz from the store had waited out back until the old man was lifted to a stretcher and driven off. Fritz had wadded a jacket under Tomasson's head, squatted by him saying, "You just lie still there, Oscar." McCutcheon stood back. The wind had shifted, blowing a downdraft of putrid smoke into their eyes—finally McCutcheon had to tip the can over and roll it, dribbling ash, out of range. And there, still staring from the corner of the building, was one of those two paperboys. McCutcheon began to shoo him off, but then thought, *Goddamn it, no, have yourself a good long look.*

Monday he took a call from Hy Glendinning, long ago Hazel's doctor, and heard the prognosis on Tomasson: bleak, no real chance he'd get back what he'd lost, other strokes sure to follow.

What McCutcheon knew about Tomasson amounted to this: He'd shown up one fall day years ago, asking about a room. McCutcheon had been hoping for a younger man, one with a regular paycheck, but let Tomasson the room anyway, and that winter hired him to do light cleanup for a knockoff on the rent. Mornings after some function upstairs Tomasson could be seen sweeping among the chairs, herky-jerk, cap wedged down over his eyes. The next spring he came to McCutcheon and asked if he might be permitted to sharpen knives and saws. McCutcheon set him up in the cellar.

From his office McCutcheon would catch sight of Tomasson's narrow overalled back disappearing down the shaft of stairs, and find himself wincing at the thought of him down in that rathole, running his files over the sawteeth. In all the time since, McCutcheon managed to learn exactly three items of fact about the man: that he'd migrated here from Mountrail County, North Dakota; that he wouldn't take a drink if you held a gun to his temple; and that the finger gone from the left hand had been snagged in a gear sprocket when he was a boy in Sweden. This last, McCutcheon wouldn't have learned at all if he hadn't just asked one morning. The point was, never did he acquire the least fondness for Tomasson, never could he see past his revulsion for the sort of man Tomasson was.

McCutcheon listened to the blather issuing from the Zenith and stood glaring at the threads in the carpet. An instant later he heard the Buick's door, then the engine firing under his daughter's foot.

• • •

SMALL TO START WITH, Tomasson had turned into a wizened child, frozen down the right side. McCutcheon had never seen him capless, was startled at the hummock of bald scalp peppered with liver spots.

Lila had shoved a chair beside the bed. She stopped talking, smiled, mock-cheerful. "Look who's come," she said. "Wonder of wonders."

McCutcheon frowned and edged to the foot of the bed, holding his hat. He was flushed from walking, already far too hot.

Tomasson's eyes looked out, rheumy, one blinking like a rooster's eye, the other tearing over and wetting his cheek. Lila dabbed at it with the corner of the sheet.

McCutcheon undid his collar and inventoried the room. A huge weight of a patient lay mounded up in the far bed—

asleep, nobody he recognized. The other bed, flanking the window, had been stripped to bare ticking.

Lila went back to asking Tomasson things, leaving spaces for him to answer. McCutcheon assumed he could no more do this than backspring down the hall, but suddenly words came—pushed out one at a time, like bits of broken teeth.

"He's worried about his money," Lila said.

McCutcheon palmed the sweat off his temples, and thought, *What money's that?* Tomasson would be the kind who'd trust his backup to a Bugler tin, jammed into loosened chimney bricks, down where he sharpened saws.

But what Tomasson was laboring to say had to do with a bank account. Not in Sperry, it turned out, but back in North Dakota. Thirty-three hundred and some dollars.

"Shh, now," Lila said, touching a finger to his lips.

McCutcheon fled to the hall and slipped into the sunroom for a smoke. He stood with his face aimed at the blackened panes, and thought, *Jesus, don't let me ever get like that,* but choked this sentiment off before it could fester, broke away to the stairwell and down to the car. The fog was back, deep as wool. He shut his eyes. Then Lila was glaring at him through the window, rapping on the glass with her ring.

"I'm walking," she said.

"Get in," he said. "Come on now, Lila," but she was off, striding into the fog.

McCutcheon started after her, but balked. He drove instead to the hotel, where he took a whiskey, then a second, tossed off before anyone could buttonhole him about the state of the world, or (more likely) the state of Sperry's woeful football team. He crossed to the store, rooted in his desk for the master key, climbed the front staircase, and made his way back across the expanse of Opera House. It was cold as sin up there. His breath puffed against the tall, street-lit windows.

238 🌲 David Long

The burnt flooring had long since been pry-barred up and
flung down to a truck, along with the remains of Old Malcolm's maroon velvet curtain, and every window propped
open to the winter air for days, but still it stank of smoke.
Why in hell did he put himself through this?

He swung open Tomasson's door and snapped on the overhead light, expecting . . . he didn't know what. An old man's
room, a raft of pathetic debris he and Lila would have to box
up and then fight over what to do with. He couldn't have
been more wrong. It was sparse as a monk's. Bed made, spare
blanket folded at the foot. Razor, hairbrush, styptic pencil laid
out by the sink. Good pants hung by the cuffs from the top
dresser drawer.

Staring, McCutcheon shivered down the length of him,
and didn't venture to touch a thing.

$$\bullet \quad \bullet \quad \bullet$$

HE CAME DOWN NEXT MORNING to an empty kitchen.
There was coffee on the rear burner, a trace of Noxzema in
the air, but Lila was already gone. Five past seven. *What now,*
he thought, but he guessed he knew well enough, and was
not at all surprised, a little past noon, when she appeared in
his office and slapped down a brown-covered statement book
retrieved from Tomasson's sock and long-john drawer.

Plains Guaranty Trust, Stanley, No. Dakota. The last balance dated March 1930, in the amount of $3,306.03.

"Ye of little faith," Lila said.

McCutcheon let the book fall, laid a hand on his daughter's
shoulder. "What's a man with money doing sweeping floors?
An old guy, ask yourself."

Lila scanned the clutter for a place to sit, made a face, then
shrugged out from under McCutcheon's arm. "I can see
about it myself," she said.

"You know what you're going to find out?" McCutcheon said. "There's not a chance on God's earth that book's any good. It's just something he held onto, you understand?"

Lila looked at him as if he'd invented all this.

"Lila, his mind's not right . . . you can't pay attention to what he says," McCutcheon said. But he wasn't up to debating her. "Look, go back to work," he said. "I'll take care of it, I'll get the story, okay?"

It took even less time than he imagined, one call to his snotty brother-in-law at the Cripps Bank. Tomasson's bank had bellied up, like so many. "You know when?" McCutcheon said to Lila that night. "The Monday after his last deposit. Can we drop it now?"

Lila ignored that, said, "I'll tell you what else I found. He owned a bunch of land over in North Dakota." She fanned out a handful of papers for him. "Old tax stuff."

"I wish you'd put that away now," McCutcheon said.

"And look here." She thrust out a letter in front of him. The stamp was watery blue, old King Gustav, the handwriting inside minute, spiderish.

Neither understood a word of it. "Except, look," Lila said. "'Broder Oscar . . .'"

"Well, okay," McCutcheon said. "There's a sister." He squinted at the postmark. "This is way old," he said.

"I asked Mrs. Haugen over," Lila said.

Before McCutcheon could say once more, with greater gusto, how it was none of their affair, the chimes rang.

McCutcheon recalled Mrs. Haugen as the fussily braided woman who held forth at music recitals, cantilevered over the lip of the stage, a voice densely Scandinavian. Remembering that, he remembered a Sunday afternoon when Lila (thirteen, fourteen?) had stopped dead a page into her piece. All you heard were folding chairs, pigeons cooing and scratching in the roof gutters. Lila swiveled on the bench and announced, "I've had a change of heart." She'd play Chopin instead. McCutcheon felt his wife's hand on his knee, heard her whisper, "That's not ready yet." True enough, but Lila stormed through it. McCutcheon sat grimacing, feeling a grudging admiration (maybe she'd grow up with enough of Old Malcolm's effrontery to get by), and also, of course, a wild embarrassment. And he remembered how this Mrs. Haugen had come to the house after Hazel's death, how she'd wept and coughed to the point where McCutcheon had been obliged to wrap an arm around her shoulder. Mourning had been an utter bafflement. The one time he wanted not to see *anyone*, the house was crawling with sympathizers.

McCutcheon straightened and managed a greeting.

Lila hurried her to the table and cleared a place under the light. Mrs. Haugen pulled up a pair of half-lenses and glanced at the envelope. "Oh, Söderhamn," she said. "My brother knew a girl from there." She offered a momentary, close-mouthed smile, cracked back the folds of the letter, and started to read.

"She's telling the kind of summer they were having . . . quite a long part about an anniversary party. *'Etthundra gäster,'* a hundred guests. She wishes he had come."

Mrs. Haugen looked up to check what special meaning this had for her hosts, and asked, "Do you want to hear it all?"

McCutcheon opened his mouth to say, "God, no," but Lila said, "My father was hoping you could take down a letter to her."

Thus, moments later, McCutcheon found himself standing, hands on the chair back, dictating, while Lila rattled out cups and saucers and a plate of Fig Newtons.

"I'm sorry to be the one to give this unhappy news," McCutcheon started in, faltered, then pushed ahead, detailing

Tomasson's hopelessness. Mrs. Haugen dug into the paper with a wild, looping script.

"There's also," McCutcheon said, "the business of Mr. Tomasson's doctor bills. I'm afraid he's not in any position to take care of them."

McCutcheon avoided his daughter's eyes. He waited for the writing to stop, added, "As well as other matters you should advise us on."

"Sign it yourself," Lila said.

McCutcheon bent to the table and scratched his name.

"Pieter met this girl on the train coming from the capital," Mrs. Haugen said in that unmoored voice he recollected.

"Your brother," Lila said.

Let's not encourage her, thought McCutcheon.

"She was in a choir," Mrs. Haugen said. "That's all I remember—she'd sung in the capital and was going home. He was in love with her from the first time he saw her. He came into my room, 'Tell me what I should write her . . .' He was so shy, I had never seen him like this. He was asked to her family's house once, it was on the water, a great stone house, so old."

She sought out McCutcheon's eyes, which had been wandering. "Who can say what it's like now?" she said. "Who knows if people even get their letters?"

"They're neutral over there, aren't they?" McCutcheon said. "There's no fighting."

Mrs. Haugen lowered her glasses, folded them into her hand. "I should go," she said.

"Your brother and this girl—?" Lila asked.

Mrs. Haugen rose and accepted her coat from McCutcheon. "It came to nothing," she said. "It was just when we were coming to this country."

Once he'd shut the door on Mrs. Haugen, McCutcheon

stepped around to the kitchen, poured milk in his cup, and dosed it with Seagram's. Lila would be on him now, about the money. He drank, bracing himself. But when he glanced back through the arch he saw her stranded in the foyer, one hand buried in her hair.

"What?" McCutcheon said. "What is it?"

"I don't think I can take another winter in this valley," Lila said.

"Oh, it's that song, is it?" McCutcheon said.

"Go, then," he was used to saying, believing she wouldn't no matter what he told her. But he didn't know anymore—she and the car could just turn up missing some morning.

"Sit down, Lila," he said. "I'll play you some cribbage."

"Maybe I'll go and see some people," Lila said.

"Who?"

"Oh, nobody."

"Why don't you not," McCutcheon said.

Lila shrugged him a smile and didn't go for her coat, but drifted about downstairs and, shortly later, up the front staircase.

Finally McCutcheon killed the lights and hauled himself up to his own room. Hours later, he woke twisted in his clothes, aware of having dreamed. He'd been in an airplane—hard-rushing wind, sunlight pounding off snowfields. He loosened his shirt and listened to the house: nothing but air purring from the register. He scuffed out into the hall, passed Lila's door without slowing, without letting his hand swing it open so he could see in to the curved walnut of her sleigh bed and the tossed, vacant covers. But he stalled on the landing, found himself staring out the octagon of leaded glass his wife had so loved, down through the birch limbs to the driveway and the drier, blacker rectangle of pavement where the Buick wasn't. His neighbors' houses crouched under their dark trees, porch lights off. A car inched through the fog, headlamps weak as punks—McCutcheon felt his heart rise, but the car continued past.

That wasn't dreaming, he realized.

Old Malcolm had known a man named Turley with a three-seater Swallow, and one July day they'd rendezvoused up the West Fork road at Cole's Meadow, where bootleggers were said to land by night. Goggled, paired-up behind Turley, they bumped along the strip of beaten-down field grass, lifted up, and banked into the mountain thermals. Old Malcolm with Hazel. McCutcheon's sister, Eve, with her husband, Connie Cripps. Lila with McCutcheon. A deep blue sky, *empty as a baby's heart*, Old Malcolm announced. A day with nothing wrong in it, is what McCutcheon remembered. Here was Hazel clearing the hair from her face, her free hand slipping into Old Malcolm's as she climbed from the Swallow, smiling and breathing hard, her eyes finding his, then Lila's. And later the hampers of food, Old Malcolm astride his camp stool pestering Turley for flying lessons, and Lila, uncontentious for once, trailing off with her aunt to pick early huckleberries in a Maxwell House can. Such a brilliant, mortal day, McCutcheon thought.

Downstairs, he tore off a chunk of ham in the icebox, told himself to skip the drink, but didn't. It was going on two. He sat and shuffled up the old papers of Tomasson's and tried stuffing them back in the packet they'd come from. Title and tax statements, old receipts, letters in exhausted carbon. Worthless as the bank book, McCutcheon imagined, as futile a pile of papers as you could find. But then he was looking anyway. Four hundred twenty acres, Tomasson had owned, half a section, plus another hundred. Wheat and barley and hay, a steam thresher . . . McCutcheon stared, stupefied. What was more: The taxes had been kept up all the time

Tomasson had been gone from it, all that time he'd lodged behind the Opera House.

Up until a year ago, McCutcheon saw. There was a first notice of delinquency, then a second, and another bunch of envelopes Tomasson hadn't bothered to open.

•   •   •

LILA WENT FIRST, whistling, wearing a slippery rayon number. Blue as a bluebird, as wrong for the hospital as you could imagine.

Tomasson's room was like a Turkish bath.

The big man was gone. Tomasson had inherited the window, but there was nothing to see. Sweating steam on one side of the glass; on the other, night and acres of fog.

"We've written to your sister," Lila said. She loomed over Tomasson, her legs squeezed against the bed linen.

Nothing from Tomasson.

"Juditta? Your sister?"

McCutcheon looked at them, back and forth, his only child and this ruin of a man who was nothing to him. He knew suddenly what foolishness that letter had been. He broke in, "Your sister's passed away, hasn't she?"

Lila gunned him that wild, off-kilter look; it didn't matter, he was right about this. She tugged at her shoulder pad, stepped back, putting a little gap between herself and the bed.

McCutcheon thought, *Isn't life a swell piece of business?*

"When'd you come to this country?" Lila asked Tomasson. "I want to picture it. You were how old?"

"Look now, he's not going to get into a big conversation with you," McCutcheon said. "Don't you see how he is?"

"I'll tell you what I think," Lila said. "I think it took some courage to come over here." Her voice had risen, it would now be carrying out into the hall. McCutcheon's head had begun to pound in the heat.

"Mr. Tomasson," she was saying, "some people, I'll tell you, they never do anything like that. Not a thing."

"Lila, come on," McCutcheon said. "You're going to get one of the sisters in here."

"No, I mean, *goddamn it*. Picture you start with nothing—"

"*Enough*," McCutcheon said.

Lila let up for a second, glanced at McCutcheon, then Tomasson. Then said, "He's going to take care of all your bills."

"No, now Oscar," McCutcheon said, "I don't know where she got an idea like that."

Lila turned on him. "You're going to," she shouted. "You're fixing it, you're fixing everything."

And then McCutcheon's hand was in the air, fingers balled.

Flushed, chin jutting, she didn't make the first move to cover up, only gulped in a breath, and watched.

But before McCutcheon could learn what his hand would do, there came an upheaval in Tomasson's bed, an eruption of covers, a white stick of arm raking across the nightstand. Water plumed in the air, then slapped down across the front of Lila's dress; the pitcher crashed broadside against the radiator and blew into thick curls of glass that fell spinning to the linoleum.

•　　•　　•

LILA FLUNG HER COAT ONTO THE CAR SEAT and got in beside McCutcheon. He turned the key and grabbed for the starter button but let his hands fall.

"I'll tell you another thing," he said. "It takes some goddamn courage to stay where you are, too. It takes a goddamn hunk of it."

Lila looked out the window, not letting herself touch the wet place on her front.

"You listen, Lila, we're not all of us Old Malcolm. Some of us—"

"Some of us are stuck tight," Lila said. "Tight as corks."

"That's not what I meant," McCutcheon said. But what did he mean? He couldn't bring himself to dig it out. He drove home, creeping, hardly able to see. Over the rise on Third, down crunching into their alley, fingers clamped on the wheel.

"Honey—" he started, but Lila jerked the handle and slid out, the rayon sighing across the upholstery.

McCutcheon didn't budge. Soon the lights came on in Lila's dormer. He broke his eyes away, crammed his fists under his armpits and thought, *You goddamn fraud. What courage does it take a rock to stay where you drop it?*

Unbidden as ever, the stations of Old Malcolm's migration sprang to his mind: Marquette to Denver to Leadville to Butte, and finally, an August evening in 1900, to the raucous steamboat landing at the head of the big lake—now just rows of stranded pilings. He'd stepped off and stood beside his trunk and seen the twilight ravishing the mountains to the east, the bottomland running north past the townsite, flat, dusted with haze, and told himself, *Here*, dead certain—this being the heart of all the retellings, all the bluster: his certainty and the bounty that had come of it. Then, dear God, McCutcheon thought, there was Tomasson. How could you not think of him, too? Tempted farther and deeper into this new world, already not new anymore, until he had nothing, and what was the point of all this feverish setting out?

Or, for that matter, of McCutcheon's own *not?*

A nauseating embarrassment flashed through him. How could a man live so long—almost into his *fifties*—and know so little of greater consequence than who owed him for sixty days, and who for ninety, and who'd owe him into the grave? McCutcheon sat frozen, running his hand on Lila's jacket, on the cold fur of its trim. He shot his eyes back up to Lila's window and thought, *Swear to God, I wish it was your mother up there instead of you.*

•   •   •

THE SIXTH OF MARCH, 1941: A windy day, almost warm, smelling of saturated earth. Dewey Fritz was there, jowly in his loose-hanging suit; next to him was Lila, then Mrs. Haugen, and finally a big-bottomed waitress from Currier's Café. One short psalm, *The afflicted shall eat and be satisfied*... a half-minute of silence for prayer or what-have-you. McCutcheon watched a convocation of gulls light on the sodden grass, flashing like whitecaps among the grave markers. He'd been back to the old man's room after all, by himself, had sat there other nights, reading from the paper or talking as the spirit moved. There were more strokes; it was hard to know if Tomasson was there at all. McCutcheon lingered in the heat and stillness of the hospital room, watching, as if Tomasson might suddenly arise from this oblivion and regard him with a howling intelligence.

The Monday following the service, McCutcheon slipped over to the First Northern Bank and pocketed the last of Old Malcolm's bequest, long buried where it could achieve some anonymity, specifically not under his brother-in-law's nose. He walked three blocks south and paid $988 cash for a DeSoto coupé, placed the hardware store in the temporary custody of Dewey Fritz, settled Tomasson's accounts, returned home and composed a one-page note to Lila, mainly instructions, signed it *M. McC.*, struck that out and wrote *Your father*, climbed into the new car, took Idaho west past the sawmill where it became Highway 2, and kept going, spending the first night in Sandpoint, the next in Walla Walla, then on to Portland, and south on Highway 1, aimed for California.

Except for scale, it was like when he'd fled to the Gladstone in Missoula—or so he told himself, driving. The car was a dream. Rocket-shaped, the color of kidskin, not a whimper of a body squeak. He cranked down the windows, freed his waist button and drove with a straight back, fingers drumming, delighted by the bright strip of beach below the highway, the sight of breakers furling and throwing spray. The radio poured out a flotilla of swing-band tunes. Late morning, shy of the California line less than an hour, he heard the King Sisters come on. *Huuun-gry for your kisses, honey,* Louise King sang. *Huuun-gry for your touch . . .* The harmony behind her was silvery, sharp as engraving. McCutcheon found himself trembling, struck with a violent, unaccountable longing.

He crossed into the city limits of Brookings, Oregon, pulled up and killed the engine. His heart was banging high in his chest. Across the way stood a diner, the Grand Union Luncheonette, chrome and red tin. McCutcheon thought, well, he was just hungry—that was all. Afterward, stuffed with the dollar-and-a-quarter, all-you-can-eat sea bass special, Platte County pie following, he stepped into the air and ruled out pushing on, drove instead to a bluff overlooking the water, crawled into the backseat and fell asleep, both doors open to the wind.

He took his supper at the same place, the Grand Union, and whereas at home he'd no more cozy up to strangers than vote for a Democrat, here he found himself trading conversation with people at the next table, a woman roughly his own vintage (her name was Silvie Markle), and her son John, roughly Lila's.

McCutcheon said he'd noticed them here at lunchtime.

Silvie Markle laughed. They'd eaten every meal there for a week. "Kitchen's all torn to pieces," she said. "Utter chaos."

She had a wide, olivy face fringed with pewter bangs, silver-rimmed glasses that rode down her nose. He thought, *What the hell is it about her?* and realized, besides the friendliness, it was that she didn't remind him of a soul. The son added a nod, mouth full of French bread. He'd toweled his face clean, but the tops of his ears were still furred with plaster dust.

McCutcheon offered a few words about himself, mainly true. He watched the woman drink her coffee, and after she and her son had left, he found himself staring at the tracing of lipstick on her cup.

Next morning, after idling over his sweet roll in the hotel's airy, near-deserted breakfast room, McCutcheon forced himself to rise and get on with the day, a Friday, bright. He toted his bag to the DeSoto, eyed the street for a filling station, saw a Flying A down two blocks, and thought, *Fine, gas up there.* The trunk slammed with a rich, secure thump. But an instant later he abandoned the car, and took off on foot, back into the grid of neighborhoods.

He was struck by how far along spring was. Tulips were up, the grass shone with shoots of deep color—where Sperry's yards were lifeless yet, mushed-down, lumps of pitted ice under the drip lines of the shrubs. It took him the better part of an hour to locate the Markles', one of two white-painted relics alone at the end of their street, smothered in lilacs and ivy.

He maneuvered over a berm of torn-out lath on the walkway, and stuck his head in the kitchen door. John Markle was peering into a hole in the counter.

One evening, much later, McCutcheon told Lila: *That was the second time I saw John. . . . He'd just cut the hole for the sink—it was way off. I said, "Too narrow you can fix," and he laughed at himself as if a man's own mistakes were something to marvel at. I suppose I liked him right then. Silvie came out through this drop cloth they'd tacked up to keep the dust confined—they didn't either of them act the least bit surprised I'd turned up at the house. Silvie made some coffee on a hot plate. Funny what you remember.*

The same family had built both houses, McCutcheon learned that morning. He trailed after Silvie, getting his feet wet, listening, looking back and forth between the green-shingled roofs.

"Quite the family," Silvie said. "Sent someone to the legislature, the whole bit. People named Gilmartin."

"What happened?"

Silvie threw a hand up. "Oh, what happens to people? One thing and another. They petered out."

"Don't they now," McCutcheon said.

"So anyway, John heard these places were going for taxes, and I thought, *Lord hates a coward . . .*"

"You took *both* of them?" McCutcheon asked.

Silvie shaded her eyes, laughing up at him. "What an idiot, huh?"

· · ·

IF ANYONE, IN HIS OLD LIFE, had asked McCutcheon, point-blank, what he had against Tomasson, he would've brushed the question off as nonsense and intrusion. "Jesus," he might've said, "I can't be picking up everybody's tab," as if that was all it was, money. He would not have touched on how Tomasson stirred up a host of the rankest feelings in him, or what this disgust (or fear or whatever it was) had to do with his winding up in that freezing Buick, loathing the touch of his daughter's coat, loathing so much as the thought of her gliding around her bedroom peeling off that blue dress . . .

Until one evening, his first June in Oregon: He and Silvie were at work on the porch of McCutcheon's newly acquired place (later to be guest house), McCutcheon installing fresh screening, Silvie in dungarees, down on the floor prying up rotten jute with a putty knife. Matter-of-fact, her back crossed by bars of shadow, Silvie was telling McCutcheon about her sister's troubles, and happened to say: "You just get to where you can't love anything where you are anymore. You get a crimp."

McCutcheon laid down his tack hammer as if it were made of glass, amazed at how correct this sounded, even more amazed that a run of words could ring in his ears like the blow from a cold chisel.

You get mean and stingy, he thought. The funny thing was, he didn't feel at all that way now.

The barn swallows had come out. Along the edge of the property, the blue spruces were flattening into silhouettes. He watched Silvie's elbow flying to the side, bare and tanned, heard a satisfying rip as the old floor covering tore loose. He felt he knew what would happen next. He'd climb down and touch the shoulder of her workshirt. She'd sit back on her heels, she'd nudge her glasses up and look at him, her lips apart in curiosity, then he'd make his first stab at kissing her, and it would come off with a little grace, or else not, but it gave him an unholy thrill to think of it, even for a second.

"What're you laughing about?" Silvie said.

"Nothing," McCutcheon said. "Can't a man laugh?"

"No, now *what*?"

"Nothing, nothing." He could hardly contain himself.

What if the King Sisters had been crooning "Red Sails in the Sunset" and not a song that left him desperately hungry?

What if the Markles had dressed up and gone instead to the Brookings Club, or suppose McCutcheon had downed his supper as usual, without a word, face bent to newsprint?

What if Tomasson had fallen straightaway dead?

Imponderables, Old Malcolm would say, which only meant he refused to think of them. But what amazed McCutcheon was his own amazement. That the man he'd become, so late in the game, could wonder at things, his mind bright, not swamped and close.

What if Lila (her heart every bit as crimped as his) had read that gingerly letter he'd banged out on Silvie's machine, and fired back, *Thanks for leaving me all this mess. Listen, Dewey's running the store straight into the ground. . . . We had a big wind last night, that split limb on the Norway maple came down on the Woodcocks' bay window. . . . What kind of stunt are you pulling down there??*

Instead of the reply that had come, a sheet of Hazel's old cockleshell letter paper: *How would you feel about my coming down there for a few weeks. . . . What do you think about August?*

And his own, *Yes, come.*

It occurred to McCutcheon one day—after the war, the house finally reclaimed from vine and damp rot and vacancy—that he'd grown to be a man older than Old Malcolm. And he realized that the rancor had gone, leached away in the time he'd been with Silvie. It was even possible to daydream about Hazel, to remember her as a young mother, and no longer mire himself in such memories as reaching into their closet and slipping a dress off a hanger—the navy organdy with the white silk flowers—to fold into a bag and give the undertaker.

A good joke on McCutcheon: Brookings turned out to be a town famous for fog. It rolled off the water prodigiously, dingy as five A.M. He could smell it before he'd opened his eyes, could hear the muffling of boat horns and the shrieks of gulls. A walk from the car to the house was enough to glaze the glasses he was now required to wear. He'd stand at the kitchen door, drying them on a shirttail. *"Look* at this!" he'd tell Silvie. "I'm moving to the desert."

"Oh, no, you're not," Silvie would tell him.

Because there were days like this one, too—breezy, the air scoured and warming. McCutcheon stepped outside, circumnavigated the house, checking the plum trees, the perennial beds. All was quiet. His boarders were off on their morning rounds. John Markle was framing houses up the coast road, Lila was downtown in the station wagon buying groceries. Silvie had come out onto the porch to dry her hair in the sun.

McCutcheon wandered over, hands in his pockets. "You know what I was remembering?" he said.

"The time I seduced you at the luncheonette."

McCutcheon smiled, touched her shoulder. "I was thinking about the Opera House," he said. "I was remembering how Old Malcolm would ribbon us off a string of seats. Right in front, naturally. He'd have us wait in the anteroom so we'd have to parade down the aisle—as if the show couldn't possibly start until everyone got themselves a good look at all of *us*. Hazel and Lila and me, my sister and her girls."

McCutcheon unbuttoned his cardigan and tossed it over the railing.

"It was exactly how he acted if he'd dragged me off to some big gathering with him. He kept booming out, *You know m'boy here? Maal-com?* I was thinking how much I used to hate it . . . I used to wish I'd never hear it again as long as I lived."

He sat on the step beside her. "What a numbskull," he said.

"You're forgiven," Silvie said. "Here." She slapped the comb into his hand and turned her back to him.

And what if he'd never figured out that simplest injunction. *Enjoy your life, take a little goddamn pride* . . . He worked the comb through the silvery hair, shook the water off, started again at the crown of her head, teasing out the snarls. He could do it all morning. He looked up, past their yard, past the spruces and the tangle of vines, and could see clear out to where the horizon shimmered, faintly blue, empty as a baby's heart.